SOON SHE'D KILL. . . .

What Jasmine needed now was one more really good mark. Then she'd have enough to start her new life. She opened the door and stepped onto the balcony that ran around the outside of the motel. She surveyed the beach ahead—Venice and Marina del Rey to the south, Pacific Palisades and Malibu to the north. *Somewhere,* she told herself, *he's out there. Or maybe it will be a woman. A rich old person, someone alone, someone ill or injured and close to death.* The last one. The one who will finally buy Jasmine's freedom.

Tomorrow, the day after, next week, she thought, *I will find my last patient. My last victim.*

DEADLY COMPANION

NANCY BAKER JACOBS

A DELL BOOK

Published by
Dell Publishing Co., Inc.
1 Dag Hammarskjold Plaza
New York, New York 10017

Dell ® TM 681510, Dell Publishing Co., Inc.

ISBN: 0-440-11766-6

Printed in the United States of America
July 1986

10 9 8 7 6 5 4 3 2 1

DD

DEADLY
COMPANION

Chapter 1

The young woman squeezed the plastic bottle and watched the thick mud-colored jelly ooze onto her head. She worked it through her hair with rubber-gloved fingers, carefully covering each strand. Her eyes watering and her breathing shallow as the stench of ammonia filled the air, she checked meticulously to be certain that she hadn't missed a single hair before removing her gloves. In just over twenty minutes she'd be a brunette. The new hair color, coupled with yesterday's haircut and perm, would leave her with little resemblance to red-haired Jane Burden of St. Louis and even less to her real self, ashy blond Jasmine Kennedy of Minneapolis. She had a new driver's license, a nursing school diploma, and freshly forged employment references. Here in Santa Monica, nearly 2,000 miles away from the city where the police sought her, Jasmine Kennedy, alias Jane Burden, alias half a dozen other young women, was ready to start over. She was now Gretchen Hedberg, nurse-companion for hire.

While she waited for the dye to take, Jasmine lowered herself onto the hard motel bed and looked up a number in the telephone directory. She pulled the phone off the small bedside table and dialed the classified advertising section of the *Los Angeles Times.*

A bored-sounding woman with a whiskey voice answered. Gretchen told her what she wanted. "Your name and billing address, please," the woman said.

"Jas—" She caught herself. She must remember, she must *become* her new identity. "Gretchen Hedberg. That's H-E-

D-B-E-R-G. Room thirty-six, Seacrest Lodge, thirteen thousand Ocean Avenue, Santa Monica." She listened to the woman's unenthusiastic rendering of the *Times'* various ad rates and terms, quickly computed the best for her, and decided to run her ad for a full week with the right to cancel if she got a job more quickly. She read the woman the copy she'd written, copy that would appear in Section 2144, "Jobs Wanted—Nurses," beginning tomorrow.

She hung up the phone feeling hopeful. She was superstitious about Santa Monica, the town where she'd been born just over twenty-five years ago. She hadn't been back since she was four, since her mother had died; still, she had a sense that she was coming back to something that was hers. Earlier today she'd gone exploring; she'd walked the beach and even driven into the hills above Topanga Canyon, where she had vague memories of happy picnics with her mother. The place gave Jasmine a feeling of coming home or at least of having found her roots. What she needed right now was a refuge, a place to hide while the St. Louis trouble blew over. And she also needed a place where there was big money available to those clever enough to grab it. The West Side of Los Angeles seemed to promise her these things.

Jasmine checked her watch. Five more minutes. Her scalp was beginning to feel warm and itchy beneath the chemicals, but she resisted the urge to scratch. She moved to the sliding glass door that led onto the balcony and looked over the rooftops to the beach beyond. The late-afternoon sun hit the water at an angle, creating a sparkling backdrop for the joggers, strollers, bikers, and roller skaters on the Santa Monica boardwalk. Dogs ran free; kids holding surfboards in the parking lot dragged openly on their marijuana cigarettes; lovers held hands and kissed; drunks sprawled in intoxicated sleep. The effect was an odd combination of resort and big city unique to Santa Monica. Each person, each group on the beach, Gretchen thought, looked oblivious of the others nearby. It seemed to symbolize this society; a person could be free here, a person could be different, and nobody would even notice, never mind care.

She wondered for a moment what she would have been like if she'd been reared in this town, reared as a beloved daughter of young Eileen Kennedy. Maybe even as the eldest of several children. Here, in sight of the Pacific, instead of in Minneapolis, where she'd been only the despised and resented responsibility of an old-maid aunt. If her mother had lived, would she still have become . . . But she was too old for a game in which the only payoff was using up the time consumed in playing it.

Whatever forces had formed her, Jasmine had chosen the path her life was taking now. She had a lucrative "business," and she told herself that nobody really got hurt by it. The potential for that was there, of course—as in St. Louis—but such was never her intention. Her clients could well afford to lose the things that she "liberated" from their households. They were old, sick, close to death anyway. They had no need anymore for their treasures—the old-coin collections, gold-plated picture frames, diamond rings, bundles of cash stashed in home safes. Not when they'd be dead in a week, a month, a year.

And if their relatives, their heirs, really deserved the entire inheritance, there'd be no reason for a private-duty nurse in the first place; instead, the potential heirs themselves would be caring for Grandma and Uncle. Jasmine certainly had done that for her aunt Sylvia. For years. Years filled with bedpans, soiled linen, irrational demands, special diets. Years of being cooped up with a crazy, dying old woman who hated her. Years that should have held high school dances, boyfriends, summers at the beach. No one could say that Jasmine hadn't earned every cent she'd taken when Sylvia finally died, hadn't earned it three times over. Sylvia never should have left her things to the church in the first place; what had the church done for her in her old age? If there was a regret there, it was only that Sylvia had taken so long to die.

Today, of course, the people Jasmine—no, she *must* remember to think of herself as Gretchen. The people Gretchen nursed now all were much richer than Aunt Sylvia had been. Most were so wealthy that their heirs didn't even miss the things she took; there was too much to distract them, what with dividing up the real estate and the stockholdings.

And if a few of her patients succumbed slightly before their intended time, what did it matter? They were in pain, suffering, probably grateful to be free of the burdens of living. Some might even argue that putting them out of their misery was a kindness. St. Louis was different, but that hadn't been her idea. She had never liked using violence against anyone, particularly not against an eighty-year-old woman with a terminal illness. If Stan hadn't been so impatient, Gretchen was sure she'd have managed, finally, to convince Mrs. Pickett to tell her where the negotiable securities were hidden. She'd warned Stan that the old woman might not survive a beating, but he hadn't listened. In the end they never did find the valuables. And because her bruises were visible, there had been an autopsy, an autopsy that had shown that Ellen Pickett had died of her injuries, not of cancer.

But that was all history now. The police were looking for Jane Burden, not for Gretchen Hedberg. She felt safe enough. And Stan Greenwood was behind her, too. She knew now that she never should have gotten mixed up with a man. Not one like Stan, who knew how she worked and would only want to get in on the deal; pretty soon he'd want to run it. And it would be even more impossible to have any kind of relationship with a man who *didn't* know. The time would invariably come when she'd have to move on, have to change her identity again, and then what? Maybe someday, she thought a bit wistfully, maybe someday, when she'd accumulated enough to settle down and go back to being Jasmine Kennedy. . . .

Gretchen dunked her head into the small bathroom sink, letting a running stream of warm water from the faucet rinse the dye from her hair. Rivulets of muddy brown water swirled down the drain, gradually becoming more and more clear. When her hair rinsed clean, she shampooed it, rinsed it again, and toweled it damp dry. Her new hairdo required no blow drying or setting, a time-saver, she thought, but definitely not the most becoming style she'd ever worn. She smiled ironically at her new image in the mirror. A few years ago any woman born with hair this frizzy would have been

frantic to iron the curl out of it. But for her, for now, the
style served its purpose.

Not for the first time Gretchen felt grateful that her looks
were average; it was much easier for her to appear different
with minimal changes than it would be for a strikingly beautiful woman. She was neither fat nor thin, her height just
under five feet six, and her face attractive but not beautiful.
Her one memorable feature, about which she'd long felt self-
conscious, was the gap between her front teeth. When she
stopped her nomadic life and when she could afford it, she'd
have it corrected. She'd been obsessed with her teeth as a
girl, had believed that people laughed behind her back. But
Aunt Sylvia had refused to allow orthodontia—"Be grateful
the good Lord gave you teeth at all!" Sylvia Loggins had
firmly believed that beauty was evil, its only purpose to en-
tice the devil. Gretchen had always felt secretly that such a
tenet was a particularly handy one for a woman who'd
looked like Aunt Sylvia. But she'd never dared say so. Offering such an opinion would only have gained her bed without
dinner, a beating with the strap, or imprisonment in the
closet that smelled overpoweringly of mothballs. And by the
time Gretchen was old enough and big enough to have sub-
dued any physical threat Sylvia had to offer, the old woman
had come up with other deterrents that were equally successful.

Gretchen peered closely into the bathroom mirror as she
made up her face to go with the new hairstyle. She stroked
tiny dark hairlines over her naturally light eyebrows, making
them appear fuller, then blacked her eyelashes with mascara.
She frowned at the effect. The dark hair against her naturally ivory complexion made her look pale and anemic. She
added extra pink blusher, which helped, and finally a slash
of bright red lipstick. There. Even Stan would have trouble
recognizing her now. A tan would help even more. Tomorrow she'd spend time lying in the sun on the balcony. She'd
have to stay at the motel listening for the telephone anyway.
She'd pick up a paperback book or two and some suntan oil
tonight after dinner and spend a leisurely day tomorrow in
her room.

Gretchen pulled a yellow T-shirt dress over her head and

put on sandals. The afternoon was still warm, though refreshingly cool in comparison with the temperatures she had endured on her drive across country. She put the room key in her shoulder bag and grabbed a sweater for later, when the blazing sun had dropped into the ocean. She had her evening mapped out. First, the newsstand in Century City, where she could pick up the latest St. Louis newspaper; it seemed important to know whether or not she was still in the news there. Then dinner alone in some small, economical place, maybe Italian. A stop at a drugstore for the books and tanning lotion and home.

Home. The motel room, cramped and tiny as it was, a place filled to capacity by its double bed, the nightstand, and one straight-backed chair, was as much of a home as Gretchen had had since her teenage years. There had been the nursing school dormitory, then a series of rooms in other people's houses, interspersed with hotel rooms like this one in city after city as she changed identities and clients. And in St. Louis there had been a few stolen nights at Stan's. For Gretchen, home had long been transient and elusive, and her possessions had spent more time in storage lockers than with her.

But that would soon change, she promised herself. Her cache of property had grown, if not into wealth, at least to a size that approached what she would need to open her own small business. She'd been careful with the valuables she'd taken, selling them gradually and in a variety of places so that she never aroused suspicion and earned top prices, too. She now had close to $50,000 in bank accounts in six cities, and when she'd sold off the items in her storage lockers, she might have close to double that. Maybe she'd even open an antiques store and sell her things direct to the public. She'd become quite an expert on valuable china, glass, silver, curios. Why not eliminate the middleman altogether? And the element of danger had its appeal, too. But that decision would have to wait. What she needed now was one more really good mark. Then she'd have enough to start her new life. A life in which she'd never again have to be dependent upon another person. Not on Aunt Sylvia. Not on some sick old man or woman endlessly hanging on to life's last thread.

Not on a lover. Gretchen Hedberg, Jane Burden, all the other false identities would die forever. And Jasmine Kennedy would finally be free.

Gretchen opened the door and stepped onto the balcony that ran around the outside of the motel. She pulled the door shut behind her, checking to see that it was locked. The view from the balcony was wide and impressive, the thing that made the cubbyhole room worth the $55 a night she was paying for it. She surveyed the beach ahead—Venice and Marina del Rey to the south, Pacific Palisades and Malibu to the north. *Somewhere,* she told herself, *he's out there. Or maybe it will be a woman. A rich old person, someone alone, someone ill or injured and close to death. The last one. The one who will finally buy me freedom. Tomorrow, the day after, next week . . . I will find my last patient. My last victim.*

Chapter 2

Estelle pushed the bowl of chicken and rice soup to the edge of the tray, her appetite dulled by a single taste. Obviously Paula had merely opened a can, added water, and heated the vile mess to lukewarm. Estelle nibbled on a cracker, found it stale, and tossed it into the soup bowl. She felt bored and irritable, and she ached all over. So this was what it was like to be old and bedridden. For the first time in her seventy-three years Estelle Edwards felt her age, felt it thoroughly and completely. She'd had her pains now and then, of course, she'd slowed down a little, slept a little less well than a few years ago, but who didn't? Generally, until now Estelle had lived up to her publicity—still taking a daily swim in her pool overlooking the Pacific, still active in charity work, looking and feeling ten years younger than she was. But now, here she was, pinned down in bed by a cast that reached from foot to crotch on her left side, her entire leg throbbing with pain. And feeling very sorry for herself.

She told herself that her blue mood was just the pain pill wearing off. Estelle didn't know which was worse: the nauseated, dizzy feeling she had when the codeine was working or the pulsating pain when it wasn't. And it had already been two days. How much longer dared she use the pills? She decided to hold off an hour, see how bad the pain became. If it were bearable, she'd do without the medication.

Keep your mind on something else, she told herself. Her still-bright blue eyes moved to the crystal clock on her nightstand. Nearly noon. On a usual day she'd be sitting on the patio—the morning fog would have burned off by now—

reading the trades. Estelle hadn't acted since 1946, but she still read the trades every day. She knew what part Jack Lemmon had just signed for, what picture Woody Allen had most recently released, which films had broken records at the box office. Her late husband, Zachary Zimmerman, was part of the reason she'd gotten into the habit. You married a director, you kept up with his business, or you didn't keep him. Since Zachary's death in 1975 Estelle had continued her morning ritual, partly as a tribute to him. In her mind she read Zach the news, the rumors, the publicity plants. And she knew just what his response would have been if he'd been there. But Paula hadn't brought the trades with Estelle's lunch tray.

A cup of tea. That would kill a few minutes, maybe raise her spirits. She lifted the small pot, part of her French china tea service, and poured some of the amber liquid into a cup decorated with delicate hand-painted pansies. The set had six cups and saucers, each pair adorned with a different flower. Estelle's favorite was the violets. She added a sugar cube and stirred, then brought the cup to her lips. Cold. For God's sake, couldn't Paula at least manage to boil the water before she dumped in the teabag? Was that too much to ask? Estelle suspected that the odious lunch was Paula's way of letting her mother-in-law know that she resented having to make it. But no one wished that weren't necessary more than Estelle did.

The throbbing in her leg grew worse, vibrating from the knee in both directions. Suddenly the weight of the lunch tray was oppressive on her lap. She tried to lift it off, but it was too heavy for her to handle at that angle. A corner dipped, dishes slid, and a combination of soup and tea flowed onto the bedcovers. Estelle swore under her breath as the greasy liquids soaked her prized quilt. Her wardrobe mistress on one of her favorite pictures, *The General's Lady*, had made it for her. Maisie Gilroy. Estelle had given it this place of honor on her bed for more than forty years.

"Paula!" she called. "Paula! Quick!"

Nothing. Where *was* she? Estelle frantically tried to wipe up the spill with tissues, but almost immediately she could feel the wetness soak through to her skin.

"Paula!" she called again, her voice filled with impatience and irritation. Still no response. Nonetheless, she stopped herself before she screamed the name in impotent rage. Her breath caught, and her eyes filled. It wasn't Paula's fault she was in such ill humor; she had only herself to blame. And it wasn't Paula's ineptitude or even her slowness that bothered Estelle so much. It was the indignity, the blasted indignity of having to ask another human being—particularly her daughter-in-law—to bring her meals, to clean up this mess, even to half carry her to the bathroom. Never before in all her seventy-three years—and she was seventy-three even though all the old movie bios listed her as only seventy—had she been unable to care for herself. Even when Seth was born and it wasn't fashionable for new mothers to leave their beds for days, she'd been up and about quickly, never once using the bedpan the nurses insisted that she keep by her bed. Until a week ago Sunday she'd done most of her own housework, driven her own car, handled her own finances.

Estelle shifted her slight body away from the wettest part of the bed, wincing as she moved the heavy cast. Two months like this, the doctor predicted. And when she'd protested, young Dr. Baxter had told her she should count herself lucky that it was only her leg, not her hip, she'd broken. Many older women didn't survive a broken hip.

At least, she wished, the accident could have been something dramatic, something that would make a good story at cocktail parties. A hit-and-run driver or foiling a mugger or something. But no. She'd simply fallen from a wobbly chair while she'd been trying to take down her favorite set of Spode china from the top shelf of a kitchen cupboard. Besides her leg, the casualties included three cups, a saucer, and a dinner plate. The dishes were irreplaceable antiques, and Estelle felt nearly as bad about their loss as she did about the fracture of her left leg. *Come to think of it,* she told herself, *you're something of an irreplaceable antique yourself.* She forced a half smile. *Keep your sense of humor, old girl. Look at the funny side of this. There is a funny side . . . isn't there?*

Five minutes later Paula shuffled listlessly into Estelle's room. Estelle had always found the younger woman to be an irritating companion, a dull woman given to slow movements and plodding conversation. Slightly overweight, Paula Zimmerman was essentially colorless, in looks as well as in personality. Her unstyled hair was a close match to the tan of her complexion; her wardrobe tended toward beiges and grays. Many times in the past sixteen years Estelle had tried to get Paula to liven up, suggesting that she buy a red dress just once or try a tint in her hair. Estelle kept her own hair the auburn of her youth, and her wardrobe was a veritable rainbow. None of those old lady costumes for her. Yet here was Paula, only forty years old, allowing herself to fade into the background. Perhaps even preferring it.

But Paula was no doormat. In her quiet, unobtrusive way she generally managed to do precisely what she wanted to do. Her way was often to act indirectly or not to act at all when others imposed their needs and ideas upon her, but the result was the same as if she had opposed them head-on. Recently Estelle had bought Paula a blue sweater, just the shade to match and enhance her one good feature, her eyes. But she never wore it. The loan of a best-selling book that Estelle had enjoyed virtually guaranteed that Paula would never get around to reading it despite her professed desire to do so. Often Paula would accept Estelle's invitation to a concert, a film, or the ballet. But at the last minute something would come up to prevent Paula from going—a headache, a previous appointment—and she'd miss an event she hadn't really wanted to attend in the first place. And when asked to do a favor, Paula often agreed, then "forgot" or performed the task so poorly that she was never asked to repeat it. Today's lunch, Estelle felt, was a prime example.

Estelle felt a recurrent desire to take Paula by the shoulders and shake some life, some action, some honesty into her. But today not only couldn't she do that physically, but she knew she couldn't afford even the luxury of prodding Paula verbally. She needed her daughter-in-law's help, and that meant keeping her mouth shut and acting grateful for everything that Paula did for her. She dared not complain that Paula was too slow or that the lunch was inedible.

"I'm afraid there's been an accident," Estelle said carefully, keeping her voice neutral. "I called you earlier, but evidently you didn't hear me. Now I think it's wet clear through to the mattress."

"I heard you. I was on the phone. I couldn't come any faster."

It's a damn good thing I wasn't having a heart attack or being throttled by a cat burglar, Estelle thought, but she kept her irritation from altering her expression. If she complained, Paula might leave. Estelle couldn't afford to stay in the hospital for two months. Her Medicare benefits wouldn't last that long; they certainly wouldn't pay for a private room. Indeed, she wouldn't have wanted to stay in the hospital even if she could have afforded it. If she was going to be bedridden, she wanted to be home, in her own bed, in the house she loved more than anything, the house she'd furnished with hundreds of mementos of her life as an actress and her nearly forty-year love affair with Zach. Estelle felt that she'd had one of Hollywood's few good marriages, and this house was where it had blossomed and grown. Everything that surrounded her, in all fourteen rooms, held a special memory for her, from the set of Spode she'd been given as a bride to the now-soaked quilt, from the Degas hanging over the four-poster bed to the photo album in the nightstand drawer. The place was expensive to keep up, of course; she'd just replaced the pool heater, and a new roof for the south wing was planned for next month. And the trust fund Zach had left her no longer went as far as it once had. But by letting the servants go and watching her expenses with utmost care—no two-month hospital stay for her—Estelle still managed to keep her home.

Paula and Seth simply didn't understand that the house was what made life worth living for Estelle. Innumerable times Seth had said, "You really should get rid of this old relic. It's got to be worth a million five, maybe two million in today's market. Buy yourself a condo in one of those high-rises, be around people your own age."

"They have nurses on duty in case you get sick. Meals you can have brought in if you don't feel like cooking. Everything you'd want." Paula had chimed in eagerly.

"How would you know what I'd want?" Estelle had shot back. "I have what I want right here."

If Paula were in her place, Estelle knew, she would agree verbally that the house should be sold, then never get around to putting it on the market or set the price so high that no one would buy it. But Estelle's manner was more direct, sometimes brutally so. Seldom was anyone left wondering what Estelle Edwards's opinions or intentions were. "This is where I've lived for the past forty-six years," she'd said, "and this is where I fully intend to die. So if you think you're going to file me away in some home for has-beens, think again. When I leave my house, it'll be in a pine box."

But Seth never let up. He claimed she was a prisoner to the house; she couldn't afford to travel, to entertain often, to go out very much. But that was the way Estelle liked it, puttering around the house, keeping her things nice, spending the day in the pool and the garden. She didn't mind not being around people her own age; she found them boring, all talk about their arthritis and their blood pressure. If she was often alone, so what? She hated cardplaying and basket weaving and all those phony, organized activities everyone thought were so wonderful for "seniors." And it wasn't as though she never went anywhere. She had invitations, a circle of younger friends. It didn't matter to Estelle that she was considered a "character," invited to those parties almost as part of the entertainment. At least those friends didn't expect her to be able to throw that kind of party in return, and Estelle thrived on being the center of attention, whatever the reason. Essentially, she thought, her life as a prisoner of her house was pretty damned good. Especially considering the alternatives.

But that, of course, was not really Seth's point. The real point was that her son thought she'd give him a good chunk of the money she'd make if she sold the house. She knew Seth blamed her that he was in Italy right now directing a spaghetti western instead of giving Spielberg and Lucas and Coppola a run for their money here in the States. "I just need a chance to show what I can do," he'd begged. "If I raise some of the financing myself, I know I can get my movie made. I'll get my chance to direct. You'll see. I'll set this town on its ear with this thing. Then there'll be no more directing idiot-box commercials for Seth Zimmerman." Seth had optioned a screenplay, lined up an actor. All he needed was money. A mere million or two would do. Estelle's mere million. All her son needed to make a mark like his father's —the way Estelle saw it—was to take away her house and risk everything she had on a stupid science-fiction movie.

She'd refused, over and over again. Truth was that Seth had never had his father's talent. And he never would have it. The money Estelle had tied up in her house wouldn't make him into Zachary Zimmerman. But her relations with her son grew more and more strained as he began to see her as the cause of his thwarted ambitions. The reason he wasn't a big-name director at forty was no longer that his name wasn't on the list of bankable directors; it wasn't that Paul Newman wanted to direct his own pictures instead of acting under Seth's direction; the blame no longer was assigned to Seth's having been typecast during the many years he'd spent directing commercials. No, now the reason he wasn't making it was solely that his mother wouldn't give up her house.

And now, when precisely what Seth and Paula had warned her about—that she would become ill or injured and be unable to care for herself—had actually happened, Estelle was frightened and worried. Seth's tone with her had become increasingly hostile. Before he'd left for Italy last month, he'd said, "I honestly wonder, Mother, whether your attachment to this house is quite normal. You know, your insistence upon living in the past could be a sign of senility." He'd paused to let his carefully chosen words sink in. "Possibly you're no longer able to make the best decisions about your future."

That statement had rolled off Estelle's back last month. He was threatening to have her declared mentally incompetent to handle her own affairs, of course, but Estelle knew he'd never be able to pull that off. No judge or jury would dare declare her, Estelle Edwards, incompetent. Not Estelle with her daily swim and her library of well-read and thoroughly understood books. Just last month she'd gone up in a hot-air balloon for the first time, and a couple of times each year she gave a lecture on motion-picture history at UCLA. Why, every few years some young movie-buff newspaper reporter did a feature story on her and her still-active life!

Today, though, her confidence was shaken. She didn't have the ability to get out of a bed soaked with chicken soup. She couldn't get to the bathroom. Or the grocery store. Or the kitchen to cook her meals. She'd become helpless simply by falling off a chair. And if Seth were successful? If he could have himself appointed . . . what did they call it? Her guardian? Something like that. Then what? Could she be stashed away in some cut-rate nursing home while her son wasted her money trying to be a movie director?

Paula helped her mother-in-law into the bathroom adjoining the bedroom, and Estelle perched on the side of the bathtub while Paula changed the bedding. Estelle pulled her nightgown over her head and carefully sponged herself off. She covered her nakedness with a towel, patiently waiting for her daughter-in-law to bring her a clean gown. She dared not show the least impatience, she told herself as she shivered against the clammy porcelain. For the next few weeks she'd have to show Paula appreciation for everything she did, even when it wasn't truly deserved. She'd figuratively tiptoe through her recovery period and get herself back in shape, back to independence. By the time Seth returned from Italy, she'd be beyond his greedy grasp once again.

Without Seth around, Estelle felt, Paula could be managed. All Paula really wanted was to stay married to Seth, whether he was a famous movie director or a truck driver; she apparently adored the man and had for the sixteen years they'd been married. Paula wanted the man, not the money. Estelle wondered what it was in her son that inspired such devotion. She couldn't see any way he'd ever earned it. She knew Paula had overlooked numerous affairs Seth had had with actresses, models, script girls. She'd borne countless separations as he'd traveled around the world. She'd allowed him to abuse her publicly. But whenever she was allowed to, Paula tagged along behind him like a faithful dog. And if Seth booted her aside now and then, the only effect was that Paula became more and more devoted to him.

Estelle pulled the clean gown over her head, and she and

Paula began the painful half carry back to the bed. Pain shot through her leg as it bumped across the Oriental rug. "I'd swear this cast must be three sizes too small." Estelle winced. Her toes, blue, swollen, and throbbing, protruded from the end of the cast. "I feel like my leg's in a vise."

"If you'd stayed in the hospital, you wouldn't have to be carried back and forth like this," Paula said. "It's probably just making things worse."

"You know I couldn't afford to spend a couple of months in the hospital, Paula. Truth is I'm very lucky—and grateful —to have you to help me."

"Only till Thursday. You know I'm going to Italy on Thursday."

"But I thought—"

"That I'd cancel my flight? It's not that I wouldn't like to; you know that, Estelle." Paula's expression was smug and self-satisfied as she lifted the old woman onto the fresh bed. "It's that Seth and I have commitments in Italy."

"You could stay. You know you could stay if you wanted to. Seth doesn't need you in Italy. He's busy all day. . . . He wouldn't even miss you."

"I just talked to him. He wanted to be sure I'd be there on schedule. He sends you his love."

"Sends me his love! I could have been killed, and my only son can't even pick up the phone to ask how I am."

"I told him you were much better."

"I'm *not* much better. I'm terrible. I can't even get out of bed." Estelle heard her voice taking on the panic she was feeling.

"You're just feeling sorry for yourself, Estelle."

"Somebody ought to."

"Nonsense. Seth feels very bad about your accident. So do I. But you can't expect other people to rearrange their lives completely just because—"

"And how many times did I rearrange my life for him, I ask you? How many times does a mother give her—her *blood* for her child?"

"I'm sure that Seth appreciates all you've done for him, Estelle. As I do. But this is impossible. If I were going to be here, of course, I'd help you out, but I'm going to be in Italy. It's that simple."

Estelle bit her lip to keep it from quivering. Paula was enjoying this. She could feel it. She was having the time of her life. Estelle would not give her the satisfaction of seeing her cry. She would not. She would die first. "What do you want me to do here all alone? Huh, Miss Compassion? What do you and that goddamned ungrateful son of mine expect me to do?"

Paula picked up the soiled quilt from the floor and rolled it into a ball. "I'd say that's entirely your choice. There's the hospital, a nursing home, a private-duty nurse. Take your pick."

"You know I can't pay for those things. Seth knows it. What are you trying to do to me?" Estelle felt as though her entire body, her entire life were encased in a cast.

"Don't be melodramatic, Estelle. Seth says that he's sure the trust fund will loan you enough money to pay your medical bills. You can pay it back when the house is sold."

"Damn it! This house is not going to be sold!"

Paula wrinkled her nose at the bundle in her arms. "I really doubt that this old thing is going to take another washing. Look at it. Practically in tatters now." She turned her back on the old woman.

"You're not going to get a dime!" Estelle screamed. "If I have to sell this house, you and Seth are not going to get a dime from me. I don't care if his next job is directing— directing traffic! You call him in Italy and tell him that, why don't you? And this time you pay for the call yourself."

"Why, Estelle," Paula said with studied calm, "you're beginning to sound awfully crazy. I wouldn't say that was very smart of you."

So that was the game. If they couldn't get her one way, they'd use another. "Give me back my quilt," Estelle said. "I want your filthy hands off my quilt."

Paula tossed the soiled bundle onto Estelle's lap, turned,

and stalked out of the room. "Just a crazy old woman," she
called over her shoulder.

Shaking with rage and fear and pain, Estelle hugged the
reeking quilt to her chest, seeking comfort from the past as a
child does from its mother.

Chapter 3

Faith Sanford plucked the key from its hiding place behind the holly bush and opened Estelle's back door. "Hello! It's me!" she called.

"No need to shout, Faith. I hear you." Paula entered the kitchen, carrying a trayful of dirty dishes.

"Oh, sorry. I brought Estelle a present," the girl said. Her left hand held a damp paper bag.

"Well, bring it up to her. She's in a real snit today. Maybe you can cheer her up."

Faith opened a cupboard and pulled out two bowls, then took two spoons from a drawer. Estelle's house had been a second home to her for most of her life, since she was a small child, and she knew where everything was kept.

Estelle was still clutching the quilt, her face red and streaked, when Faith entered the bedroom. If Faith didn't know better, she'd think that Estelle had been crying, but she had never seen Estelle cry in all the years she'd known her. "Hey, I brought you some Häagen Dazs," Faith said in greeting. "Honey vanilla."

Estelle forced a smile. "You may well save me from slow starvation, my dear." She tossed the soiled quilt aside and grasped the girl's hand warmly.

"I brought up bowls and spoons. I walked all the way from Main Street with it, so I think we'd better eat it fast. It's getting soupy." Faith scooped half of the pint of ice cream into each bowl, handed one to Estelle, and plopped her long frame onto a chair beside the bed. "I'd ask you how you're feeling, but I can see. It's that bad?"

"Hurts like hell if you really want to know. I think I'll give in and take another pain pill if you'll get me a glass of water." Estelle washed down the pill and felt its numbing effects begin almost immediately. "So much for another good intention." She returned her attention to the ice cream and felt her spirits rise as she licked the creamy honey-flavored concoction off the spoon. "This is perfect, just perfect," she said, taking another bite. "I only wish my own children were as thoughtful as you are, Faith, dear."

"Yeah, well, tell my dad how wonderful I am. He probably wouldn't know who you're talking about."

"Come now, that's not true."

"That's what you think. He's always either out of town or spending his time with some girl. *I* never see him."

"You can't blame him for being lonely, Faith. Your mother's been dead four years, and a man needs female companionship."

Faith shrugged her slender shoulders. "Companionship, huh! You should see the tootsies he picks, Estelle. It's downright embarrassing. The last one had a chest out to here and so much makeup on she couldn't smile without cracking it."

Estelle chuckled. "Are you sure you're not exaggerating just a tiny bit, Faith? Maybe you're a little jealous."

"I wouldn't be if he'd choose a woman like my mother. Somebody with a little class, a little style. Somebody his own age, for God's sake."

"Oh?"

"You know how old his latest one is? Twenty-two! Only six years older than I am! That's obscene."

"Not exactly obscene. Perhaps a bit unseemly."

"But he's *old*, Estelle. He's nearly fifty."

"Thanks a lot."

Faith blushed. "I'm sorry. I didn't mean—"

"I know what you meant. Forget it. Truth is I agree with you. Your father ought to find a woman more suitable, someone who could be more of a mother to you. But my guess is he won't. He's looking for something else just now."

"I wish I didn't have to know about it. He brings these— these tramps to the house and expects me to be polite to them. Or he goes to their places, and I never know whether he's coming home or not—"

"You're not left alone."

"Ever since he hired Mrs. Wattman, he thinks I'm taken care of. Filed away like one of his business projects. I can't stand her, Estelle." Faith's lower lip protruded in a childish pout. "She drinks and she smells."

Estelle patted the girl's hand. "This has been very hard on you."

"No lie! But I'm not going to take it much longer. As soon as I get an acting job, I'll be able to afford my own place. Then I won't care whether he pays any attention to me or not. Just wait until he wants to talk to me and *I'm* not home."

"Don't be in such a hurry, dear. One thing I've learned is that we always think life is going to get better, but usually it's just a rerun of the same old thing. At least your father still provides for you financially. I'm sure he cares for you. He's just going through a hard time."

"Why does it have to be *my* father who's so messed up, Estelle? He's making a fool of himself." Faith nervously stirred her remaining ice cream until it was soupy.

"If we could choose our relatives, life would be a hell of a lot more pleasant. . . . I can guarantee you that."

"Things aren't going so well for you either, huh? Paula said you were in a—a snit, I think she called it."

"Humph. That ungrateful woman is a model of understatement. She's going off to Italy on Thursday and leaving me here helpless. Not exactly the kind of news you'd expect to put me in a good mood."

"Can't you get someone else to stay with you? I wouldn't want her taking care of me. She's worse than Mrs. Wattman." Faith scooped the last drop of melted ice cream from her dish and swallowed it.

"You've got a point there. My daughter-in-law is not on my list of all-time favorite people. I certainly would never pick her for a relative. She's a lousy cook, too. But I'll have to pay someone else to stay here, and I haven't got the money. Paula and Seth want me to sell my house, and this is one way of making me do it."

Faith's jaw dropped. "But, Estelle, you can't sell your house. Where would you go?" The house had been Faith's sanctuary for a long time, particularly since her mother's death. Estelle's was the place she came to cry, to get advice, to be accepted.

Estelle smiled at the girl's chagrin. "I'm glad someone else sees it the way I do. Where would I go? Probably to my grave in short order. And I'm not entirely kidding." She shifted her cast-covered leg, which under the effect of the codeine now seemed merely unwieldy, no longer the source of blinding pain. "But the bottom line is that I'll have to hire someone to take care of me. Either that or go into a nursing home, and I don't dare do that. I—I have a feeling that the house wouldn't be here when I got out again . . . *if* I ever got out."

"They can't do that to you. We won't let them. I know . . . I'll move over here and take care of you. That would solve both our problems!"

Estelle felt a rush of warmth for her impulsive young friend. "You know, I believe you really would take care of me." She blinked back tears before Faith could see them. "But your father would never let you do that."

"My father wouldn't notice I was gone."

"Of course, he would, Faith. He cares about you. Besides, you've got to go to school, and I need someone here full time."

"School's out—except for my driver's ed class—unless I have to take remedial math." Faith made a face. "Listen, Estelle, we'll think of something. I know. I'm trying out for this part in a new play." She rose from the chair, pulled her mop of reddish blond hair to the top of her head in a makeshift knot, and assumed a seductive pose. "Do you think I can pass for thirty? The part's a thirty-year-old woman. If I get it, I could help you pay for a nurse or somebody to come stay with you."

Estelle laughed out loud, unsure whether her mirth was the result of Faith's mugging or the codeine. "That felt good," she said. "I haven't laughed since I fell off that damn chair. You're very good for me, Faith Sanford. Somebody ought to figure out how to bottle you and market you to all sick old people."

"Don't say that. You're not sick and you're not old. I didn't mean what I said before. What do you think, huh? Can I pass for thirty?"

Estelle thought that Faith had about as much chance of passing for thirty as she herself did. "In about ten years maybe."

The girl's face fell. "I can't win. I'm too tall to play teenagers, and I look too young to play older women."

"Oh, to be young enough to think that thirty is an older woman . . ."

"That's not what I meant."

"I know what you meant." Estelle's eyes surveyed this girl, who often seemed more like her own child than Seth did. Or at least the grandchild that Seth and Paula had never given her. In a few years Faith would be a beauty, but now her face was creased with the impatience of sixteen, and she needed a dose of maturity. The girl was already five feet ten inches tall and couldn't weigh more than 110 pounds in her T-shirt and designer jeans. Not a curve in sight. But with another 15 or 20 pounds in the right places and the gracefulness that would gradually replace her adolescent gawkiness, she would be what used to be called a heartbreaker. "I know you won't listen to a word I say, Faith, but you really don't have to be in such a headlong rush to grow up. The theater will still be there in a couple more years."

"Wait, wait, wait. I'm sick and tired of waiting." Faith pouted. "All I ever got from waiting is taller." She folded herself back onto the chair and held her chin in one long, slender hand. "I don't even know if I'm through growing yet. Is there some kind of medicine you can get to make you stop? Maybe I'll take up smoking. . . . It's not fair. How come all actors are so short anyway?"

"Not all of them are. Look at Rock Hudson, James Arness. Gregory Peck."

"Look at Paul Newman, Robert Redford, Dudley Moore. They're all *inches* shorter than I am."

"The movies can fix that quite nicely, dear. Don't worry. Sophia Loren walked in a trench to costar with Alan Ladd.

And some of Ingrid Bergman's leading men stood on boxes
to measure up to her."

"Really?"

"Would I lie to you?"

"I'm going to try out for the part anyway. It'll be good
practice. My drama teacher at school says you have to learn
to take rejection or you'll never make it in show business."

"You have a very wise drama teacher, Faith." Estelle well
remembered her own days as an actress, starting when she
was younger than Faith was now. She'd enjoyed acting at
first, all except for the constant don't-call-us-we'll-call-you
attitudes of the agents, the directors, the producers. Then,
after she had been able to get almost any part she wanted,
she began to find the whole thing boring. She hoped that
Faith would make it big if that was what she really wanted
out of life, but she also hoped that she wouldn't find her
victory to be hollow, the way Estelle had. After years of
introspection Estelle now realized that what had attracted
her to the movie business was not the opportunity to create a
character, not the chance to bring art to the screen, but
merely the glamour that surrounded the business. She'd
hated learning all the lines, the interminable costume fittings
and makeup sessions, waiting around the movie set while
camera angles were selected and lights positioned. Truth was
she'd been happy to retire once Zach's directing salary allowed it. The one film she'd made after Seth's birth had
simply been too energy-draining. After that, thanks to
Zach's success, she'd been able to stay home with her baby,
avoid working so hard, yet still be part of the glamour.

"I've tried out for fourteen parts," Faith said. "I read
somewhere that the average actress gets hired once out of
twenty auditions when she's starting out. So I figure six
more tryouts and I'll land a part."

Estelle chuckled. "That's one way to look at it. But don't
rush things, Faith. A girl your age ought to be spending her
time thinking about clothes and boys, not about making a
living."

"Sure." The girl rose to her full height and gestured from
her head to her feet. "Look at this body. The tall sizes are
for old ladies, and the regular sizes are way too short for

me." Faith's jeans hit well above her ankles. "And boys! Oh, Estelle, what's wrong with me? Here I am almost seventeen and I've never even been french-kissed. A girl in my class, Elizabeth Warren, she's already got a baby—"

"Well! Be grateful you're not in her place."

"I didn't mean that. It's just . . . the only boy taller than me in the whole junior class is Bobby Blankenfeld. We've gone to the movies a couple of times, but it's like going with my brother. I like Bobby, but he's just a pal. . . ."

"What's wrong with that? I married my best pal, and it was probably the smartest thing I ever did."

"Really?"

"Absolutely. Never underestimate the value of friendship, Faith. It's not that easy to come by. Especially these days, when everybody seems to be looking out for number one. Keep Bobby's friendship even if you fall hard for someone else one of these days."

"I wish I had more friends sometimes. Marcia Palmer was about my best friend, but she got in with the Bugsy Johnson crowd, and I think she's turning into a pothead. I told her she was stupid to fool around with that stuff, and she hasn't spoken to me since."

"She'll probably be back when she grows up a little. You've got one very good friend here, my dear." Estelle clapped her forehead with her hand. "Look at me, will you? Break my leg, and all of a sudden I get maudlin. You'd think I was on my deathbed. But I mean it. We are good friends, Faith, no matter that I'm old enough to be your grandmother, and—what the hell, truth is that I wish I were your grandmother. You'd be a credit to me."

Faith blushed with pleasure. "If I were your granddaughter, maybe I could do more about your problems." She began to tidy up, stacking the bowls and spoons and putting the empty ice cream carton into the paper bag.

"I think maybe you have done something about them."

"I don't get it."

"A new perspective, dear. Here I sit griping about other people's being self-centered and selfish, and I've been doing exactly the same thing." She silenced Faith's protest with a gesture. "I used to have friends, quite a lot of them. Know where they are now, most of them? Some are dead. Smokey Levine is in the Motion Picture Actor's Home. Gladys Baxter—her son, Cullen, is my doctor now that old Dr. Cunningham is retiring—Gladys had to move in with her daughter in Toledo. Toledo, for God's sake. Who else is alive? Maisie Gilroy. She was a great friend in the old days. She made this quilt. Last I heard about her, she was living in one room in Venice, taking in sewing to stay alive. George Kelly still has his money; he made millions investing in some new kind of movie camera. George had a stroke three years ago. Can't walk by himself; nobody can understand half of what he tries to say. His fourth wife left him, said she couldn't stand it any longer.

"Point is, Faith, I'm lucky. Spoiled really. I've still got my home. I've still got my health; at least I'll get it back again when I get out of this goddamned cast. I can't expect my children to wait on me hand and foot. They've got their own life, and God knows it's not an easy one either. My son lives with disappointment in himself every day of his life. He drowns it in liquor and young girls and a vile temper, and his wife has to live with that. Paula doesn't need my vile temper too.

"You got me thinking, Faith. What you said about rejection applies to everyone, not just to actors. I've had things my way for a long, long time, and when you're not used to being rejected, you can get pretty full of self-pity when it happens."

"So what are you going to do?"

"I have to figure out my priorities. I want to keep my house. That's the most important thing right now. After my health, of course. It hurts to part with anything here. . . ." Her eyes surveyed the room, cluttered with keepsakes. "But I'll have to. I've got a couple of thousand dollars set aside to patch the roof next month. I'll start with postponing that . . . and praying that it doesn't rain. Then I'll decide what to sell first—some of my silver, maybe, or the Picasso print. I haven't any idea what they're worth anymore, but they'll bring in something. Those picture frames, for instance." Two tables and a dresser were covered with silver-framed photos. "I could put those pictures in an album and sell the frames . . . if I have to. You can help me if you will, dear."

"Sure. What can I do?"

"First bring me a telephone book and today's want ads. I'm going to find myself a live-in nurse. Then, later, you can be my legs. You can sell some things for me."

"Okay. That could be fun."

"Bring me a paper and pencil, too, will you, dear? May as well start making an inventory."

Faith brought them.

"Thank you." Estelle's eyes drifted to the window opposite the bed. The jacaranda tree outside was a riot of purple blossoms, some of them dropping to the patio below and into the pool. It was a messy tree, but she loved it. Its beauty justified its existence. The ocean beyond was a brilliant blue, speckled here and there with whitecaps. "What's it like out there?" she asked.

"Breezy. But it's getting warmer. Maybe seventy-five."

"I do miss being outside. It seems unhealthy to spend a day like this cooped up in here. Why don't you take a swim, dear? Somebody should get some use out of the pool."

"Thanks. I wouldn't mind. There's nobody to talk to at home anyway."

Estelle smiled and squeezed Faith's hand. "Don't worry too much, dear. You'll outlast this girlfriend, and the next one too."

Faith leaned over to plump Estelle's pillows and impulsively kissed her friend on the cheek. "At least you understand," she said, picking up the dishes and starting downstairs.

Estelle paused for a moment and reached for the newspaper.

Chapter 4

Dr. Cullen Baxter left his home late. Like every other morning that week, an argument with Laura had held him up. He was getting very tired of waking up to her complaints and self-pity, and something in him couldn't, or wouldn't, just ignore her. He *had* to answer back, to defend himself, and then they were at it again. Another quarrel was started, and more of his valuable time was gone.

It was true that she was stuck at home every day with the babies; he'd give her that one. But whose fault was that? Laura, not Cullen, was the one who had wanted kids right away. It wasn't that he didn't like children. He did, and he was really crazy about the girls now that they were here. But he'd wanted time to buy his practice before they took on the responsibilities of parents. He'd envisioned time to pay off his medical school debts, time to enjoy life a little. It wouldn't have hurt if Laura'd gotten herself a job, if she'd helped hasten their freedom from the overwhelming bills. But no. Laura didn't want to get a job, and the next thing Cullen knew, she was announcing that she was pregnant.

She'd done the traditional bit—candlelight and champagne ready to celebrate the moment after she'd told him he was going to be a father. If he'd shown how disappointed, how angry he'd really felt that night, their marriage might well have ended right then. Even three years later Cullen still felt that Laura had tricked him, that she'd deliberately gone against his wishes, and he bitterly resented her wanting him to be elated about it.

Laura hadn't had the sense to stop with one baby either.

"Meggie needs a sister or brother," she'd insisted. "Only children are too lonely, and they're easy to spoil." So now there were too little girls. And once the kids had arrived and Laura had learned that full-time mothering of two babies was really no easier than taking a full-time job, she'd become bored and resentful. Now she complained—constantly, it seemed—that she needed more adult time, both for herself and with her husband. She wanted to hire sitters so she and Cullen could get away for intimate weekends, so she could have her hair and nails done, so she could meet Cullen for lunches at romantic seaside restaurants. But with a wife and two babies to support and a practice to pay for, Cullen had neither "more adult time" to give Laura nor the money to pay for the luxuries she wanted so badly.

"I may as well have *three* babies," he muttered out loud. "It's about time Princess Laura grew up."

He glanced at his watch. It was already nine o'clock. His first patient was coming in at nine-thirty, and he'd promised to stop by and look at Estelle Edwards's leg on his way in this morning. House calls were a pain—almost no doctor would do them these days—but Estelle was a sprightly old girl, and she'd been a close friend of Cullen's mother for more years than Cullen had been alive. Besides, Estelle Edwards had helped influence old Dr. Cunningham to take Cullen into partnership. He owed her a debt of gratitude, even if Cunningham was getting top dollar to let him buy into the practice. Cullen had to admit that Santa Monica was a lot more pleasant a place to open shop than some of the others he'd considered. Small towns, places hundreds of miles away from the ocean he loved, even other parts of Los Angeles County, where smog obscured the horizon and his kids would have to grow up breathing the putrid stuff. He knew that Doc Cunningham could have had his pick of hungry young doctors, yet he'd chosen Cullen Baxter. And Estelle Edwards was part of the reason why.

Cullen revved the engine of his Honda Civic, taking some of his frustration out on the machinery. It would probably be years before he'd have his Mercedes at this rate, years before he'd look like a successful young doctor instead of a struggling medical student. He put the car in reverse, screeched out of the parking space, then shifted into first and pulled out of the apartment garage. If he stepped on it, he could spend ten minutes at the Edwards house and be only a few minutes late for his first patient. The little car's tires squealed as Cullen turned into the street and headed north.

By the time he'd reached the northwest corner of town, some of the edge had worn off his anger. He loved being a doctor, helping people. And it wasn't his nature to let an early argument with his wife ruin the pleasure he took in his work. So, by the time he reached the Edwards mansion, Cullen had become a satisfied physician; the harassed husband had been left behind.

The morning had an eerie feeling as Cullen pressed the bell. The fog, typical for a June morning, gave everything a hazy quality, like an impressionist painting. Impatiently he pressed the bell a second time, and the massive oak door opened.

"Oh, Dr. Baxter. How nice to see you." It was the daughter-in-law—Stella, Pamela, Paula, that was it. "Estelle's been waiting for you," she told him.

"I'm running late, but I've got time to look in on her quickly."

"May I get you some coffee?"

"No, thanks. I haven't got an extra minute," Cullen said, sprinting for the stairs.

Estelle, wearing a fuchsia negligee and a matching satin ribbon in her improbably bright hair, was propped up in her old-fashioned four-poster bed, reading the *Hollywood Reporter. Estelle Edwards really is from another era,* Cullen thought, smiling to himself. It was easy to see why his mother had never forgotten Estelle, why few people who'd known her ever did.

"Cullen, how nice," Estelle said, folding the newspaper and turning her heavily rouged cheek toward him in expectation of a kiss. "Come to see the invalid, have you?"

"If you'll be an invalid for long, Estelle, I'll be the next pope. You're looking prettier than ever." He gave her a quick peck.

"Not if you look at my foot." She pulled the covers back

and pointed to her toes. "I've seen plums a lighter shade than these."

Baxter examined the foot. "Perfectly natural. The color will improve in a few days. Pain giving you any trouble?"

"I'm still using those pills you prescribed. I do hope you're not going to make me into an addict, Cullen." Estelle wagged her finger at him.

"You needn't worry yet, but you should start cutting back. See if you can make do with aspirin by later today or tomorrow." He pulled the bedcovers back over her foot and asked, "How's your morale? Mother asked about you the other night."

"Tell her I'm muddling through. This isn't exactly my idea of a good time, though. My daughter-in-law is deserting me too."

"Oh?"

"She's afraid my darling son is cheating on her with all those earthy Italian beauties, so she's going to Italy to check up on him."

Paula barged into the room, betraying the fact that she'd been listening outside the bedroom door. "That's not true, Estelle!"

"It *is* true, and you know it, Miss Eavesdropper. I ought to know my own son's failings." Now that she'd made the decision to hire a nurse, Estelle didn't much mind telling Paula what was what.

"Now, ladies, ladies. Let's not quarrel," Baxter chided. He'd had more than enough of petty family fights in his own home for one day. It was getting late too. "The important thing is not *why* your daughter-in-law is going, Estelle, but what you're going to do without her. Do you want me to reserve you a hospital bed? You won't be able to stay alone."

"I know. I'm going to hire a nurse to stay here with me, for a few weeks anyway."

"Maybe Dr. Baxter knows someone who would take the job," Paula said. "We can't waste time. My plane leaves on Thursday, and I intend to be on it."

Cullen furrowed his brow. "I don't know anyone right off hand. There are home nursing services, of course. I'll ask Doc Cunningham if you wish."

"That shouldn't be necessary, Cullen," Estelle said. "I found several ads in yesterday's *Times,* and I have three women coming to interview today."

"Estelle! Hi, Estelle!" a voice called from downstairs, followed by a thundering on the stairs. Faith barged into the bedroom, clutching a bunch of daisies in her hand. "Oh, excuse me. I didn't realize you had company. I didn't see anyone downstairs, so I thought I'd just come up. I—I'll come back later." She turned to leave.

"Don't be ridiculous, Faith. Get back in here. Cullen's not exactly doing a pelvic exam on me. You can come in." The girl reentered the room shyly. "Faith Sanford, this is Dr. Cullen Baxter. His mother is my old friend Gladys Baxter. I've mentioned her to you."

"Uh, yes. I remember. Nice to meet you, Dr. Baxter."

"Faith. How do you do?" Cullen picked up his bag. "Well, ladies, I've got to run along. My first patient has already been waiting for me a good five minutes. I'll never get caught up if I don't get a move on. Good to see you again, Paula. No need to show me out. Nice to meet you, Faith. Estelle, you keep your spirits up, hear? Mother will never forgive me if you don't recover in record time, and you know what's she's like when she's mad. You don't want that on your conscience."

"You're just as charming as your father was, Cullen. That wife of yours is a very lucky young woman. I hope she knows it."

"So do I, my dear." He leaned over and gently kissed the top of her head. "Now you behave yourself. No dancing until that cast comes off. Promise?"

Estelle chuckled and winked at Faith as Cullen swung out of the room and took the stairs two at a time.

Chapter 5

Gretchen Hedberg—she was beginning to think of herself as Gretchen now, not as Jasmine—squinted as the microfilm pages of the *Los Angeles Times* raced past on the screen. Her eyes ached as they tried to focus on the blur, and she had a dizzy feeling of motion sickness. But she swallowed the bile that rose momentarily in her throat and continued, determined to find anything in print about the woman with whom she had her interview appointment this afternoon.

Gretchen had been waiting on the Santa Monica Library steps before the building opened this morning—along with an assortment of street dwellers anxious to use the bathroom facilities the library had to offer. She stood apart from the others, three men and a woman. It was the woman, who stood with her earthly possessions in two shopping bags at her feet, who most repelled Gretchen. She looked about seventy and exuded a rank smell, as though she hadn't bathed in weeks. Yet Gretchen noticed that she didn't smell of liquor, as she would have expected. Dressed in a ragged sweater and a cotton housedress faded to an undistinguished gray, the woman looked mainly tired. Her eyes lacked the wild look of the total misfit. But Gretchen thought that the woman must be crazy. To believe that sheer bad luck could have led someone to this life-style was to recognize that Gretchen herself could end up like this someday. And that was unbearable.

For Gretchen the world was filled with those who had wealth and those who, like herself, were entitled to help

themselves to some of it if they were smart enough. She
could not—would not—include in her world people whom
life and luck had defeated. That was one of the reasons why
she had dropped out of nursing school. She couldn't stand
being around the sick and destitute, whom she was forced to
serve. The sick and wealthy were another matter; she could
force herself to care for them because they represented an
opportunity for easy material gain. Their infirmities became
an asset to her. Nowadays Gretchen had become able to
ignore the fact that people like the bag lady outside the library even existed. If they didn't exist, their fate could never
happen to her.

But face-to-face with this unfortunate, poverty-stricken
woman who obviously *did* exist, Gretchen felt suddenly
compelled to explain away her plight. The woman had to be
crazy, Gretchen told herself. She lived as she did simply
because she was insane. It was her own fault. Since there was
nothing crazy about Gretchen, she didn't need to worry. It
could never happen to her.

A library clerk unlocked the glass doors at exactly ten
o'clock, and the bag lady barged through first, a sack in each
hand, heading for the stairway at the rear of the building.
Gretchen looked away and asked directions to the reference
area. She made herself comfortable at one of the long oak
tables and examined the last few years of the *Los Angeles
Times* index. If the woman who had called yesterday in response to her ad, Estelle Edwards, were important in this
town, there would be some mention of her in the *Times*,
Gretchen was sure. And according to how often the woman
was mentioned and in what context, Gretchen could get a
pretty good idea of her financial status as well as the number
of her nosy friends who might be expected to be concerned
about her.

By the time Gretchen climbed the stairs to the periodicals
room, she had noted three entries for Estelle Edwards. That
was promising. At least she would have some information
before the interview. Gretchen hated interviewing "cold"
with a prospective employer. She'd made a few mistakes that
way in the past, and she couldn't afford to this time, not
with the police looking for her.

She remembered once turning down a job with an old woman in Philadelphia because she'd been unable to find any published information about her. Later Gretchen had found out that the old woman had simply believed in an axiom of the old rich: The only times a lady's name should appear in the newspaper are when she's born, when she's married, and when she dies.

Another time, in Chicago, she had run out of cash and become desperate to be settled somewhere with a likely mark. So she'd accepted a position nursing an old man who'd appeared to be well-to-do, although she'd been unable to check him out in advance. She soon learned that his apparent wealth had been all show. Shortly after she had moved into his house, most of the old man's furnishings departed in repossessors' vans, and in less than a month even her paychecks began to bounce.

This time she'd have to be more careful. Of course, she had to move quickly, to get away from hotels, where she might be tracked down too easily by an ambitious cop. Once she was hidden away in an employer's home, safely masked by her new identity, she could breathe again. She'd be safe there until she could stash away enough to find her own hiding place. But she had to make sure that she found the *right* employer.

She slowed the microfilm as the date she wanted approached on the screen and adjusted the focus. There it was. That day's Westside section of the *Times* had a half page feature on Estelle Edwards, reminding readers about her long-ago movie career and bringing them up-to-date. An old movie star. That could even be fun, Gretchen thought, although the old girl was probably a bitch, used to having everyone's undivided attention. But she'd handled that type before. A few of the right pills, and their demands completely disappeared.

There were two photos with the article, one of the former actress sitting poolside in a patio chair overlooking the Pacific. The place looked like real money. The second photo showed Estelle Edwards in a parlor type of room, peering over some old photo albums. The room was cluttered with framed photos, paintings, figurines, antiques. From the look of it Estelle Edwards was well fixed financially. She had to be to afford a place like this.

The newspaper story also detailed the history of the house: In 1938, twenty-seven-year-old actress Estelle Edwards was married to movie director Zachary Zimmerman, thirty-two, and the newlyweds moved into the house. In later years it had been the scene of some of Hollywood's legendary parties. Clark Gable had spent many an afternoon beside this very pool, Miss Edwards was quoted as saying. The house was considered a Santa Monica landmark by local historians, and she had kept it almost a shrine to the memory of her late husband. So that was the reason for the clutter and the thirties bric-a-brac, Gretchen thought.

She deposited fifteen cents and pushed the button to make a photocopy of that page of the *Times,* then folded the copy and put it in her bag. She found the other two stories about Estelle Edwards—one noting her seventieth birthday and the other an anniversary of Zachary Zimmerman's death—and made photocopies of them as well.

Gretchen rewound the microfilm and returned it to the periodicals desk, feeling elated. Maybe her luck had finally turned. She ran through her mind the facts that the old woman had told her on the phone yesterday. Her only son was out of the country, and his wife was leaving to join him in a few days. That meant no relatives nearby to check up on her. Estelle had broken her leg and would be laid up for another month or two. One month would be plenty of time to strip the house—and Estelle Edwards—if Gretchen's plans proceeded as she expected. Edwards lived alone in the house, and she needed someone who could do more than nursing duties, someone who would cook, shop, help with the details of her daily life. Most private-duty nurses would balk at a request to double as a cook or a maid in addition to nursing, but the situation was precisely what Gretchen wanted. It meant that there would be no interfering servants to deal with. Her first fear had been that Estelle Edwards's living without a staff of servants might mean that she was broke, but it certainly didn't look like it, to judge from those newspaper photos. She was probably just an eccentric old woman who wanted her privacy, someone who didn't want servants invading the virtual museum she'd created in her husband's memory. All the better for Gretchen.

As she left the library, she noticed the bag lady sitting on the front steps, her bags beside her. She was reading a John Irving novel. Gretchen averted her eyes and focused her concentration on her interview appointment.

She walked down Santa Monica Boulevard to Ocean Avenue and then south toward her hotel. The haze had burned off, and the sun shone on the blue Pacific beyond the palisades. With the sun warm on her back, she felt good. Everything was working well for her. She knew she would get that job with Estelle Edwards this afternoon. At the interview she would be the walking, breathing answer to every one of Estelle's prayers.

By the end of the week she would be running that household. Without interference from anyone.

And by the end of another week she'd be running Estelle Edwards.

Chapter 6

In St. Louis Stan Greenwood was spending his morning in a library too. It was starting to feel like a habit with him. Each morning for the past week he'd painstakingly examined the major newspapers from each of the cities where he thought Jasmine Kennedy might have gone. He'd managed to subdue his anger for the moment; he couldn't afford to let it loose yet. He'd have to channel it into energy he would use to find her.

She'd go west, he figured. She'd already hit too many cities in the East and Midwest, and she wasn't one to backtrack. Too much chance of being recognized by someone from her past, she'd once told him. He flipped to the back pages of the *Denver Post* and ran his finger down the column headed "Jobs Wanted—Nurses." There were three ads in yesterday's paper, none of them sounding like one that Jasmine would write, but Stan noted the phone numbers anyway.

"Here're the papers from San Francisco and L.A. They just came in." A young library clerk smiled and handed them to Stan. He'd seen her here each morning and knew that she was interested in him. He couldn't blame her; he was a pretty good-looking guy. Not too tall, but plenty of muscles. The women liked that. The girl looked about twenty-two, slender, with tawny hair falling around her shoulders and oversize eyeglasses. She was cute, probably would be fun in bed. Stan was sure he could show her a good time, but time was exactly what he didn't have to waste just now. Not until he settled his score with Jasmine.

The clerk seemed reluctant to move back to her counter. "What're you doing? Looking for a job?" she asked.

"Uh, yeah." Stan turned his back on her and buried his head in the newspaper.

Undeterred, she leaned over his shoulder and watched what he was doing for a moment, breathing gently down his neck. Her breath smelled faintly of spearmint. "You a male nurse or something?"

Stan bristled and closed the pages. What he didn't need right now was this girl getting too nosy. He turned to her and pasted a smile on his face. "I just got out of prison, miss. It's rough. I'll take any kind of work I can get." Shock registered on the clerk's face as she quickly retreated to the periodicals counter. Stan chuckled with satisfaction. That prison routine hit different women in different ways. Some were turned on by a man who'd been behind bars, thought it made him macho or something. Others ran like scared rabbits. He'd been sure that the library clerk would be one of the rabbits, and he was right. He put a lot of stock in his ability to read people.

It wasn't really true that he'd just gotten out of prison. He'd actually been out for going on three years now. But if he didn't find Jasmine soon—and the money that rightfully was half his—he just might end up back there again. Not that he had any intention of going peacefully.

There was a limit to how long Stan dared stay in St. Louis. Sooner or later someone would connect Jane Burden, the woman wanted for the murder of Ellen Pickett, with Jasmine Kennedy and ultimately with him. And he didn't want to be around when it happened. Truth was he'd have moved on by now if Jasmine hadn't cleaned him out. Greedy bitch. Now he had to be careful with his last few dollars. He'd need it to follow her, once he found out where she'd gone.

Jasmine had actually drugged him as if he were one of her old fogy patients! By the time he woke up she was gone, and so was everything else: the money from her St. Louis checking account, her car, her clothes, and God knew what more. Stan never had found out where she'd stored her loot. She probably had at least one storage locker rented in every city she'd worked, figuring that she'd wait until the heat was off, then send for the stuff. She was a smooth operator, he had to give her that. A very smart and gutsy girl. His mistake was in trusting her as much as he had. That's what happened when you fell for a broad.

He'd gone through her things, of course, anything she'd left behind at his place while she nursed old Mrs. Pickett. He sometimes wondered if Jasmine knew he'd done that. He'd learned some things about her that way. He'd found her stash of stolen driver's licenses, blank nursing school diplomas, the forged stationery that she used to write reference letters for herself. But she hadn't left any clues to where she'd hidden the stuff she'd taken from the victims she'd cleaned out before he met her. She hadn't trusted him enough to leave that kind of information around his apartment. He should have been as distrustful of her.

There was a time Stan would have settled for half of what Jasmine had taken off Mrs. Pickett, although they never did find the old broad's real stash. But now he felt different. Now he felt entitled to at least half of everything Jasmine had. He'd known her only since she'd been in St. Louis, but he was owed something for what she'd put him through, wasn't he? When he found her—and he wouldn't even consider the possibility that he wouldn't, sooner or later—he might just relieve her of all of it. Teach her a lesson. And if she didn't cooperate, if she didn't hand it over, he just might relieve her of more than her money. He made a fist and pictured it smashing Jasmine's self-satisfied smile. Wham! He'd show her.

But not yet. Stan pulled in a deep breath and exhaled slowly. For now he had to keep his temper under control. It had plagued him all his life. Got him in a hell of a lot of fights, woman trouble, lost him jobs. Got him that prison sentence for breaking some guy's jaw in a barroom brawl. It had killed Mrs. Pickett. There were times that Stan Greenwood's temper seemed like a thing apart from Stan himself. It was as though he would wake up afterward and be shocked to see what his temper had done. But since the murder he'd been doing pretty well. He had to. He couldn't afford to call any attention to himself by flying off the handle.

Stan closed the *Post* and opened the *San Francisco Examiner.* Before he left the library, he would check the classified ads from yesterday's newspapers in ten western cities. Then he'd go home and dial the phone numbers, waiting for Jasmine to answer one of the calls. If he could just find out what city she'd gone to, he'd find her somehow. Getting the right city would be ninety percent of the battle.

Oh, he knew he was gambling that she would use her old MO. And that she would go west instead of, say, to Florida. But he'd known the woman intimately for the past seven months, and he figured he had a pretty good notion of how she thought. He had to trust his hunches. What else did he have?

He made some notes from the *Examiner,* closed it, and set it on the stack of papers he'd already read. Three more papers to go for today.

He reached for the *Los Angeles Times.*

Chapter 7

Estelle felt discouraged, but at least she had one applicant left. And, she told herself, if her last potential nurse-companion didn't look any better than the first two, she could always use a nursing service temporarily, just until she found someone less expensive. The first woman she'd interviewed, one Maria Chavez, had seemed pleasant and eager to please, but she had command of no more than thirty words of English. When Estelle needed to engage in a vigorous pantomime to explain to Mrs. Chavez how she had broken her leg, she realized that this would never work, no matter how reasonable a salary the woman asked. How would she manage to pantomime the preparation of her favorite meal or procedures for locating her son in Italy if there were an emergency? Just thinking of the possible difficulties exhausted her.

The second applicant, on the other hand, had spoken beautiful English. Constance Caulfield had informed Estelle —in perfect syntax—that she was unaccustomed to working in a house without servants and had no intention of doing so now. Or ever. Moreover, Miss Caulfield had declared that she would require Sundays and Mondays off, a paid week's vacation after two months of service, and a strictly vegetarian diet prepared by a competent cook. Estelle had informed Miss Caulfield that she would continue searching for the nurse-companion of her dreams.

But Estelle's spirits lifted as Paula ushered the third of the job seekers into her bedroom. This one was relatively young, in her mid-twenties, Estelle guessed, and she wore a white nurse's uniform with white stockings and shoes. Perhaps her uniform indicated that she knew her place. Constance Caulfield had been dressed in a tailored suit and a silk blouse, and she seemed to be under the impression that she was to be the superior and Estelle the subordinate. Estelle hoped that this latest young woman's attire was a positive sign. She introduced herself and invited the young woman to sit down.

"How do you do, Miss Edwards? I'm Gretchen Hedberg." Gretchen surveyed her surroundings. The bedroom, like the other parts of the house that she had seen so far, was cluttered with an almost overwhelming array of keepsakes. Miss Edwards was somewhat overwhelming, too, small as she was; she looked like a miniature old doll, dressed up in a garish negligee that must have dated back to the 1930s. Screaming pink, the garment even had ostrich feathers around its plunging neckline; its vibrant color clashed with the bedridden woman's dyed red hair. And Gretchen noticed that Estelle Edwards had managed to apply an excessive amount of makeup, despite her infirmity. This was going to be an experience. She sat down, swallowing the smile that threatened to break out.

"I'm so glad you could come this afternoon," Estelle said graciously, as though she were hosting a tea party. She outlined the requirements of the job, carefully watching the young woman's face as she told her about the many varied duties that would be required of her if she took the job—the usual nursing care of an invalid plus cooking, shopping, occasional secretarial duties, and light cleaning. "I'd expect you to be here in the house most of the time in case I needed you. I can't even get out of this damned bed, you know. But I wouldn't expect miracles on the rest of it."

"That's perfectly acceptable to me," Gretchen said.

"You wouldn't mind that there are no servants then?"

Gretchen sensed a slight suspiciousness from the old woman. Obviously she'd been prepared for a battle about the lack of servants. "No, I really don't mind, although I admit I'm not the world's most energetic housekeeper." The way dust had collected here, Gretchen thought, no one would notice the difference if she never lifted a duster. "I *am* an excellent cook, however," she added. "I love to cook. To tell you the truth, Miss Edwards, my main objective right now is to find a position that allows me some privacy and quiet in my off-duty hours. I'm writing my thesis for my master's degree. I want to teach nursing someday." She warmed to her story as she noticed Estelle's impressed look. "I just can't seem to find the time and energy to finish it when I'm working in a hospital. Or in a household with too many distractions. This job sounds ideal to me. Provided that I could have a few hours to myself each day to finish my project."

"You could do that here in the house?"

"Of course. All I need is some solitude and time for my writing. With no staff to supervise and a patient as mentally alert as you are, I don't think we'd have any problems."

Estelle had to admit that this girl seemed perfect. Maybe too perfect. But she dismissed her glimmer of doubt. Perhaps fate was finally being kind to her—making up in part for letting her fall off that chair—by sending someone seemingly ideal to help her through the next couple of months. But they hadn't discussed salary yet. Perhaps Gretchen Hedberg would prove to be less perfect when she learned what this job paid. "I must tell you that I can't afford to pay top wages," Estelle explained. "That's why I'm looking for someone through the newspaper ads instead of calling a service."

The truth is, you're cheap, Gretchen thought. But she kept her thoughts off her face. The woman who had shown her upstairs had warned her that her mother-in-law was difficult, but Gretchen could put up with a difficult personality for the kind of money she could see around here. The only reason she could see that there were no servants in a house like this was that Estelle Edwards was a miser. Well, all the better for Gretchen. If the old woman had kept her money all these years, it was only a matter of time until Gretchen found it. But first she had to get the job and send the daughter-in-law off to Italy on schedule. "If I have a quiet place to finish my school project, I can work for a reasonable salary," she replied.

Estelle named a figure that Gretchen knew was about half of what an agency in this town would charge for a nurse-companion. The old woman certainly *was* cheap. But surely she couldn't be broke, not with what Gretchen saw around her. The house was huge, with wall-to-wall antiques. She had noticed thousands of dollars' worth of period pieces just in the time it took to walk upstairs to the bedroom. The salary was really beside the point; Gretchen's eventual take from this job would be the "fringe benefits." But she could see that this situation was touchy; she dared not seem too willing to work for too little, or she would certainly increase the slight suspicion she'd sensed earlier. Yet demanding too much more would mean that she wouldn't get the job. "Does that include my room and board?" she asked, testing the waters.

"Of course. You'd have a lovely room with a view. A perfect atmosphere to write your thesis."

Gretchen could see that Estelle was beginning to sell the job to her. A good sign. "*That* part does sound perfect," she said, hesitating slightly. "You say the job would last about two months?"

"Dr. Baxter says that I'll be out of this monstrosity by then," Estelle replied, tapping her cast lightly. "If I'm not, I guess I'll just have to sue him." She laughed and added, "But you could stay on for a little bit longer, until you finish your thesis, if you wanted to. Once I'm up and about, I wouldn't be able to continue paying your salary, of course, but I wouldn't put you out on the street until you'd found something else."

Gretchen smiled. She sensed now that Estelle wanted to hire her. It was time to ram home her advantage. "I don't know. I had hoped to earn a bit more. My last job paid much better, even though salaries are a little lower in the Midwest. . . ." She paused and sized up her opponent. Estelle was beginning to retreat. Gretchen had pushed her far enough. "But of course," she added, "that job required supervising thirteen servants in addition to my nursing duties. And I didn't have a minute to myself—"

"I'm not a demanding woman, Miss Hedberg. I'm perfectly willing to allow you the time you need. Just so you take care of me adequately."

I'll take care of you all right, Gretchen thought. But she smiled as though she were convincing herself to do something that she knew was not in her best interests. "I'm certain that I could earn a higher salary, Miss Edwards, but there's something about this job . . . something about this house and, of course, you. The situation seems ideal for me in some ways. I guess I don't really need much money as long as I have a room to call my own and my meals. And I do want to finish that degree. . . . Well, why not? Why *shouldn't* I take a chance?" She smiled in acceptance. "I think we'll get along just fine."

"I assume you have references that I can call?"

Gretchen was prepared for that question. "I have better than that. I've brought letters of reference with me." She opened her oversize handbag, took out two forged letters, and handed them to Estelle.

Estelle read them quickly. "Mrs. Angeline Russell of Kansas City. She was your last employer?"

"Yes. Just before I decided to come to California and finish the thesis I'd started a couple of years ago. Mrs. Russell —she's one of *the* Russells of Kansas City, you know. Department store heiress. She was suffering from high blood pressure, and her doctor told her she was asking for a stroke if she didn't lower it. We got her blood pressure down. A new diet, massage, learning to relax. By the time I left her she was planning a trip to Europe."

"How nice for her. Can she be reached by telephone?"

So the old girl is suspicious, Gretchen thought. "She'll be back from her trip in another couple of weeks, I think. You could talk to her then."

"Oh, dear. I need someone to start right away." The letter from Mrs. Russell raved about Gretchen Hedberg, but Estelle knew that often employers wrote such letters just to make firing employees easier on their own consciences. She'd done it herself. "How about this other one—Geoffrey Parkinson of St. Louis?"

"Poor, dear Mr. Parkinson." Gretchen assumed a grief-stricken expression. "He was terminal, I'm afraid. He died not long after I left him. He had to go to a nursing home, poor man." Gretchen managed to bring tears to her eyes at the thought of the fictitious Mr. Parkinson's demise. "It got to the point where we just couldn't care for him at home anymore, although it broke my heart to see him have to go live with strangers. He was such a kind and thoughtful man; he made sure I had a top-notch reference before he went into the home. He was really more like a father to me than a patient. Mr. Parkinson even remembered me in his will with a little cash. I used it to move out here." She wiped her eyes, carefully judging the effect she was having. "I am sorry to be so sentimental, Miss Edwards. It's probably my greatest fault. In this line of work, you can't afford to begin feeling like part of the family, but I'm afraid I often do. That's one of the reasons why I want to become a teacher. I don't think I can stand too many more years of becoming involved with my patients and then having to move on. The ones who can't be cured are particularly— But I'm talking too much, aren't I?"

"Not at all. I can understand what you're saying, my dear. It must be very difficult to care for someone who is dying. I couldn't do it myself."

"Well, Miss Edwards, caring for you, knowing that you'll be up and around again in only a matter of weeks, will be an enjoyable change for me. Anything else you want to know? My nursing school perhaps? Here, I've brought a copy of my diploma from St. Lucia's. That's in Minnesota. It's an excellent school. Perhaps you've heard of it?" She handed one of her phony diplomas, recently made out in the name of Gretchen Hedberg, to the bedridden woman.

Everything looked legitimate to Estelle. She wished she could call those references, but they certainly did appear to be all right. And they could hardly be more glowing about Gretchen Hedberg's professional and personal attributes. Certainly there was nothing inherently suspicious in Geoffrey Parkinson's having died and Angeline Russell's having gone to Europe. Still, she did have a small feeling of apprehension. . . . Maybe she was just getting old or feeling frightened about obligating herself to paying a salary, no matter how reasonable it was. And she hadn't had anyone else living in the house, with the exception of Paula's current stay, in years. Estelle didn't want anyone living here now, but it had to be. Still, one couldn't be too careful. . . .

"Surely there must be *one* of your former employers I could contact," she said. "I suppose I'm being silly, but I'd feel so much better. . . ."

Estelle's hesitation made Gretchen a bit nervous, but so far, she felt, it was nothing she couldn't handle. Allaying the old woman's suspicions would require only a small risk. "Mr. Parkinson's niece might be able to talk with you," she said.

"That would be fine," Estelle replied, feeling relieved.

"I'd have suggested her sooner, but she travels on her job, and sometimes it's not easy to reach her. Let me write down her phone number for you." Gretchen pulled a piece of paper from her bag and jotted down a St. Louis phone number. "Her name is Miss Kennedy."

Estelle took the phone number. "Assuming that I can reach this Miss Kennedy, and, of course, that she backs up her uncle's enthusiasm, when would you be able to move in, Miss Hedberg?"

"If it would help, I could come tomorrow. I know you're in a bind with your daughter-in-law's leaving. Let's say I'll check out of my hotel and be here by midmorning. That way I'll be able to get my things settled in and still have plenty of time to cook your dinner." She smiled winningly. "Do you like chicken Kiev? How about a chocolate soufflé for dessert? They're my specialties. I make a mean beef Stroganoff too."

"Marvelous." Estelle clapped her hands in delight. How wonderful it was going to be to eat good food again. "I'm certain that this is going to work out perfectly for both of us, Miss Hedberg. I'll ring you at your hotel as soon as I've reached Miss Kennedy."

"Please, call me Gretchen. I'd like to think that we're going to be friends."

"I'm sure we are, Gretchen. You may call me Estelle. I'll have my daughter-in-law show you around the house when you arrive. Then she can leave to do her packing and catch her flight to Rome. She'll be delighted that this has worked out so well. May I keep this until tomorrow?" she asked, indicating Mr. Parkinson's letter.

"Of course. Don't worry about reaching Miss Kennedy.

I'm certain she'll call you back promptly if she's not in."
You'll never know just how certain I am, Gretchen thought as
she rose and extended her hand, shook Estelle's tiny one,
and turned to leave. "Don't bother your daughter-in-law,
Estelle. I can find my way out. I'll go back to my hotel and
wait to hear from you."

Gretchen smiled to herself, visually surveying the house
from the staircase as she left. There was a silver service on
the dining room buffet that should be worth close to $2,000.
An Andrew Wyeth original hung in the entryway. That
would bring a good price, although paintings were risky.
Too easily identifiable. She saw an Oriental rug, a solid jade
chess set, a Ming vase. . . . There was more here than
she'd ever dreamed of, and if Gretchen had sized up Estelle
correctly, there would be plenty of cash stashed away somewhere in the house as well.

The old woman herself was perfect too. Gretchen couldn't
have custom-ordered a more ideal employer. Estelle Edwards was tiny—probably under 100 pounds. No problem
drugging her if need be; Gretchen would have none of the
dosage problems she'd had with 250 pound Oscar Peterson
in Milwaukee three years ago. Estelle had no relatives
nearby; it was a real piece of luck that her son and his wife
would be halfway around the world. And obviously she had
no friends who cared enough to move in and take care of
her. The old cheapskate was too tight to have servants living
in. No, Gretchen could not have chosen a better employer.
She congratulated herself on her luck as she pulled the front
door closed behind her. In just twenty-four hours she would
be living here, safely hidden from the police—and from Stan
Greenwood. And in not much longer than that she'd be
adding Estelle Edwards's fortune to her own.

As Gretchen started her car and headed back to her hotel,
Estelle placed a call to St. Louis.

"Five-five-five-two-eight-one-zero," a female voice answered.

"Miss Kennedy, please."

"This is her service. May I have your name and number,
please? She'll return your call."

"Is she out of town?"

"I'm sorry, I couldn't say," the officious voice replied.

Disappointed, Estelle left her name and instructions for Miss Kennedy to return her call as soon as possible, collect.

When she reached her hotel, Gretchen Hedberg kicked off her shoes, flopped onto the bed, holding the telephone, and dialed the St. Louis number.

"Five-five-five-two-eight-one-zero."

"This is Jasmine Kennedy. Any messages for me?"

The expected instruction to call Estelle Edwards was the only one. She hung up, wadded a corner of the bedspread over the telephone mouthpiece, and dialed Estelle's number. She smiled as she gave Gretchen Hedberg yet another glowing recommendation.

After speaking with Miss Kennedy and, a few minutes later, with Gretchen Hedberg, Estelle was feeling particularly self-congratulatory. Now that she'd hired an obviously excellent nurse-companion and had resigned herself to paying the cost somehow, she was beginning to think that it might be pleasant to have a live-in servant again. She told Paula that she hoped Gretchen was as good a cook as she claimed to be. "It would be heavenly to have a chocolate soufflé for dessert tomorrow night and not have to bake it myself, wouldn't it?" If Estelle's comment was partially a barb at her daughter-in-law's efforts in the kitchen over the past few days, Paula was oblivious of it. "I tell you, Paula," she went on, "this nurse may be the answer to a prayer."

"I'm happy for you, Estelle."

For once Paula did seem genuinely happy for her mother-in-law. It was probably just that Paula wanted to leave, and now she could do it guilt-free, Estelle told herself, but she was in a magnanimous mood. She no longer begrudged Paula her freedom. Feeling as smug as she did, she was willing to bury the hatchet. "You know, Paula," Estelle confided, "I have to admit that I feel pretty damned good about myself right now. It's still pretty hard to get Estelle Edwards down, seventy-three years old or not, isn't it? You just tell that son of mine that his mother's not through fighting yet. *I'm* not giving up. I may break my leg and end up bedridden and alone, but do I let that defeat me? Not likely!" She warmed to her bragging. "Estelle Edwards not only figures out a way to live with it but finds a nurse who can cook, who has wonderful references, who doesn't charge too much money, *and* who can move in tomorrow. Not bad! How about a little glass of sherry to celebrate?"

Paula brought a tray with two hand-etched glasses and a matching decanter filled with sherry. She poured two inches of the liquid into each glass, handed one to Estelle, and raised her own.

"Let me propose a toast," Estelle said. "Here's to a safe trip for you," she said, remembering her manners belatedly. Then, before she drank, she added, "Here's hoping I'm in for a speedy and pleasant recovery. Here's to my good luck in finding my new nurse-companion. And here's to Gretchen Hedberg—a nurse who's practically too good to be true."

Chapter 8

Gretchen smiled to herself as she packed the clothes she would bring with her to her new home. She had caught a big fish this time, and she was pleased with herself. Estelle Edwards had swallowed her bait, hook and all. By this time tomorrow Gretchen Hedberg would be firmly entrenched in the old mansion overlooking Santa Monica Bay.

She savored that exhilarating sense of excitement and danger that always preceded a new job. She wanted the money, the valuables, the art objects that a new mark would bring her. But over the years this heady feeling of challenge had become almost as important to her as the material things. It was during the times when she was embarking on a new adventure like this that she felt most alive, and she loved it. Sometimes she wondered if she'd ever be able to give it up, even after she'd reached her financial goals. The part of her that longed to settle down and live a normal life, to marry and have children, was at war with the part of her that experienced an almost sexual euphoria through living dangerously. But Gretchen would not worry about that now. She'd deal with breaking her addiction to the thrill of danger when she had to. For now she'd simply relish it.

She folded her green wool sweater, smoothing it carefully, and placed it on top of the pile of clothing in the suitcase. She added another sweater and a multicolored striped shirt, then lowered the lid and latched it. There. She had a few things she needed to wash at the Laundromat, and she'd pack them tomorrow morning. If she stayed on schedule, she easily could be checked out of the hotel by midmorning.

With just a few loose ends left to tie up, her trail soon would be cold. She would be safe from St. Louis, from Stan, from her past. Gretchen reached for the telephone, dialed the *Times,* and canceled her ad—she wouldn't need it anymore. She instructed the *Times* clerk to bill her at Estelle Edwards's street and number. She would leave no forwarding address with the hotel.

Gretchen flopped onto the bed, stretched for a moment, then reached for the Yellow Pages. She turned to the heading for "Self-Storage Facilities" and ran her finger down the listings. There were three in Santa Monica. She located them on her map and chose one within easy distance of the Edwards house. The smallest locker available, 800 cubic feet, would be large enough to store the valuables Gretchen planned to remove from the Edwards house. After all, she wasn't planning to take the grand piano. Small but valuable items that would fit in her suitcases—sterling silverware, jewelry, works of art, cash, and securities—were her style. Things that wouldn't be missed immediately. Things that she could carry out of the house without neighbors' noticing and becoming suspicious. She knew from past experience that it didn't pay to be too greedy, no matter how tempting some of the larger items might be.

Gretchen jotted down the address of the storage facility on a loose piece of paper and stuffed it into the pocket of her jeans. Then she swung her legs off the bed, rose, and began loading a cardboard box with items to keep in the storage locker. A coat too warm for Santa Monica, her few books, an old photo album, her stash of false identifications and references, her address files, some items with the name Jasmine Kennedy on them. She never took more than a minimum of possessions with her to a new client's house. No sense in inviting curiosity—or discovery—by leaving evidence around. And she always had to be ready for a quick departure. She prided herself on being well prepared for anything.

She added her bankbooks and a sheaf of old letters to the box, then folded down the lid. She surveyed the compact motel room. Her toilet items, along with her nightgown, remained in the bathroom; she'd need them tonight. A fresh nurse's uniform hung on the closet door above her sturdy white shoes, ready for her to wear tomorrow morning. In a corner, ready for the Laundromat, was a pillowcase stuffed with soiled clothing. Everything else was packed and ready to go.

She grabbed her shoulder bag, then lifted the box and headed out the door. The old orange Volkswagen she'd bought for cash at a used car lot last week was parked in the lot below the balcony, not far from the room. A strong young woman, accustomed to lifting and turning patients who weighed more than she did, Gretchen wouldn't need a bellman's help to load the car.

She pulled the door closed behind her and carefully maneuvered the bulky box down the outdoor staircase. She hummed softly and happily to herself as she jockeyed the box into position beside the jack and the nearly bald spare tire in the trunk of the Volks.

As she drove away from her motel room, Gretchen's song was lost among the traffic noises, the blare of radios in the beach parking lot, and the sharp calls of the sea gulls overhead.

Chapter 9

Stan Greenwood popped the cap off his third bottle of Budweiser and downed half of it in a single swallow. He positioned himself in front of the lone window fan and futilely tried to cool off. Damn, it was hot for June. Seven o'clock and he still couldn't get cool. It was that oppressive humidity that built up before a thunderstorm. He felt sweat trickle from his armpits as he took another swig of the cold beer.

He told himself that even his physical discomfort was that bitch's fault. With the money Jasmine had taken with her, he could have bought an air conditioner. The apartment was filthy too; it had been her job to clean it, and in the last week it had become a point of honor with Stan not to do it himself. Dust balls scurried around the marred hardwood floor, propelled by the fan's artificial wind. Throughout the small apartment, drawers were pulled out and their contents scattered, evidence of Stan's compulsive searches for anything Jasmine might have left behind, for any clue to where she had gone. Wastebaskets overflowed with wadded newspapers, the remains of carry-out dinners, and empty beer bottles. The place was beginning to stink, the odor of fermenting garbage gradually overpowering the stench of beer and sweat. But Stan figured he wouldn't be living here much longer. He didn't have another month's rent, and he was sure he'd find Jasmine soon. The landlord could clean the dump after Stan had split.

He pulled his T-shirt off over his head with one hand and tossed it onto the floor. He raised his arms above his head and let the fan dry his armpits, one at a time. Then he finished off the beer and tossed the bottle savagely toward a corner wastebasket. It hit with a sound of shattering glass.

"Back to work," he muttered to himself. He slouched sideways in an overstuffed brown velvet chair, opened his notebook, and pulled the telephone into his lap. He jabbed at its buttons, dialing phone numbers in Denver, San Francisco, Las Vegas, and Phoenix.

"Hello. I'm calling about your newspaper ad," he said to each woman who answered. Impatiently he carried on each conversation just long enough to determine whether or not Jasmine Kennedy's voice was on the other end. He had to get lucky soon. He had to find her before the cops found him and before he ran out of money. Stan was down to less than a hundred bucks in cash. He still had his credit card, but he'd been using that to buy takeout food and beer and gas for his car. And he'd need the card for a plane ticket when he found out where Jasmine had gone. He couldn't hold out much longer.

He hated living so close to the edge. He hated having to be so careful about everything he did, too. In the past, when he'd been broke, he'd just lifted a wallet or managed a simple break-in. But now he didn't dare risk being picked up by the cops for any reason. Not with a murder rap hanging over his head. He even drove more carefully than before. The police might not have his name yet, but he'd bet they had his physical description from Ellen Pickett's relatives and his fingerprints from her house. Stan knew he had to get the hell out of St. Louis before they closed in on him. But before he did, he had to find Jasmine.

He began to dial the Los Angeles numbers from yesterday's ads. The first call rang. *"Buenos dias,"* a woman's voice answered.

"I'm calling about the ad in the *Times,"* Stan said.

The voice replied in a heavy Spanish accent, "For a nurse, yes. I am a good nurse, I bring very good references—"

Stan hung up and dialed the second number. It rang three times. "Seacrest Lodge," a male voice replied.

"Room thirty-six," Stan said, reading from his notes.

"One moment, please."

There was a pause, then another series of rings. After six or seven the male voice came back on the line. "Sorry, sir, Miss Hedberg seems to be out at the moment. Would you like to leave a message?"

"No. No, thanks. I'll call again." Hedberg. Hedberg. Why did that name sound familiar? Could it have been on one of the stolen drivers' licenses Stan had found among Jasmine's things months ago? He cursed himself for not having copied her false credentials. He cursed himself for ever having trusted that deceiving broad.

It was just too goddamned hot in this reeking pigsty, Stan told himself. Outside, the sun was starting to fall behind the hills. Maybe he could cool off if he went out for dinner now. He'd finish the calls later. Stan dried his broad chest with a bathroom towel and pulled his T-shirt back over his head. He double-checked his wallet for the credit card and headed for the House of Wong. He'd had Mexican food last night, Italian the night before. Tonight he felt like Chinese.

It was after ten by the time Stan returned to the apartment. It was a few degrees cooler inside as well as outside, and Stan's mood had improved in the air-conditioned restaurant. He'd also had three more beers to wash down his sweet and sour chicken, and he was staggering slightly.

But he didn't have to be cold sober to punch the telephone buttons. He looked at his watch. It was two hours earlier on the coast, just after eight. Not too late to call the rest of the ads.

He punched in a 1, then 213, then rechecked the remainder of the phone number from the ad, and pushed the appropriate buttons. "Seacrest Lodge."

"Room thirty-six."

"One moment, please."

This time a woman's voice answered the second set of rings. "Hello. Gretchen Hedberg speaking."

The short hairs on the back of Stan's neck stood on end. Drunk or sober, he knew that voice. He dared not reply; she might know his voice as well as he knew hers.

"Hello," Jasmine Kennedy said a second time. "Who is this?"

Stan slowly replaced the receiver. He'd found her. In a hotel—another piece of luck. That made it even easier to locate her. He redialed the Seacrest Lodge, posing as a tourist seeking a room. The accommodating desk clerk supplied the hotel's address and directions from the Los Angeles airport. Now it was simply a matter of reaching L.A. before Jasmine moved on.

Stan phoned for a reservation on the next direct flight to LAX; a nonstop DC-10 was scheduled for 8:00 tomorrow morning. Gaining two hours by traveling west, he'd land in L.A. shortly after 9:00 A.M. He figured a couple of hours to pick up his luggage, rent a car, and drive to the Seacrest Lodge in Santa Monica. He could be there before noon, easy. If she were there tonight, she'd be there tomorrow. She had to be. And if she were out, Stan would wait until she came back. Getting even with Jasmine Kennedy would be worth waiting for.

He took the last beer from the refrigerator and popped off the cap. This called for a celebration.

Chapter 10

The sun was sinking into the Pacific by the time Dr. Cullen Baxter pulled into the underground garage of his Santa Monica apartment complex. His last patient had been a fifteen-year-old girl with an advanced case of acne and a mother who constantly harped at her about eating too much chocolate. Cullen had spent an hour with the girl and her mother, explaining that chocolate had nothing to do with acne. And neither did potato chips or sexual fantasies. Why so many parents blamed their children for their physical ailments never failed to baffle him.

He turned the steering wheel sharply, then carefully maneuvered the Honda into the parking slot numbered 10. Mrs. Wilson's Cadillac in slot 11 was usurping a portion of Cullen's space as usual. He'd spoken to her about it a dozen times or more, but she still parked as though she were entitled to the entire garage. At least he had one reason to be grateful he drove a tiny car.

He grabbed his black bag and bolted up the stairs. As he turned the key in the apartment door, his older daughter, Margaret, dropped the crayon she'd been using onto the rug and dashed toward him. "Daddy!" she shrieked with a two-year-old's enthusiasm.

He put down his bag, scooped her up in one arm, and planted a kiss on her plump cheek. "Is Daddy ever happy to see you, muffin. I'm glad you're still up." He nuzzled her neck until she broke into a fit of giggles. Her hair was damp, and she smelled faintly of baby shampoo. Cullen glanced at the coffee table, where Meggie had been coloring in a Sesame Street coloring book.

"I did Big Bird, Daddy," she announced proudly. "See?"

The yellow wax markings extended beyond Big Bird, beyond the page, and onto the shiny finish of the oak table. "You did Big Bird all right, sweetheart. Where's Mommy?"

"Baffroom. She's giving Jessie a baff."

"Bath, muffin. *T-H,* not *F.* You can say it. Bath."

"Bafth."

"Close. Come on, let's go say hi to Mommy and Jessica."

Jessica, who had not yet taken her first steps, was engaged in trying to crawl off the dressing table before her mother could encase her feet in pajamas. "God help me when you learn to walk, kid," Laura muttered. "Hold still, Jessie!" Jessie increased her struggles, grinning as though this were a game. Laura shoved a strand of her tawny hair out of her eyes with one hand, took a firm hold of the baby's ankles, and thrust her feet into the pajama legs. She pulled the elastic waistband over the bulky diapers while Jessie screeched in protest.

Cullen entered the small, steamy room, Margaret riding on his hip. "Hey, what's going on here? Is Mommy sticking pins in you, punkin?" he asked Jessica.

"Just like always." Laura's voice dripped sarcasm.

"Come on, come to Daddy," Cullen said, scooping the baby up with his free hand. With a daughter on each hip he leaned over and pecked Laura on the cheek, noting that she was wearing her most harassed expression. He decided not to call her attention to Meggie's coffee table artwork. "Rough day, sweetheart?"

"I'm only ready to boil both of them in oil. Other than that, no problem."

"It can't be that bad."

"You try being cooped up with them all day. I'm starting to feel like a two-year-old myself."

Experience told Cullen to let that pass. "I'll put them to bed," he offered. "You break open the wine and put some romantic music on the stereo. You want to feel adult, I'll give you adult."

"Promises, promises," Laura said, but Cullen noticed that she was almost smiling.

He tucked the babies into their beds—Margaret into her "grown-up" youth bed and Jessica into her crib a few feet away—and kissed them both. He really was crazy about his girls, but he wished they weren't always at the center of some dispute between him and Laura. He knew that wasn't good for any of them, yet he didn't know how to change things.

" 'Night, girls," he said softly, closing their door behind him.

" 'Night, Daddy," Margaret called. "I love you."

"I love you, too, Meggie. Sleep tight."

Cullen changed into jeans and a sport shirt. Then he put away Meggie's coloring book and crayons and started Neil Diamond's *Jonathan Livingston Seagull* album on the stereo. Laura was puttering with something in the kitchen. "What's for dinner, hon?"

"Shoe leather."

"Same as last night, huh?"

"I'm not kidding. Look at this roast. It's ruined." Laura's voice sounded close to tears. "Damn. If you'd come home on time like a normal husband, I might know when to plan dinner."

Here we go again, Cullen thought, determined that he wouldn't participate in another fight with her. He took the carving knife from Laura and cut four slices of beef from the shrunken roast. "It's just a little well done. Some barbecue sauce on top, and we'll never know the difference."

"Sure."

"Come on, Laura. Lighten up. It's not that serious."

"Maybe to you it isn't."

The telephone rang. *Saved by the bell,* Cullen thought. Laura went into the living room to answer it while Cullen rummaged in the refrigerator for the barbecue sauce. When his wife reentered the kitchen, her mouth was set in a firm line.

"It's for you, Doctor."

Paula Zimmerman was on the line. "I'm sorry to bother you at home, Cullen," she said in her quiet yet determined way. "Estelle insisted that I call and ask you to stop by and see her tomorrow."

"Is it an emergency? I'm booked solid from eight o'clock on, Paula."

"It's not an emergency, but I'm leaving for Italy tomorrow. We've hired a nurse who will live in. Estelle wants to make sure she's healing normally before I leave the country. I think she wants your approval of the nurse before I leave too. It'll only take a few minutes."

"I'd like to, Paula, but I don't see how—"

"Maybe on your way to the office? Estelle wakes early, and I could call the nurse and see if she can be here by then."

With the mood Laura was in tonight, Cullen knew that leaving earlier than usual in the morning wasn't going to go over at all well. If he could just take the girls off her hands at breakfast . . . "Not in the morning, Paula. I simply can't tomorrow."

"I don't like having to remind you, Cullen, but Estelle has been very good to you. Without her help—"

Cullen felt his stomach knot. "All right, Paula. I'll manage somehow. Tell you what. I'll come over during my lunch hour. I can't promise what time I can get away, but I'll do my best to make it as early as possible."

"My plane leaves at three. You know I've got to be at the airport at least an hour early."

"You'll make your plane." There was a loud noise in the kitchen. "I'll do my best, Paula. That's all I can do. See you tomorrow." He hung up the phone.

Laura stalked across the living room toward the bedroom, wiping her hands on a white dish towel. Her eyes blazed at her husband. "When was the last time you spent a lunch hour with *me?* I'll tell you when. Never!" she raved. "You haven't got time for your own wife, but you've got plenty for that dried-up old actress, haven't you, *Doctor?*" She had a talent for making the word *doctor* sound as though it labeled a criminal activity.

"Laura—"

"Leave me alone." She slammed the bedroom door behind her.

Cullen considered going after her, but he knew he'd only elicit more of her venom unless he waited for her to cool off. He didn't know how many more of these scenes he could take, yet he saw no alternative. He couldn't divorce her and leave Margaret and Jessica with her a hundred percent of the time. He couldn't do that to his girls. Yet he couldn't care for them by himself either. Maybe Laura'd grow up one of these days. . . .

He turned his back on the bedroom door and went into the kitchen. The dinner, platter and all, lay in the sink, where Laura had obviously thrown it during her tantrum. Cullen took a clean plate from the cupboard and carefully picked two pieces of meat and a withered baked potato out of the sink.

He ate his dinner standing by the sink. It tasted as juiceless as his life.

Chapter 11

It was nearly 9:00 A.M. by the time Stan collected his suitcase from the baggage carousel at LAX. He'd never been in Los Angeles before, and he found the sprawling airport confusing. Everywhere he looked were portable gray plywood walls hiding remodeling and construction efforts from public view, with hastily lettered signs pointing directions to departure gates, baggage claim areas, and various travelers' services. The overall effect was chaotic.

It took him another fifteen minutes to locate the bank of telephones for the car rental agencies and to find one that had the right kind of car available. It couldn't be anything either too noticeable or too expensive—no red convertible or Corvette or Mercedes-Benz or Jaguar. A nondescript Chevrolet or Ford would do. He found one equally anonymous—a tan Oldsmobile Cutlass—at Angel City Rent-a-Car. Twenty-five dollars a day, unlimited mileage.

He boarded the Angel City shuttle bus to the rental car lot and office, where an unsmiling young woman in a yellow uniform handed him an application and examined his Missouri driver's license and credit card. Stan filled out the application and returned it to her. She looked it over and shoved it back at him. "Put your local address here," she said, pointing to a blank space with a manicured finger.

"I don't have a local address," he said. "I've just arrived, and I don't know where I'll be staying."

"Then put down your Missouri address. I can't rent you a car without an address. Fill in the blank where it asks for your employer too." She turned her back and began punching Stan's VISA card numbers into a computerized device for validating credit cards.

Welcome to L.A. Stan would have liked to put the officious bitch in her place, but he bit his tongue. He couldn't afford to call attention to himself. He picked up the pen and wrote in a phony St. Louis address; he dared not use the address he'd shared with Jasmine Kennedy. He put down the name of a major insurance company as well, listing his occupation as insurance salesman.

The clerk in the yellow uniform imprinted Stan's credit card on a charge slip, then rechecked his application form. He wondered what she'd have said if he'd listed the White House and President of the United States as his home and occupation. Probably wouldn't have noticed as long as all the blanks were filled in. "Okay," she said. "Sign here." He did. "The car's in slot fifty-five, out the front door and to the left."

"Right. How do I get to Santa Monica?"

She grabbed a map off a pile and traced the route efficiently with her pen. "Take Century Boulevard, the street in front of the building, until you hit Sepulveda. That's Highway One. Follow the Highway One signs north until you reach Santa Monica. It's about a half hour drive this time of day."

Stan adjusted the Olds's seat and mirrors and rechecked his route on the map. He rolled down the windows. The cool morning fog was still burning off, and he didn't need the air conditioning yet. The weather felt refreshing after St. Louis's heat wave. He hoped it was an omen, boding good fortune for him now that he'd found Jasmine.

As he pulled the car into traffic on Sepulveda Boulevard, the digital clock on the dashboard read 10:10. He'd make Santa Monica well before noon.

Chapter 12

Gretchen made a final survey of the motel room, assuring herself that she was leaving nothing of value behind. She threw away this morning's newspaper, some used tissues from her purse, and a paperback book that she'd finished reading. Then she emptied the medicine cabinet of its few remaining items. She checked the closet and under the bed. Nothing there.

She glanced out the window at the sea one final time, but the view no longer seemed quite so special now that she could look forward to the panorama from Estelle Edwards's house. Still, the morning fog slowly giving way to sunshine on the beach was compelling. She wondered fleetingly whether her mother, young Eileen Kennedy, had lived in a room like this in Santa Monica while she'd awaited the birth of her baby. She hoped that Eileen had been able to see the ocean, that enjoying it had lightened her mood so many years ago.

But there was no time now for speculating about that long-ago event. Eileen Kennedy's now-grown daughter had events of her own waiting to be experienced. When she had satisfied herself that she'd left none of her belongings behind, she went down to the lobby and paid her bill in cash, using nearly $300 in fifties and twenties. She'd been tempted to drive away without paying, but she couldn't risk having the local police after her. And, she told herself, soon the money wouldn't matter. Her cash supply would be replenished from Estelle Edwards's coffers, and $300 would seem like small change.

Her bill paid, she loaded her suitcase into the Volkswagen's trunk and slammed it shut. As she turned the key in the ignition, she felt a new sense of freedom. Within minutes she would be settled in at the Edwards mansion, safe from detection, her path westward from St. Louis forever obscured.

As Gretchen angled her car out of the west end of the motel parking lot, a tan Oldsmobile Cutlass pulled in from the east, its driver's glance darting from the sign that read SEACREST LODGE to a paper on the dashboard and back again. As the driver of the Olds jockeyed his car into a parking space near the front of the motel, he didn't notice the orange Volkswagen.

And as she turned north on Ocean Avenue, happy anticipation playing around the corners of her mouth, Gretchen Hedberg never looked back.

Chapter 13

The room with the brass "36" on the door was on the second floor of the motel, at the back of the parking lot. From his observation point in the Oldsmobile Stan could see a maid's cart loaded with towels and sheets on the balcony near the room. He decided to wait until the maid finished her rounds before he approached Jasmine. A witness was the last thing he needed. The maid finished with room 35, then pushed her cart to the doorway of room 36 and opened the door with a key. A short, stocky woman with overbleached hair tied back in a makeshift ponytail, she entered the room, pushing an upright vacuum cleaner. Several minutes later she came out again, carrying a blue plastic bag and an armload of soiled white linens. She took a supply of clean sheets and towels from the cart and went back into the room.

So Jasmine was out. Well, Stan could wait until she returned, whenever that might be. He'd waited more than a week already. Another hour or two wouldn't kill him.

The maid finished with number 36 and went on to room 37. She knocked on the door and called, "Maid service." When there was no response from within, she opened the door with her key and entered. She repeated her routine and ten minutes later moved on to room 38, the last one on the balcony. She knocked, called, "Maid service," and entered, using her key when she received no response.

Wait a minute, Stan thought. There had been something different about the way the maid had approached room 36. Something . . . He had it: She hadn't knocked on the door of number 36. Maybe Jasmine was always out in the mornings, and the maid knew it. Maybe she'd gotten herself a job. If she had, she might not be back for hours. He was getting hungry, but did he dare leave his post to get some lunch?

Stan climbed out of the car and entered the motel's small lobby. A young man sat behind the counter, his head bowed over a college textbook.

"Hi," Stan said, smiling. "Just wondering if you know what time Gretchen Hedberg will be back. Room thirty-six."

"Hedberg? Let's see," the clerk said, rising from his chair. He ran a finger down a page in the registration book. "Ah, thought so. She's checked out."

"But—" Stan froze. No! God damn it, she *couldn't* have checked out. Not after he'd come all the way from St. Louis. It wasn't fair. With a concerted effort he hid the anger and frustration he was feeling. "Are you sure?" he asked as calmly as he could. "I had an appointment to meet her here this morning."

"Look for yourself," the clerk said, turning the book toward Stan. "Her bill was settled not more than an hour ago."

"Did she say where she was going? Leave any forwarding address?"

"Uh-uh. Probably wasn't expecting any mail. I don't think she got any while she was here. She might've had her mail sent to general delivery, though. Lot of people do that when they first move here, until they have a permanent address. You could try writing her care of general delivery, Santa Monica."

"Sure. Thanks."

Somehow Stan managed to force his reluctant legs to carry him out of the lobby. So that's why the maid hadn't bothered to knock on the door of number 36. She'd known it was vacant. The tenant had checked out—less than an hour ago. Damn, he had rotten luck! His whole life had been filled with rotten, stinking bad luck, one thing after another, and it sure as hell hadn't improved any when he'd met Jasmine Kennedy. Stan pounded his clenched right hand into the palm of his left, over and over again, until his hands smarted. He wasn't sure whether he was symbolically pummeling Jasmine or himself.

His eyes wandered to the motel's balcony, where the maid was finishing her duties in room 38. She pushed the cart back along the balcony, then into a closet. She emerged, holding some blue plastic bags in her left hand, and descended the staircase.

Maybe, Stan thought, just maybe Jasmine, had left something behind, something that would tell him where she'd gone. He approached the maid. "Hi there," he said, smiling at her.

"Hello," the woman said suspiciously. "Something I can do for you?"

"I'm looking for the woman who just checked out of room thirty-six. My sister, Miss Hedberg. Somehow we must've crossed signals. I thought she was going to meet me here, but she's gone, and no one seems to know where."

"Yeah?"

"I wonder . . . do you think you could let me into her room? She might have left something behind that would tell me where to find her."

The maid shook her head, making her stiff ponytail bounce. "I'm not allowed to do that. You'll have to ask the desk clerk. There's nothing in there anyway. I cleaned real good."

"But she might have left a scrap of paper, an address—"

"I told you, you're not gonna find nothing in that room. I emptied all the wastebaskets, vacuumed up."

"Where'd you put the stuff you took from that room?"

"The trash?" The woman looked suddenly frightened. "I didn't take nothing else."

"Nobody's accusing you of anything. Where'd you put the trash?"

"Here. It's all in one of these bags." She indicated the blue plastic bags she had clutched in her hand. "They're going in the Dumpster."

"I'll take them for you."

She glanced at him sideways. "I dunno—"

"You got rules say you can't let somebody help you with the trash?"

"No—"

"Come on, I leveled with you, lady. It's no skin off your nose if I go through the trash. Besides, who'll ever know?"

She hesitated, clutching the bags tightly. Jobs were not that easy to find these days, what with so many people out of work. She didn't want to do anything to jeopardize the one she had.

"Ten bucks help you make up your mind?" Stan pulled his dwindling roll of bills from his pants pocket and removed two fives. He waved them in front of the maid's face.

She looked toward the motel lobby, making sure no one was observing her. "You don't tell nobody."

"You don't tell, I don't tell. How about it?"

Silently the maid took the bills and stuffed them quickly into the pocket of her apron. She handed Stan the bags and turned away.

He loaded them onto the passenger seat of his car and drove out of the parking lot. He'd go through the trash all right, but he'd do it in private. If it contained the smallest hint about where Jasmine Kennedy could be found, he wouldn't lose her again.

Chapter 14

Estelle Edwards's house was the largest on its affluent street, a massive gray frame Victorian built on a half acre bluff lot overlooking Santa Monica Bay. The first floor of the three-story structure was dominated by a large veranda of the type more common in New England than in California architecture. Above it was a balcony that ran part of the length of the second floor. On the west the house featured a three-story circular section: the parlor on the main floor, the sitting room connected to Estelle's bedroom on the second, and a round corner of a large bedroom on the third floor. This portion, topped with a witch's hat peaked roof, was the detail with which Estelle had originally fallen in love. It had seemed to her like something from a romantic novel, and she had imagined that she and Zach would spend many cozy evenings in their round chamber, watching a roaring fire in the fireplace and sipping good wine. Indeed, for more than thirty-five years, they had done just that.

The roof held three chimneys connected to six fireplaces below—one each in the massive entry hall, the parlor, the study, and the dining room on the main floor as well as one in Estelle's sitting room and another in the large front bedroom on the second floor that had once been Seth's. When the house was built, the fireplaces had served as its heating system. Years later, when they bought it, Estelle and Zachary had installed gas space heaters in several of the rooms, but the place still had no central heating plant.

When she was a young bride, newly moved into the house, Estelle had considered the fireplaces her greatest luxury. She had kept each stocked with split oak and eucalyptus logs so that she could enjoy the comforting crackle and warmth of a fire whenever she wanted one. In the summertime she'd often built a fire, then opened the windows to prevent the room from becoming too hot. It had never occurred to her not to have a fire when she was in the mood for one, the seasons be damned. In recent, more financially restricted years, however, she'd treated herself only to an occasional artificial log, the waxy kind that burned with colorful flames. These days, when she felt chilly, she generally made do by wearing a heavy sweater.

As she arrived, Gretchen Hedberg surveyed the exterior of the house, noticing that its white trim was beginning to crack and peel in places. The lawn, however, complete with two varieties of palm trees and a border of flowering bushes, seemed well tended, and when she pulled her car into the driveway and around to the backyard, she noticed the rectangular swimming pool sparkling in the noontime sun. Purple flowers dropping from a tree she couldn't identify floated on the water's surface, giving the pool a delightful tropical effect. She suspected, however, that cleaning the blossoms out of the pool was a constant chore.

Overall, the house and grounds were an eclectic and dramatic combination of elements—seashore, old New England architecture, California foliage, and poolside living—and a rather ostentatious display of wealth. It looked like something that had been assembled by movie people, using sets from a multitude of dissimilar old movies—*Wuthering Heights, South Pacific, Beach Blanket Bingo,* and a dozen others for accent. To Gretchen it represented a different kind of "class" from any she'd ever seen in the Midwest, but she thought it looked like fun.

She parked the Volkswagen in front of one of the four garage doors, removed her suitcase from the trunk, and approached the front door. Virtually before she'd finished pressing the doorbell, Paula Zimmerman opened the door, her dour expression belying her words. "Right on time. How nice, Miss Hedberg. Gretchen. Come in. Estelle's waiting for you." Gretchen entered the massive hallway and set her suitcase on the tile floor. "Leave your suitcase here for now,"

Paula told her. "Come up and say hello to Estelle. Then I'll show you around the place."

Gretchen followed the other woman up the staircase and into the upper hall. As on yesterday's visit, she was dazzled by the valuable antiques and art objects displayed with ultimate casualness: a cherry wood grandfather clock next to a Duncan Phyfe tub-back chair near the elaborate foyer fireplace, a distinctive needlepoint carpet in the parlor, a late-sixteenth-century Italian chest beneath a gilt-framed mirror on the upstairs landing, a variety of good artwork on the walls. Yet the old ruby wool carpeting on the stairway was frayed and worn, and the interior walls obviously had not been painted in many years. Gretchen concluded that Estelle Edwards must be a reclusive sort of person, perhaps one who avoided change at all costs. All the better for her own purposes.

"You'll have to learn how to handle Estelle," Paula said as they reached the second floor. "She can be quite intimidating if you let her get away with it. She'd just as soon work you to the bone as look at you. I should know. These days since she broke her leg have been hell for me. I can't wait to get on the plane. . . . But I'm talking too much, and Lord knows, I don't want to scare you off."

Gretchen wondered why her intuition told her that Paula would like nothing better than to frighten her away. "I don't scare easily, Mrs. Zimmerman. I'm used to dealing with difficult patients."

They approached the open door to Estelle's bedroom. "Estelle, Gretchen is here," Paula called.

"Well, don't keep her waiting out there," Estelle replied. "Bring the girl in."

They entered the room, and Gretchen extended her hand to the old woman. Estelle Edwards was sitting up in bed, dressed in a filmy chartreuse negligee, touching up her makeup. "I hope you're feeling better," the nurse said politely.

"At least I'm off that damned dope the doctor had me taking," Estelle said frankly, extending a tiny hand tipped with shiny fuchsia fingernails. "I expect I'll feel better as soon as you're doing the cooking. Paula won't win any citations from *Gourmet* or *Cuisine* for this stuff." She gestured at a tray of food she'd barely touched, lying beside her on the bed. It appeared to hold slivers of rubbery chicken drowning in some sort of congealed yellow gravy. "I hope you can improve on that." Now that her new nurse-companion had arrived Estelle couldn't help letting some of her frustration with her daughter-in-law creep back into her conversation. Her tongue simply wouldn't be still.

Gretchen paused. Before she could think of a diplomatic reply, Estelle broke into laughter. "Don't mind me," she said. "As Paula can tell you, sitting in this bed hasn't improved my disposition. Maybe it wasn't terrific in the first place."

"I'd be the last one to argue with you, Estelle," Paula said, "on that score."

"May I take this tray from you, Estelle?" Gretchen asked.

"Just put it on the dresser for now, and Paula will show you around the house. You can use the bedroom closest to mine. Then you'll be able to hear me at night if I need you. The room's not large, but I think you'll like it. It has a bay window with a view of the sea and a nice little desk you can use for writing your paper."

Her paper. Gretchen had almost forgotten her claim to be writing her master's thesis. "Fine," she said, removing the tray from Estelle's bed. "What's your favorite meal?" Always appear willing to accommodate in front of the patient's relatives; that was Gretchen's motto. It helped them avoid feeling guilty for staying away, and the more the relatives stayed away, the easier Gretchen's plans were to implement.

Estelle grinned mischievously. "Mussels the way they make them at Antoine's in Paris, the abalone amandine from the Chronicle in Santa Monica, blanched vegetables like those served at Tavern on the Green in—"

"Whoa! Let me rephrase that," Gretchen said. Estelle Edwards certainly had no trouble making decisions. "What would you like me to make for dinner? Something *feasible.*"

Paula snorted faintly, as if to say, "I told you so."

"Hmmm. Something to look forward to for a change," Estelle said, winking at Gretchen conspiratorily. "What do you cook well, my dear?"

"How about pasta? You seem to like seafood, and I cook a great coquilles St. Jacques on a bed of spinach pasta. Maybe some fresh fruit for dessert?"

"That sounds wonderful, but you'll have to shop first. Paula hasn't stocked up on anything that doesn't come in a can."

"I'll make a quick trip to the market as soon as I'm settled."

"Come on," Paula said grumpily. "If I'm to show you around, I'll have to do it now. I'm not going to miss my plane."

She gave Gretchen a quick tour of the main floor rooms: the parlor and study on the west side of the house; the dining room, kitchen, pantry, and laundry on the east.

"I've left you a list of emergency numbers by the kitchen phone," Paula said. "There's the doctor, the next-door neighbors—that's the Sanfords on the west side—and one or two of Estelle's friends. She doesn't have many these days. Keeps herself cooped up in this mausoleum when she could be with people her own age. It's not good for her, but she's stubborn."

"It is a beautiful house, though," Gretchen said.

"It was once. But it's way too big for a woman her age to take care of. She should get herself one of those apartments for senior citizens if you ask me. A nice, clean place with services . . . Maybe you can convince her. Lord knows she doesn't listen to Seth or me."

Gretchen made a noncommittal sound. This kind of family dispute was familiar to her, and she knew she could only harm herself by becoming involved in it. She directed her attention to the rooms Paula showed her. They were, indeed, massive and not particularly well kept. Gretchen saw a film of dust over nearly everything. Estelle hadn't been kidding when she said she didn't employ cleaning help, and Paula obviously had done nothing to improve matters in the time she'd been here.

Gretchen picked up her suitcase and carried it to the second floor, following Paula to a back bedroom. "This is the room you'll be using," Paula told her. It was a pleasant room, sunny and light, with old-fashioned yellow-flowered wallpaper. The bed was three-quarter size, covered by a pale green taffeta bedspread with a ruffle around the bottom. The same green taffeta covered a cushion for the window seat beneath the bay window. A double dresser made of cherry wood stood along the wall opposite the bed; above it was a framed mirror. The desk Estelle had mentioned was against the wall next to the bed, and a chair upholstered in a green-and-yellow-striped fabric stood in a corner of the room, near the closet door. "As Estelle told you, the room's not large, but it's quite comfortable," Paula said, moving to the window and pulling back the filmy curtains. "The view from here is pretty. The house does have *that.*"

Gretchen looked out at the swimming pool and patio in the yard below, with the blue arc of Santa Monica Bay beyond.

Paula opened the closet door. "The closet should be adequate for you." She glanced at Gretchen's single suitcase. "Looks like you didn't bring too many clothes. If you haven't enough hangers, steal some from the hall closet."

"I'm sure I'll do just fine, thanks. Most of my things are in storage."

"You can use the bathroom closest to your room, right down the hall. The only other bath on this floor, the one Estelle uses, connects to her room. These old Victorian houses are strange. When this place was built, there was only one bathroom, the one you'll be using, plus the downstairs lavatory. Yet there were ten bedrooms. Estelle and Zach remodeled one of the bedrooms into a second bath when they moved in, but that's it. There's still no bathroom on the third floor."

"Gives you a new respect for chamber pots," Gretchen said.

"Sure does—" Paula's reply was cut short by the echoing of the doorbell from downstairs. "That'll be Cullen—Dr. Baxter. I'll go let him in, and you can come into Estelle's room in a few minutes. She wants you to meet him."

"I'm on the run, Paula," Cullen Baxter said as soon as she'd ushered him into the house. "I hope Estelle realizes I can't stay and visit."

"You tell her," Paula replied. "She never listens to me."

Cullen took the stairs at his usual hurried pace, then dashed into Estelle's bedroom. "Hello, gorgeous," he said to her.

"How nice, Cullen. You noticed that I got all gussied up for you."

"You're more beautiful than ever. Now let's see that leg. I sneaked out on three patients in my waiting room. I've got to get back into my office before they realize I'm gone."

Estelle threw back the bedcovers, then pulled up her nightgown to display the cast. Cullen leaned over to examine her. "How does it feel today?"

"It still twinges, but I'm off the dope—" There was a knock on the bedroom door, and Estelle saw Gretchen peek in. "Come in, Gretchen. I want you to meet someone. Gretchen Hedberg, Dr. Baxter. Gretchen's my nurse-companion, Cullen."

"I'm delighted to meet you, Doctor," Gretchen said, smiling. "I must say I'm impressed."

"Oh? Why?"

"I didn't realize that you California doctors still made house calls."

"Only for famous movie stars like Estelle," he said, giving Gretchen a surreptitious wink.

"Only for Jane Fonda and me, right, Cullen?" Estelle asked. She caught Gretchen's eye. "He thinks I'm too senile to know he's teasing me, but there was a time when I really was just as famous as Jane Fonda. You two are just too young to remember it. I was nominated for the Academy Award twice, you know. Thought I had it in 1939, when I played Marion opposite Gary Cooper's—"

"You'll always be more famous than Jane Fonda and Gary Cooper combined—in my book," Cullen interrupted, patting her cast as he might pat one of his daughters' heads. "I wish I could spend the afternoon with you, sweetheart, but I've really got to get back to my more mundane, ordinary patients."

"Gretchen's going to live with me until I'm able to get by on my own," Estelle said, ignoring his effort to leave. "She's a real nurse too. Aren't I lucky to have found her?"

Cullen observed the young woman in the doorway. She was in her middle twenties, brunette, with a slim figure and firm, well-rounded breasts. She was certainly attractive, if a bit on the pale side. Perhaps it was the effect of the stark white uniform and almost black hair against her ivory skin. Yet her paleness made her brilliant blue eyes more striking. "Have you been doing private-duty nursing long, Miss Hedberg?" he asked her.

"A number of years, back in the Midwest. But I've just moved to California, so this is new for me."

"How lucky you happened upon Santa Monica, Miss Hedberg."

"Please call me Gretchen, Doctor." She smiled at him warmly, meeting his eyes directly and holding his gaze. "Why don't I walk you to the door and you can give me any special directions you have for Estelle's care? I want to be sure I'm doing things your way."

Cullen lowered his eyes a bit self-consciously as he felt a charge of emotional electricity travel down his spine. Damn. He knew that his troubles with Laura were making him vulnerable to other women, and he didn't need that kind of complication in his life just now. "Uh, sure. Of course," he stammered. He regained his composure quickly, leaned over, and kissed Estelle on the forehead. "Be a good girl. No more surfing for you this week. Roller skating is out too. See you in a few days."

"Thanks for coming by, Cullen," Estelle said. She watched the young doctor and nurse as they left the room. "You watch out for him, Gretchen," she called after them. "He's already married."

Cullen felt his face grow warm as he headed down the stairway. Senile, indeed. Estelle Edwards was about as senile as he was. Virtually nothing got past her unnoticed, and she'd never had the least problem expressing precisely what she was thinking. "Don't let her give you a hard time, Gretchen," he said. "What she needs is bed rest, some decent food, and to stop feeling sorry for herself. She's a tough old gal, and she'll mend. The question is whether or not she'll drive everyone around her batty before that happens." Cullen gave Gretchen a quick verbal list of instructions for

Estelle's care. "I'm sure you'll do just fine as long as you don't let Estelle run you ragged."

"Thanks for the advice," Gretchen said. "I'll call you if there's any problem, but I don't think there will be." She opened the front door for him.

"I'm sure everything will be fine, but just in case, here." Cullen held out his card. "If it's after my office hours, be sure to tell my service that you're calling for Estelle, and they'll track me down right away. Better still, try me at home." He pulled out a pen and wrote his home telephone number on the back of the card.

"Thank you, Doctor." Gretchen took the card and shook Cullen's hand. "It's been a pleasure to meet you."

"I'm delighted to meet you too," he replied. "And call me Cullen. Don't hesitate to let me know if you need anything." Their parting handshake lasted a fraction of a second longer than necessary.

As she went back upstairs Gretchen hoped that she'd handled Cullen Baxter correctly. A little flirting with the doctors who'd treated her previous patients had always served to flatter them into trusting her abilities. But they had all been much older men; Cullen Baxter was not more than thirty. He'd obviously been impressed with her, and that was good. She'd wanted to reassure him that Estelle would be all right without his dropping in to check on her too frequently. But had she overdone it? Gretchen didn't want him coming around to see her instead of the old lady. And she'd sensed something lonely, maybe even desperate, about Cullen Baxter. She'd have to play this one very carefully.

"Gretchen, come in here, please," Estelle called. When the nurse entered the bedroom, Estelle told her, "Here's a check for fifty dollars I've made out to the market on Montana. I've called Scotty, the owner, and told him that you're going to be doing my shopping for the next few weeks, so he won't give you any trouble about cashing my checks. After you've unpacked, run down there and pick up whatever groceries we'll need for the next couple of days. If you hurry, you can get back before Paula leaves to catch her plane."

It took Gretchen only a few minutes to hang up the meager wardrobe she'd brought with her. Then she stepped inside the small closet and stood on her tiptoes to push aside several old hatboxes lying on the shelf. She took a deep breath, focusing her attention on the boxes, not on the closet. Ever since childhood going into a closet had made her feel claustrophobic; within seconds she would begin to think she smelled mothballs and feel the door closing on her. She'd studied enough psychology to know that her reaction was a psychic memory of the fear she'd felt as a child. Aunt Sylvia's idea of punishment for some small infraction of her rules had been to lock her niece in a closet. Often for hours. But understanding the fear's source and overcoming it were not at all the same thing. Controlling Gretchen's reaction sometimes took every ounce of concentration she could muster. When she had her own home, she vowed, all the closets would be the shallow kind with sliding doors—the kind that no one could be locked inside of.

Gretchen grasped and shoved one of the hatboxes, then another one. There. She cleared a spot at the back of the shelf, just large enough for her small duffel bag. It would be out of sight yet easily accessible whenever she needed it.

Before stowing the bag on the shelf, Gretchen rechecked its contents. It held her working tools—those items that would ensure her power over Estelle. The medications were most important: a variety of tranquilizers, sedatives, hypnotics, and stimulants in both pill and liquid form as well as a supply of syringes and sterile needles. She had stolen her cache a little at a time from various patients as well as from hospitals where she'd worked until she had accumulated enough drugs to control a dozen women the size of Estelle Edwards. And for any situation that drugs could not handle, Gretchen kept another kind of tool in her bag: a compact pearl-handled pistol. She examined the gun to see that it was loaded, then put it back inside the duffel bag and placed the bag on the shelf. She wouldn't need her working tools for a while, at least not before Paula Zimmerman was well on her way to Italy and Estelle was alone in the house.

Some four hours later Gretchen was congratulating herself for having everything efficiently under control. She'd finished the grocery shopping. Paula had gone in a cab to LAX. By now she would be en route to Italy. And Estelle was happily settled in front of her bedroom television set, watching Miriam Hopkins and Bette Davis in *Old Acquaintance.* "Henry Blanke and Vincent Sherman offered me the lead in this picture, but I turned it down," Estelle had told Gretchen, her eyes riveted to the small screen. "My son was just a baby, and I'd already decided to retire from acting. Bette Davis did a wonderful job, though, don't you think? I always liked Bette. Everyone used to claim we were bitter rivals, but that was just publicity."

Gretchen had refilled Estelle's crystal water pitcher and excused herself to begin preparations for their dinner. Now she had everything ready to be cooked. She'd minced the onions, pressed the garlic, sliced the mushrooms, and measured out the wine, scallops, heavy cream, and butter. A large pot of water for the pasta was ready to be heated.

Estelle would be occupied with the movie for at least another hour, so Gretchen had plenty of time to get a better look at the treasures the house held, enough time to begin an inventory of the many things that would soon belong to her. She would begin with the living room and then inspect the study behind it. Gretchen rinsed and wiped her hands before checking to see that the back door was securely locked. Then she began her private tour of the house, like a greedy child in a toy store at Christmas.

Chapter 15

Faith Sanford sat on the back steps of her house, her bare legs doubled up under her chin, feeling like a whipped puppy. She hadn't really expected to get the part in the play, but she hadn't expected to be dismissed quite so readily, either. The director had taken one look at her and gone into his don't-call-us-we'll-call-you routine. He hadn't let her recite a full line of her character's dialogue before he'd dismissed her. "Thanks, honey," he'd shouted at the stage. "We'll let you know. Next, please." *Honey*—as if she weren't important enough to have a name. She hadn't even been worth enough of the director's valuable time for him to glance at his audition list.

Had her acting been that bad? Was she that lacking in talent? *Of course not,* Faith told herself. She hadn't been given a chance to act. It was her appearance that had hurt her. As usual she hadn't "looked the part." She clenched one fist and absentmindedly punched herself on the knee. She was sure the problem was her long legs. She stretched them out before her and evaluated them cruelly, right down to her size nine feet. She felt like a female Ichabod Crane.

After the fateful audition she had come home, kicked off her shoes, changed into shorts and a T-shirt, and flopped down on the back steps to lick her wounds. What she needed most was a warm hug and a vote of confidence, but neither was easy to come by in her sixteen-year-old world. Her mother was dead, and her father disapproved of her acting aspirations. Or he would disapprove if he were around long enough to be aware of them. Faith's girlfriends focused their attention on boys and clothes; they wouldn't understand her disappointment. And she had no boyfriend of her own. Estelle was the only one Faith could count on to understand what she was feeling. She told herself that she should visit Estelle in any case. She would take her some of the roses that grew in the backyard, some of her mother's beloved roses.

Faith bent over the rose bushes, her mop of copper-penny hair glowing bright in the late afternoon sun. She chose two yellow blossoms that were just beginning to open and, placing her fingers carefully to avoid the thorns, cut the stems. She plucked off two of the leaves and one of the outer petals, all of which had tiny holes in them. Aphids were beginning to invade the garden. Faith's mother never would have let that happen, but now no one cared very much about gardening.

Faith left the scissors on the steps and carried the fragrant blossoms next door. Following her habitual route, she walked down the long driveway and around the back of Estelle's house. She plucked her hidden key from behind the holly bush and let herself in the kitchen door.

The smell of garlic permeated the room, overpowering the sweeter smell of the roses she held. Faith noticed the dinner preparations sitting on the cutting board and wrinkled her nose appreciatively. Paula must be shaping up, she thought. Real food for a change. She went into the pantry, pushed aside Estelle's portable stepstool, and reached up to the shelf where Estelle kept her vases. Faith could reach all but the highest shelf without standing on anything. Being tall did have one or two advantages, she told herself—if you searched hard enough to find them.

She selected a cut glass bud vase, filled it with water at the sink, slid the flower stems into it, and wiped off the excess water with a dish towel. She had begun to feel better already, just by doing something for someone else.

Faith carried her gift out of the kitchen, through the passageway to the foyer, and toward the stairway, her bare feet silently slapping against the chilly tile floor. As she passed the archway to the study a flash of white caught the corner of her eye. She backed up and looked in. A woman in a white uniform was searching through Estelle's desk. "What are you doing?" Faith demanded boldly.

Startled, Gretchen straightened bolt upright and turned to see a skinny teenage girl staring at her. Who was she? How much had she seen? Momentarily speechless, she dropped the papers she'd been examining into the drawer and struggled to regain her composure. Then she did what she always did when caught red-handed: She attacked. "Who are *you?* What are you doing in this house?" Gretchen's eyes blazed at Faith.

"I—I'm Faith Sanford. I live next door. I brought these for Estelle." She held out the flowers.

"How did you get in here? The doors were locked."

Faith swallowed and regained her composure. She'd been intimidated enough for one day; now she was beginning to be angry. "I used a key," she said. "How do you think I got in? You didn't answer me. Who are you, and what are you doing going through Estelle's desk?"

Gretchen reassessed the situation and forced herself to smile. "Forgive me," she said. "It's just that you startled me so. I'm Gretchen Hedberg, Estelle's nurse-companion. You're misunderstanding . . . Faith, is it?"

"Uh-huh." Faith did not return the smile. "I don't see what I can be misunderstanding. You were looking through Estelle's things. I saw you."

"I'm just looking for a phone number, dear—"

"My name is not *dear.*"

This girl promised trouble. "Sorry, Faith. The truth is I'm looking for the doctor's phone number. There are a few things about Estelle's situation that I'd like to discuss with him—"

"I'm sure Estelle would give you the phone number if you asked her."

"I'm sure she would too, but then she'd worry, wouldn't she? She'd be afraid that something was wrong."

"Is something wrong?"

"I'm concerned about her, yes. She looks too pale, and her daughter-in-law told me that she hasn't been eating properly. I think the doctor should know. Those things might affect her recovery."

The nurse looked earnest enough. It was possible that she was telling the truth, Faith thought, although she still didn't think it was right for her to be searching Estelle's desk no matter what her reason. "Well . . . maybe. But I don't think Estelle would like it."

"Perhaps you're right. I was only trying to help my patient. I'll take your advice and ask her for the phone number." Gretchen moved away from the desk.

"All right then," Faith said. She turned away and started up the stairway.

Estelle was engrossed in an old movie on TV, and to Faith, she didn't look pale. It was hard to tell, though, with the amount of rouge she was wearing. Faith bent over and kissed the artificial pink circle on one of the older woman's cheeks. "Brought you a present," she said.

"Oh, how lovely," Estelle said, taking the vase. She nuzzled the golden blossoms under her nose and sniffed. "Ah, my favorite perfume. Turn that thing off, will you, Faith?" She gestured at the television set with the vase.

"Are you sure? I didn't mean to interrupt."

"Don't worry about it. I've seen this film at least fifteen times already. I was dying for some company. Paula's left—not that she was much company anyway—and my new nurse is cooking me a gourmet meal. You must have met her on your way up." She set the flowers on her bedside table.

Faith turned off the television set and sat down. She avoided Estelle's gaze. "Uh, yeah. I met her."

"Well?"

"Well what?"

"What did you think of her?"

"I don't know. What am I supposed to think?"

"Whatever you want to think, Faith. When have I ever told you what to think?" Estelle noticed that the girl's gaze was concentrated on her bare feet, as though she expected her toes to speak for her. "Something's wrong, Faith Sanford," she said. "What is it?"

Faith fidgeted uncomfortably.

"Well? What's wrong, young lady?"

"I—I don't want to be the one to make you worry, Estelle," she said. "I want you to get well."

"I have every intention of getting well. Now what's going on here?"

Faith worked up her courage. "She told me—the nurse told me that you were too pale and you weren't eating right. That's why she was looking in your desk for the doctor's—"

"She was what?"

"When I walked by the study, she was going through your desk. At least that's what it looked like to me. I asked her what she was doing, and she said she was looking for the doctor's phone number, that she didn't want to ask you for it because you'd worry."

"I don't understand. Cullen was here only a few hours ago. Gretchen walked him to the door. What could she have to say to him now that she didn't say then?" An ugly suspicion crept into Estelle's thoughts. "What exactly was she doing in the desk when you saw her, Faith?"

"I—I'm not sure exactly. I think she was looking at some papers. I was so surprised to see someone standing there that I guess I blurted out something and startled her. She might have been looking for a phone number. I don't know."

Estelle thought a moment. "She might have been snooping too. Or stealing from me. Try to remember, Faith. What exactly did she tell you?"

"She said that she was looking for the doctor's phone number so she could call him without your knowing. She said that you looked sick—too pale and you weren't eating."

"Well, Cullen saw me not five hours ago, and he didn't say I was too pale. It's true that I haven't been eating much. Who could eat that slop Paula kept shoving under my nose? I told Gretchen that. I can't think what she'd have to say to him unless—"

"Unless what?"

"She did seem to be flirting with him. I remember now. I warned her that he was married, but maybe she's the type who doesn't care—"

"Or maybe, like you said, she was snooping." Faith rose and started to pace back and forth. She began to appreciate the drama of the situation. "I'd get rid of her if I were you,

Estelle. You can't have someone you can't trust living in your house. That's terrible! Now that I think of it, why couldn't she just look in the phone book if she *really* wanted Dr. Baxter's phone number? She didn't have to go through your desk. I wonder what she was really looking for."

"But I can't just fire her. Paula's gone, and there isn't anyone else—"

"I'll stay with you until you find someone else, Estelle," Faith said, warming to her self-appointed role as her friend's savior. "It's a good thing I caught her at it before something serious happened, that's all I can say."

"Hold on, Faith. Don't go off half-cocked. Gretchen is entitled to an opportunity to defend herself. And practically speaking, I'm dependent on her, at least for now." Estelle turned the situation over in her mind. "Gretchen is a nurse. What if there really *is* something wrong with me?"

"I think you look fine. I can take care of you, Estelle, honest I can."

At her listening post outside Estelle's bedroom door Gretchen decided that she had allowed this to go on long enough. She entered the room abruptly. "Estelle, it's time we got you cleaned up for dinner," she said. "Faith, you may visit Estelle another time."

"But—" Faith protested. "I don't think Estelle wants me to leave. Do you, Estelle?"

"Estelle and I have some things to talk about," Gretchen insisted. "Some adult things. You can come back another time."

Estelle considered the situation, then said to Faith, "Go ahead, dear. I'll be all right. I'll give you a call later."

"Well . . . I suppose, if you're *sure* you'll be okay," the girl said.

"I'm sure."

After Faith had reluctantly left the room, Gretchen faced Estelle. "I suspect that girl told you that I was looking on your desk for the doctor's number. I want to tell you why," she said.

Estelle noted that the nurse used the words *"on" your desk* not *"in" your desk*. Had Faith's imagination taken over, or was Gretchen lying about the extent of her search? "All right. Why?"

"Your daughter-in-law told me that she was leaving a list of emergency numbers for me, and I can't find it. I had a question for Dr. Baxter—nothing of earthshaking importance, but I wanted it to be a surprise."

"You certainly managed to surprise me, Gretchen. I'll give you that one."

"I really am sorry. I guess I used bad judgment."

"You certainly did." Estelle wagged her finger scoldingly at Gretchen. "Paula left those numbers posted beside the kitchen phone. At least that's what she told me—"

"Oh, of course. Now I remember."

"Tell me why you wanted to talk to my doctor, young woman."

Gretchen shrugged her shoulders in mock resignation and smiled at Estelle. "I guess I'll have to tell you about it so you won't think I was snooping. I just wanted to ask him about a wheelchair—"

"What wheelchair?"

"I thought that if I could rent a wheelchair for you, you could be a lot more mobile."

"I don't understand. You told Faith that I was too pale and that I wasn't eating—"

Gretchen forced a laugh. "Oh, dear. Poor Faith. She misunderstood what I meant. I'd been thinking about Mr. Parkinson, my former patient. I used to lift him into his wheelchair and wheel him outdoors into the fresh air. It would always put some color into his cheeks and improve his appetite. As a nurse I know that it's not good for people to be cooped up indoors all day, especially flat in bed. I couldn't manage to get you downstairs, but if we could get a chair that supported your leg properly, I could wheel you out on that upstairs balcony. You could enjoy the sunshine and fresh air from there."

"So that's it." Estelle began to find Gretchen's explanation plausible and the idea of a wheelchair appealing. "The wheelchair could be a good idea, as long as renting one doesn't cost too much. But next time ask me. I don't appreciate people plowing through my personal belongings."

"I honestly am sorry, Estelle. I promise it won't happen again. Let's get you cleaned up." Gretchen placed her strong hands under Estelle's arms and lifted her off the bed.

"All right then," Estelle said, putting most of her weight on her good leg. "We won't mention it again. You call and ask Cullen about the chair."

"Here, lean against me and use my body like a crutch. That's right." Gretchen proceeded slowly toward the bathroom, half carrying Estelle. "I have to admit, Estelle, that I almost had heart failure when Faith suddenly appeared behind me in the hall like that. Does she carry her own key to the house?"

"You'll have to get used to Faith's hanging around here, Gretchen. She's been in and out of this house since she was a toddler. Years ago I got tired of running downstairs and answering the bell every time Faith decided to visit, so we devised a hiding place for a key. That way she wouldn't lose it, and she could let herself in whenever she wanted. You'll get used to it."

Not if I can help it, Gretchen thought. They reached Estelle's bathroom, and Gretchen lowered her gently onto the side of the bathtub, then turned on the water in the sink. Efficiently she helped Estelle use the bathroom facilities and manipulated her back into bed. "It will take me about twenty, twenty-five minutes to finish the dinner preparations. Anything I can bring you in the meantime?"

"No, dear. I'll just go back to my movie if you'll turn on the TV."

Gretchen turned on the heat under the pots and pans. While she waited for the water to boil and the butter to melt, she inspected the area outside the back door. Within minutes she had located the key in its hiding place behind the holly bush and pocketed it. She reentered the kitchen and locked the door securely behind her. There would be no more surprise visits from that teenage snoop.

As she added the garlic and onion to the melted butter and watched it sizzle, Gretchen smiled with relief. She had managed to recover nicely from what could have been a fatal setback. She added the sliced mushrooms to the garlic and onion mixture in the frying pan and stirred, then poured salt into the boiling water in the large kettle.

The grandfather clock in the foyer chimed six times. With luck Gretchen might still catch Cullen Baxter in his office. He sounded pleased to hear her voice as she explained that Estelle had visions of renting a wheelchair. "I think it's probably a bit early for that yet," Gretchen told him, "but I promised her that I'd ask you—"

"Maybe next week, when her healing process is further along. That's a very nasty break she's got."

"That's what I thought. Just one more thing. Paula told me that Estelle isn't sleeping very well, and I thought we should have some sleeping pills on hand in case she continues to have trouble."

Cullen agreed to call in a prescription to a nearby drugstore but cautioned Gretchen against using the pills unless it was absolutely necessary. "And be sure that she doesn't mix them with the codeine I gave her for pain or with any kind of alcohol."

"Of course, Dr. Baxter—"

"Cullen."

"Sorry, Cullen. I don't like to use sedatives particularly, but if a patient needs one occasionally . . . Well, I like to be prepared."

"I can't argue with that approach."

Gretchen thanked him and returned to cooking dinner. She would watch her step more carefully for the time being, working hard to seduce Estelle Edwards, and maybe even Faith Sanford, into trusting her. She poured white wine into the frying pan and added seasonings, then added half a pound of fettucine to the pot of boiling water. The pungent aroma of the sauce was beginning to make her hungry. She poured herself a glass of the wine, sipped it, and began to relax. Her earlier fright was almost gone now. There was nothing—nobody—in the Edwards household that Gretchen Hedberg couldn't handle as long as she retained control of the situation. She added the fresh scallops to the sauce and, when the seafood was sautéed to perfection, some heavy cream. She lowered the fire under the frying pan and turned her attention to the pasta. She removed one long green strand of fettucine and tasted it. *Al dente*—just the way it should be. After draining it, she mixed the pasta with the seafood and mushroom sauce.

She quickly finished preparing Estelle's dinner tray—the seafood pasta dish, accompanied by fresh sourdough bread, sliced oranges dusted with nutmeg, and a glass of wine—and carried it up the stairs. With a good dinner, a professional back rub, and a sympathetic ear, Gretchen would lure Estelle Edwards into trusting her with her life.

Chapter 16

Faith Sanford sliced off a sliver of rare roast beef, pierced it with her fork, and pushed it around her dinner plate listlessly. Tension had sapped her appetite, yet she knew she had to force some food down if she didn't want to become even thinner. She clamped the piece of meat between her teeth, then forced herself to chew it. One, two, three . . . she silently counted the number of times her teeth ground at the tasteless morsel. Then she washed it down with a swallow of milk.

As she glanced across the dinner table Faith's face betrayed the resentment she was feeling. She had counted on using the dinner hour to discuss the problem of Estelle's nurse with her father. Since discovering Gretchen Hedberg snooping through Estelle's things, Faith had felt confused and fearful. She needed to talk over the situation with someone level-headed, someone authoritative, someone who could help her help Estelle. She needed someone who could help her make a decision about what to do. She needed her father. Yet he had brought a guest to dinner, a date, who now occupied him completely. Candace Blake, a stunning blonde in her mid-twenties who claimed to be a model, was attracting both Theodore Sanford's gaze and his daughter's animosity.

"Horseradish sure brings out the flavor of the meat, doesn't it, Teddy?" the blonde gushed. "I don't remember ever having it like this back home in Arkansas."

Faith's meager appetite died completely. She observed—not for the first time—that being attractive to men seemed to

require no giant intellect. Maybe no intellect at all. Candace
Blake—Faith figured her name was about as genuine as her
hair color—looked as though she could barely manage to
identify the food on her plate or to find her way home. *Vacant* was far too subtle a term for the look in her heavily
mascaraed eyes. But then, although Faith would have
wished for better from her own father, it clearly wasn't
Candace's brains that had attracted him. Theodore
Sanford's eyes were focused on the milk white shoulders and
mounds of cleavage that rose from Candace's red off-one-
shoulder dress. Occasionally his gaze wandered upward to
the young woman's lipsticked mouth and perfect teeth. If
Candace were a model, Faith thought, she must work at
Sexy Lingerie. She felt like throwing up. Instead, she decided to attack.

"Tell me, Candace," Faith asked nastily, "what effect do
you think this latest rise in the prime rate will have on the
economy?"

"The what?"

"The prime rate. It went up to twelve and a half percent
yesterday. You must have heard about it." Faith herself had
no real idea what to expect from this economic development,
but she'd read an article about the prime rate in today's
newspaper. She'd known that bringing up the subject at dinner would make Candace uncomfortable, and anticipating
that had pleased her greatly. Faith also hoped that her tactic
would make her father realize what a young airhead he was
dating. He had to be shown just how inappropriate a woman
like Candace Blake was for him.

"Uh, I guess I don't . . ." Candace stared at her plate, as
though concentrating harder on her food might supply her
with an answer to Faith's question. Her thick black eyelashes fluttered spastically, silent evidence of her discomfort.

Faith brought in more artillery. "Well, don't you think the
federal budget deficit is what's really at fault? Certainly any
intelligent, educated person has an opinion. . . ."

The model raised her bare shoulders slightly and
squirmed. Suddenly a bright smile lighted up her features as
she found a solution to her unease. She turned to Faith's

father and asked her in her tiny, childlike voice, "What do *you* think, Teddy?" When in doubt, ask a man.

"I think Faith should finish her dinner," Sanford replied, scowling. "She and I will discuss the national economy privately. She can count on it."

"I'm not very hungry," Faith said.

"If you've finished, I'm sure you must have some homework to do."

"School got out last week, Dad," she said, staring him down. "I'm sure I told you, but I guess you're far too busy to pay attention to unimportant little things like—"

"That will be quite enough, young lady."

Faith rose from her chair, picked up her dinner plate, and stomped into the kitchen. As the door swung closed behind her, she heard the airhead asking her father, "Teddy, what's the matter? Did I say something wrong?"

The Sanfords' housekeeper, Clara Wattman, sat at the kitchen table, washing down her own dinner with a mugful of something that Faith was sure was largely gin. A portly woman with frizzy brown hair, Mrs. Wattman ate while leaning over her meal, both her plump elbows on the table. She looked up at Faith, her right hand grasping her brown mug and her left curled around her fork. Her eyes zeroed in on the girl's dinner plate. "What's the matter? You didn't like your dinner?"

"I'm not hungry tonight, Mrs. Wattman."

"Roast beef's your favorite, Faith. I made it special because you like it."

Faith turned and observed the housekeeper. She didn't much like Mrs. Wattman, mainly because she never knew what to expect from her. She was one Mrs. Wattman sober, another slightly tipsy, still another dead drunk. Sometimes she was pleasant, sometimes weepy, other times silly. Faith could put up with those personalities. But occasionally Mrs. Wattman was vicious and mean, mocking Faith or exploding in irrational rage. Often Mrs. Wattman ignored Faith's behavior. Yet if the girl did the same thing on another day, the housekeeper might launch one of her tirades. It all depended simply on how far in the bag the woman was. Underneath her chameleon exterior, however, Faith believed that Mrs. Wattman meant well. Probably she really had prepared the roast beef because she wanted to please Faith, and the girl felt a little guilty for not having eaten it.

"It's not the food, Mrs. Wattman. Honest. I'll have a roast beef sandwich for lunch tomorrow. I'm just upset tonight. . . ."

"It's that woman, isn't it?" Mrs. Wattman leaned forward, as if to include Faith in a secret conversation. "You don't like to eat with that phony blonde, do you?"

Faith was startled by Mrs. Wattman's sudden perception. Were her feelings that obvious? "Why do you say that?" she snapped.

"Any girl would be jealous, Faith, her father seeing a floozy like that, bringing her into their home."

Faith had no intention of confiding in Mrs. Wattman her feelings about her father's love life. Who knew if the woman could be trusted to keep her mouth shut? "I don't care who he dates. Let him make a fool of himself if he wants to. It's none of my business."

"Then what are you moping about, girl?" The portly housekeeper gestured at the chair next to hers with her fork. "Come and sit a minute. Tell me what's eating you."

Faith hesitated, then sat down. She would never trust Mrs. Wattman enough to reveal how she really felt about her father's behavior, but the housekeeper might be helpful in solving Estelle's problems. She seemed to be in a decent mood at the moment, and she certainly had long experience working in other people's households. She might add some perspective to Gretchen Hedberg's behavior. "I'm worried about Estelle Edwards," Faith began. "I think she's in real trouble, and I don't know what to do about it." Faith told Clara Wattman about having caught Estelle's new nurse-companion snooping through the old woman's desk and about Gretchen's reaction to being caught.

"So what can you do about it, Faith? Seems to me like Miss Edwards's problem, not yours."

"Well, maybe. But Estelle can't do anything without *some*body to help her. With her broken leg she can't even get out of bed. What if this nurse person is dangerous? What if she hurts Estelle or something?"

"So the nurse snoops a little. She's probably just keeping herself entertained. Think how boring it is for her, cooped up with an old lady like that."

"That's no excuse for what I saw her doing."

"Maybe not, but you don't know how hard it is, living in somebody else's house. Nothing ever your own. Everything off limits. Everybody suspicious of what you do . . ."

"Who wouldn't be suspicious of something like this? I caught her red-handed, Mrs. Wattman. That woman's a snoop and a thief, I just know it." Faith rose and began to pace the kitchen floor, waving her long arms to emphasize her words. "I have a feeling. I don't think Estelle's safe with that nurse in the house."

"Faith, stop and listen to yourself a minute. You have no real reason to think that woman is dangerous. She could have been looking for a phone number, just like she said. Either way it's nothing."

"I don't think it's nothing," Faith replied. "Estelle told me that Seth and Paula are trying to make her sell her house. What if they got this Hedberg woman into Estelle's house to spy on her? Maybe she's being paid to make a case that Estelle can't handle her own house. Or maybe she's supposed to find some secret to blackmail Estelle into sell-ing—"

Suddenly Mrs. Wattman broke into a belly laugh, her heavy body shaking with mirth while her frizzy brown head bobbed. When she regained control, she wiped tears from her eyes, cleared her throat and took another swig from her mug. "Ah—you kill me, Faith Sanford. Such an imagination on a young girl. Danger. Blackmail. Spying. You're better than my soaps!"

"*I* don't think it's funny."

"Oh, don't dramatize everything so much, girl. Know what I think?" As the housekeeper took another swig of her drink, her speech began to slur slightly. "I think Esh—Esh —I think that old Miss Edwards is a bad influence on you. Acting, movies. All make-believe. Some actress you're going to be, can't tell real from pretend. Some actress . . ." Her shoulders began to shake once again.

"I should have known better than to talk to you, you stupid old drunk!" Faith shouted. She stalked out of the room, using the servants' stairway at the back of the house to avoid passing the dining room. By the time she reached the landing the sounds rising from the kitchen had begun to sound more like tears than laughter.

Chapter 17

Estelle sat up in bed, turning pages in an old scrapbook. Feather pillows propped behind her back and her injured leg jutting out in front of her, she felt as comfortable as circumstances allowed. Her leg now gave her little pain, and thanks to an excellent dinner and a professional back rub from Gretchen last night, she'd enjoyed her first full night's sleep since the accident. Yesterday's doubts about the new nurse now seemed to be the silly paranoia of a teenager who loved to overdramatize life and of a previously active woman who'd become trapped and bedridden. Just because Estelle had lost some control over her life was no reason to overreact to Gretchen's display of poor judgment. The nurse had meant well, and her wheelchair idea could result in Estelle's having more freedom as early as next week.

Estelle turned another page, gave her memory free reign, and immersed herself in nostalgia. During her years as a motion-picture actress she'd saved publicity photos from dozens of films—some in which she'd acted and others in which friends had performed or directed. Then, when Seth was a baby, she'd spent many, many evenings fitting little black photo corners on the pictures and mounting them in her albums. Nowadays she often used the books for a few pleasant hours of reminiscing and reliving old times.

The book she held on her lap was a large leather-covered album with the number 1940 engraved on its cover in gold. A good year for Estelle, 1940. She and Zach had been married only two years, Seth's birth was still four years away, and both their careers were blossoming.

For perhaps the thousandth time Estelle inspected the yellowing photos of old friends: Pat O'Brien, Bette Davis, Ann Sheridan, Andy Devine, James Cagney, Olivia De Havilland. There Estelle was with Humphrey Bogart on the set of *It All Came True.* She touched Bogart's picture tenderly for a moment. He'd been so full of life in those days. They all had been. Another shot showed a young Estelle, her fashionably coiffed hair then naturally auburn, standing between Zach and Charles Boyer on the set of *All This and Heaven Too.* Charles had been so suave, such a ladies' man; Estelle had always suspected that Zach was a little jealous. A small photo with cracking edges showed Estelle chatting with David Niven at a studio party. If she hadn't married Zach, she thought, she'd have liked to marry David. He'd been so marvelous to talk to, such a clever man, a true natural wit. Now David, too, was gone.

Estelle brushed away the beginnings of a tear. If she didn't watch herself, she'd become maudlin. In recent times, when she still felt half her age, she had thoroughly enjoyed looking over her photos. But now everything seemed changed. In her invalid status, looking at photos of old friends and realizing how many of them were dead was more depressing than fun. She closed the album and set it on the nightstand, then picked up today's *Variety.* She'd keep herself busy reading about what was happening in today's movie world.

When Gretchen returned from the drugstore, they'd play some gin rummy, Estelle decided. She wasn't crazy about card games, but there was only so much television and nostalgia that one person could stand.

She checked the bedside clock. The nurse should be back soon. Estelle mused about what prescription Cullen had ordered for her. She was off codeine completely, so it wouldn't be a pain-killer. Maybe some sort of vitamins or calcium tablets. She should have asked Gretchen. Goodness knows Estelle didn't need to spend unnecessary money, not at the rate her small cash supply had been shrinking.

She turned to an article detailing a power struggle within the ranks of the Screen Actors Guild and was engrossed in it when the bedside telephone rang. She picked up the receiver and recognized the voice of Claudia Morrisey on the other end. "Hello, Claudia," Estelle said without enthusiasm. She'd known Claudia from the thirties, when they'd acted together in several of Zach's films, and she had barely been able to tolerate the woman since then. Claudia had been married to Peter Morrisey, Zach's first assistant director, so Estelle had had to maintain a civil relationship with her. There was no justice, Estelle thought privately, when so many nicer people, in and out of show business, died young while Claudia Morrisey just kept on inflicting her irritating personality on the world.

"Estelle, I just heard about your accident," Claudia said in her loud, nasal voice. "I couldn't wait to call and see how you are. You've just got to give me all the details."

"Actually I don't," Estelle replied.

"What?"

"I don't have to give you all the details, Claudia." One of Claudia's greatest pleasures in life, one that drove Estelle wild, was gossiping about her friends' misfortunes, particularly their physical misfortunes. Herman Weiss's colostomy had dominated the woman's conversation for weeks.

"Estelle, you are a stitch, you old thing." Claudia cackled. "Always kidding around."

"I'm not kidding, Claudia. I have no intention of becoming grist for your gossip mill."

"Well, don't get huffy. I only called to be nice, Estelle. I was concerned about how you're getting along all by yourself."

"I'm not all by myself. I've hired a nurse to live in, so I'm doing just fine, Claudia. You needn't worry about me."

"You still must be lonely."

"I'm surviving. At least I'm not in the hospital. I'm able to be in my own home with my things around me. The situation could be a lot worse."

"That's certainly true. Did you hear what happened to Sue Justin?"

Estelle cringed. She knew that if she said that she had not heard about Sue, Claudia would tell her. If she lied and said she knew all about Sue's troubles, Claudia would want to discuss them. If she said she didn't care what had happened to Sue Justin, she would appear to be unfeeling. She braced herself for a morbid story and confessed, "No, I didn't hear about Sue Justin."

"Pancreatic cancer," Claudia said with a triumphant tone in her voice. She loved to be first with the news. "They thought she had gallstones, opened her up, and there it was: tumor the size of your—"

"Claudia, *please!* I'm not in the mood to hear about cancer just now."

"I just thought you'd like to know, Estelle. There was a time when you and Sue were pretty thick, as I recall. The poor woman's dying. They found cancer cells everywhere. Her innards looked like rotting—"

"Claudia, I will hang up unless you shut your mouth about poor Sue Justin's insides. I'm sure she wouldn't appreciate your talking like that either."

"You've certainly gotten touchy since you broke your hip, Estelle."

"I only broke my leg, Claudia, and I never liked to hear about ghoulish things. It turns my stomach."

"Just be thankful you're not in Sue's place, that's all I can say."

"I assure you I'm infinitely grateful. Now I really must go."

"Wait a minute. I called to find out when I should drop by. I'm sure you can use some company."

Estelle groaned silently. When she was mobile, she was adept at avoiding people she didn't want to see, but what excuse could she use now? Claudia knew she would be home. "To be honest with you, I don't know if I'm up to having company, Claudia." It was worth a try.

"Nonsense. You're just feeling sorry for yourself, Estelle. Lying there all alone, not making any effort to be social, you end up wallowing in self-pity. Next thing you know, you'll be in a full-fledged depression. Look what happened to Cliff Tully after he had his heart attack. Got depressed, refused to see anybody, dead in two months—"

"I am *not* depressed, Claudia. At least I wasn't until you called."

"What you need, Estelle, is somebody to talk to. A nice social evening. Tell you what. I'll pick up a dessert and bring it along. That way I won't be any trouble. There's this marvelous new bakery on Fourth Street; they make heavenly cream puffs stuffed with chocolate mousse. . . ."

Claudia droned on about her second favorite subject, food. Fattening food. No wonder the woman had gained a good forty pounds since Estelle had known her.

"Claudia, I can't eat that kind of food. I'm bedridden, and I have no way to burn off the calories."

"Then I'll bring something less fattening, although I don't see the point in watching your figure at your age. We've got to get *some* pleasure out of life, don't we? But that's your business. Tonight all right, Estelle? Eight o'clock?"

Estelle sighed and capitulated. It was clear that Claudia Morrisey was determined to visit, so she might as well get it over with. "All right," she said. "Eight o'clock. But it will have to be a short evening. I go to sleep very early these days."

"We'll have a nice visit, Estelle, just the two of us. And I'll bring you something special."

By the time Estelle had extricated herself from her conversation with Claudia she felt thoroughly deflated. In the past she had simply tolerated the woman, sometimes even mocking her behind her back. Over the years Claudia Morrisey had become the stereotype of older people that Estelle hated most: a woman obsessed with bodily functioning, in her case illness and eating.

When Estelle was a child, she remembered, her grandmother had always turned to the obituary column as soon as the newspaper arrived. Gran had wallowed in the bad news whenever a friend or acquaintance was listed there. She would gossip over the cause of death, the disposition of financial assets, whether or not the family had looked adequately grief-stricken at the funeral. Observing her grandmother, young Estelle had vowed that she would never be like that when she got older. She realized now that was what drove her crazy about Claudia: The woman was so much like Gran.

Yet, because of her accident, Estelle was afraid that she, too, was beginning to fall into that old woman's trap. Now she gauged the success of her days by the lack of pain in her body. Her world had narrowed to the four walls of her bedroom. She whiled away hours and hours with mindless television programs. And God knew, she had become obsessed with food. In her invalid's life her next meal was the main thing she had to anticipate.

Estelle knew she was stuck in that world for at least another month. She'd have to find some way to keep herself from going crazy . . . and from growing old. She would have to find something other than her infirmities, her meals, and her memories to keep her mind occupied, or she'd end up just like Claudia and Grandma.

Chapter 18

For the dozenth time Stan Greenwood examined the discarded items he'd taken from the maid at the Seacrest Lodge. Among the things he had spread out on the worn chenille bedspread there had to be some clue to where Jasmine Kennedy had gone. There *had* to be—he had nothing else—yet he couldn't seem to find it.

He'd gone over and over the items since yesterday, when he'd checked into his room at the Pleasantview Inn. The inn's one attraction was its price—a hundred a week, single, for a room with a Spartan bed, a lone chair and table, a hot plate, and a bathroom with a stall shower. Everything was shabby and dingy. The windowsills were covered with soot. The toilet flushed only with coaxing. The pea green linoleum floor was pitted and cracked. And, if the Pleasantview Inn had ever offered a pleasant view, it had now been replaced by the Santa Monica Freeway, which ran a few hundred feet away. Unlike at the Seacrest Lodge, here the sea air was tainted with exhaust fumes, and the roar of automobiles offended the ears.

Stan had taken the obviously useless things from the three brown plastic bags—used tissues, a plastic razor, yesterday's newspaper, some orange rinds, gum wrappers, an empty Cutty Sark bottle—and thrown them away. He examined an empty hair dye bottle—midnight black—carefully, then discarded it, too, noting that he might well now be looking for a brunette.

There was not much left. Some bits of paper—he'd tried each of the four telephone numbers written on them, and

Jasmine's voice had not answered any. One number belonged to a restaurant in West Hollywood, the second to the
Universal Studios tour; they could be discarded. The other
two were residences, but whose and where? He could keep
calling those phone numbers periodically and hope that Jasmine eventually answered one. But Stan realized that even if
she was staying at one of these places, she still might never
answer the phone. Perhaps he could find someone at the
phone company who'd be willing—for a little cash or the
right kind of attention—to give him the corresponding ad-
dresses. It might be worth a try.

The remaining items included a parking lot claim check,
not likely to be of help unless he wanted to hang out at the
lot and hope Jasmine returned. Then there was a dry-clean-
ing receipt. Chances that the dry cleaner would remember
Jasmine and also know where she had moved were roughly
nil. Stan did not even know which of the trash items had
come from Jasmine's room. The parking lot check and the
cleaning receipt could well have belonged to another
Seacrest Lodge guest.

Frustrated and angry, Stan crumpled the receipts into a
ball and threw them at the wall with all his force. Damn! It
was just goddamned unfair. What was he going to do? If he
gave up and went back to St. Louis, he might find the cops
waiting for him. By now they'd probably figured out that
Jane Burden, the nurse they sought for Ellen Pickett's murder, was really Jasmine Kennedy and that Jasmine's boyfriend was Stan Greenwood. They could be camped on his
doorstep, waiting for his return.

If he stayed here in California, how was he going to find
Jasmine? If he didn't find her soon, he'd be flat broke. He'd
been so close to her yesterday, Stan told himself for the
hundredth time, so close. His luck—no, his logic in finding
her through the classified ads had been brilliant. He'd located her from nearly 2,000 miles away. He'd come so damn
close. Now she was probably within a mile or two, and he
couldn't think where to look next. If only she'd run another
ad . . .

Maybe she would, Stan thought. Maybe Jasmine had just
been playing it safe, moving to another hotel to keep her

trail from being too easy to follow. That would be like her. He bolted from the bed, threw open the door, and ran to the news box in front of the motel. He plugged a quarter into the slot, lifted the door, and removed a copy of this morning's *Times*.

As he walked back to his room he turned to the back of the paper. His eyes searched the columns of advertisements. Nothing. Yesterday Jasmine's ad with the Seacrest Lodge phone number had still been there. If she was continuing to look for work and had simply changed her home base, she hadn't managed to have another ad started yet. Maybe tomorrow.

Stan tossed the newspaper onto the bed and flopped down beside it. The ad had been such a lucky lead—*Wait a minute,* he thought. The ad. The ad still might be the connection he'd been seeking. Would the newspaper know where she'd gone? If another ad were scheduled to begin tomorrow, it'd have to have a billing address. And if Jasmine had found a position and moved on, it was possible that the *Times* would know where she'd gone. It was worth trying.

By the time Stan reached the *Times'* west side office, he had formulated his plan. A matronly clerk behind the counter waited on him.

"I want to pay the bill for my wife's ad," Stan told her, flashing a smile. "We're moving out of our motel, and I want to make sure the bill is paid."

"The name and classification?"

"Hedberg. Gretchen Hedberg. Section two-one-four-four."

The clerk disappeared for a few minutes, then returned with a file folder. "Sixty-one fifty," she said. "It's a good thing you came in. The billing clerk was about to mail the bill."

"Sixty-one fifty sounds awfully high," Stan said. "Let me make sure you've got the right file there." He reached for it.

The woman held on to the file but opened it and laid it on the counter. "This is Gretchen Hedberg's ad all right." She read it aloud.

"Let's see," Stan said, turning the folder around. A computerized invoice itemizing the number of lines and days that the ad had run was clipped to the folder. At the top of the invoice was the name Gretchen Hedberg, and—he was in luck—the Seacrest Lodge address was crossed out in blue ink, and another was handwritten next to it: 23 Adelaide Drive. Stan's heart began to beat faster. He'd found her. He knew it in his bones. "Uh, I didn't realize it was going to be quite that much," he told the clerk. "I'll have to go get some more cash and come back."

"We're open until four-thirty. I'll keep the file pulled."

"Thanks," he said, smiling genuinely. "You've been wonderful." The clerk would never know just how wonderful.

Chapter 19

By early evening Gretchen was bone tired. Nursing Estelle Edwards reminded her of caring for Aunt Sylvia all those years ago. Estelle was more pleasant, of course—Idi Amin would be a more pleasant patient than Aunt Sylvia—but in her polite way Estelle was extremely demanding. She had kept Gretchen running up and down the long staircase all day. The old lady had wanted playing cards from the parlor, an iced tea from the kitchen, her address book from the study, her photo albums from her sitting room, her checkbook from her handbag. . . . If Gretchen had climbed those stairs once today, she'd done it twenty-five times. And when Gretchen wasn't running and fetching, Estelle wanted her to play cards, chat, carry her to the bathroom and back again, or rub her back.

Gretchen had actually begun to look forward to the telephone's ringing—that pesty girl from next door had called twice, and some other friends had phoned as well—because a call kept Estelle busy for a few minutes. While she was on the phone, she couldn't be asking Gretchen for more attention. The trouble with Estelle Edwards was that she just wasn't sick enough. Gretchen was used to nursing patients who lay in bed quietly, grateful for a minimum of her personal attention.

During her many treks around the house Gretchen had begun a mental list of things she would remove from the old Victorian house. She planned to take the valuables to her storage locker gradually, in small, inconspicuous loads.

Then, if she ever had reason to flee quickly, she'd still have a
stash of Estelle's possessions for her trouble.

She decided to begin with the dining room. There was a
lovely old tea and coffee service on the buffet—solid silver.
And in the flannel-lined silverware drawer was a sterling
service for sixteen. If the silver items were as valuable as
Gretchen estimated, they could bring her upward of $5,000
from the right dealer. She would load the things she had
earmarked into her suitcase tonight and transport them to
the storage locker as soon as Estelle was asleep.

That wouldn't be long now. Gretchen had served Estelle
another choice dinner—baked chicken with apple and raisin
stuffing and buttered fresh asparagus spears. And she had
added a special finishing touch to the meal: a glass of white
wine in which she'd dissolved enough crystals of Dalmane to
keep Estelle snoring all night. By shortly after seven Gretch-
en's patient was doing exactly that.

Gretchen sipped an undoctored glass of wine as she
loaded the silver items into the open suitcase on the dining
room table. She wrapped the coffee and teapots in newspapers to protect them from being scratched and carefully
packed them. She placed the creamer and sugar in the suitcase's side pockets. Then she wrapped the heavy serving tray
and packed it gingerly.

As she turned her attention to the silverware drawer, the
front doorbell rang. Gretchen froze. If it was that damn girl
from next door again . . . She hurriedly closed the suitcase
and carried it to the pantry. The bell chimed a second time
as she hurried to answer the door.

A fat gray-haired woman in her sixties, holding the string
of a white bakery box, stood on the porch. She smiled at
Gretchen. "Hi. You must be the new nurse. I'm here to see
Estelle."

As the woman began to push her way into the house,
Gretchen partially closed the door, preventing her entry.
"Estelle is sleeping. She can't be disturbed."

"Nonsense. We have a date. I'm right on time. My name is
Claudia Morrisey."

Gretchen stood her ground. Estelle had said nothing

about a guest tonight, and Gretchen could hardly let the woman in. Estelle was drugged unconscious. She couldn't be roused before morning. "Sorry. Miss Edwards didn't say anything to me about expecting a guest and she's already sleeping. I'm not going to wake her." She closed the door a few more inches.

"One moment, young woman." Claudia firmly planted her sturdy shoe in the door's path. She raised the hand that held the white box. "I brought dessert," she said, adding indignantly. "It took me twenty minutes to choose. I brought a whole selection—a slice of carrot cake, some Viennese torte, a cherry tart, some German chocolate cake. I went to a lot of trouble to make sure there'd be something Estelle likes."

"That's most thoughtful of you, but Estelle was exhausted this evening. She's a sick woman. I put her to bed more than an hour ago. She's sleeping and I'm not going to wake her. If you want to leave the dessert, I'll give it to her tomorrow."

Claudia Morrisey stared at the stern young woman in the nurse's uniform. She could see that she was not going to win this battle, not short of coming to blows. She looked wistfully at the bakery box. She'd anticipated eating most of its contents herself. Estelle would hardly touch those goodies; she'd never been much of an eater, not at around a hundred pounds. Yet, if Claudia didn't leave the dessert for Estelle, she knew she'd appear cheap. "Well," she said angrily. "This is a fine surprise! Estelle is going to hear about this tomorrow, you can bet on that. The least she could have done was call and tell me not to come." Claudia shoved the box at Gretchen. "Here. I hope Estelle enjoys it." Claudia's tone made it clear that she really hoped Estelle would choke.

"I'm certain she'll be delighted," Gretchen said, keeping her voice coolly polite and her temper in check. She took the box and firmly closed the door in Claudia Morrisey's outraged face.

Gretchen carried the bakery box to the kitchen and tossed it onto the table. She sat down for a moment and tried to calm herself. The encounter with Claudia Morrisey had shaken her far more than she had shown. If the woman had been able to force her way into the house, if she had found out Estelle was drugged . . . Gretchen did not want to think about the consequences. It was clear Estelle could not be allowed to set up another of these engagements, not without Gretchen's knowledge and control.

She took the kitchen phone off the hook and let the receiver dangle. There. From now on the phone would stay off the hook except when Gretchen felt like dealing with calls. Estelle would not place or answer another phone call without Gretchen's knowledge.

Her hands still shaking slightly, Gretchen finished loading the silver pieces into the suitcase. Before carrying it out to her car, she scanned the grounds carefully to make sure no one was about. Then she walked calmly to her car, opened the trunk, and locked the suitcase inside. She dared not visit the storage locker tonight, not without knowing whether that Morrisey woman might return or what other plans Estelle might have made. But somehow, Gretchen decided, she would manage a trip tomorrow. In the meantime, her loot would be safe enough locked in the Volkswagen.

As she locked the back door behind her Gretchen eyed the bakery box on the kitchen table. She broke the string and looked inside at the sugary confections. No wonder Claudia Morrisey was so heavy if this was her idea of dessert for two old ladies. Gretchen wrinkled her nose and closed the box. A second glass of chilled wine would do more for her battered nerves. She sipped it slowly as she coaxed her exhausted body upstairs to bed.

Chapter 20

When Estelle awoke, sunshine was already pouring through her bedroom windows. She felt unusually groggy, even slightly nauseated, and as she lifted her head from the pillow her temples began to throb. She lowered her head again and tried to think. It must already be late morning to judge from the sunlight brightening the colors of her bedroom rug. She raised her head again, this time more slowly, and saw that her bedside clock said nearly 11:00.

She was confused. The last thing she remembered was finishing her dinner, sipping the last of her wine. Although her food had been excellent, she had eaten lightly because . . . Because . . . Why?

Of course. Claudia. Claudia Morrisey had been coming to visit and planned to bring a dessert. Estelle had known she'd at least have to taste it to avoid offending the woman, so she'd cut back on dinner.

But what had happened? Had she fallen asleep before Claudia arrived? That wasn't like her at all. Despite what she'd told Claudia yesterday, Estelle usually had trouble falling asleep and stayed up late, reading or watching television. Certainly it was unprecedented for her to fall asleep before eight and not to wake until late the next morning. She must be sick.

Estelle shifted her cast and carefully pushed herself upright. She realized that she felt hung over, as though she'd had too much to drink. Yet she didn't remember drinking anything after dinner. Had she and Claudia been imbibing? Could she have spent the evening with Claudia and now be unable to recall it? Had Claudia ever arrived? Damn, but her head hurt. Estelle needed some coffee, and she needed it quickly. "Gretchen!" she called as loudly as she could. "Gretchen, come here!"

A few minutes later Gretchen entered Estelle's bedroom, carrying a tray laden with coffee and freshly baked blueberry muffins. "Good morning," she said cheerfully. "You certainly must have been tired."

Estelle groaned and looked away. The white of Gretchen's crisp uniform was so bright it hurt her eyes. "I feel terrible."

The nurse looked at her with apparent concern. "What's the matter?"

"My head is throbbing; my stomach is upset; I feel like an army has marched through my mouth. If I didn't know better, I'd say I'd hung one on last night. I haven't felt like this in years."

Gretchen laughed. "Have you been nipping behind my back, Estelle? Are you hiding a bottle under your mattress?"

Estelle tried to respond to the nurse's humor, but her head hurt too much. "Maybe I've got the flu. But I don't know how I could have caught it. I haven't been around anybody sick. . . ."

"I suppose you could have picked up a bug while you were in the hospital. Or your daughter-in-law could have passed something on to you." Gretchen laid her hand across the old woman's forehead. "No fever, though. If you've got the flu, you can't have much of a case."

"Maybe you'd better call Cullen and have him come over and take a look at me."

Gretchen's face froze momentarily. Her voice took a patronizing tone. "Come on, Estelle. It's Saturday. Let the poor man rest."

"He won't mind. We're old friends."

The nurse shook her head. "I'm going to have to be brutally honest with you, Estelle. When I spoke with Dr. Baxter, he told me that he couldn't keep running over here all the time for nothing. He feels that you've been imposing on his friendship far too much."

"Cullen said that?"

"Sorry to be the one to tell you, but he's a busy man, and

he's got patients far sicker than you. You don't want to be a
pest."

"But I really do feel awful, Gretchen. Something's wrong
with me."

"Don't forget I'm a nurse. I'm perfectly capable of keeping an eye on you. If I think it's really necessary, I'll call Dr.
Baxter. For now I'll bring you some aspirin." Gretchen
ducked into the bathroom and returned a moment later, carrying a glass of water and two white tablets. "Here. Sit up
now and swallow these. Then have a sip of coffee. You'll feel
better in no time." She lifted Estelle into a sitting position
and adjusted the pillows behind her back, helped her with
the aspirin, and then raised the coffee cup to her pale lips.
"All these days in bed are starting to get to you; that's all it
is. Your mind can start to play tricks on you after a while.
Particularly as you get older."

Estelle stiffened. Was her mind playing tricks on her? She
certainly was feeling confused and disoriented. What had
really happened last night? She wondered whether Claudia
had been here, whether they had visited, whether Estelle had
somehow forgotten. Maybe Paula was right, and Estelle really was becoming senile. "Gretchen," she said cautiously,
"last night . . . When I spoke with a woman friend of mine
yesterday, we made plans to get together last night. . . ."

"Yes?"

"I—I wondered if she had . . ." Estelle took another sip
of the coffee Gretchen held for her. It was difficult to find a
way to word her question without sounding as though she
were losing her mind. She might as well just blurt it out.
"Did Claudia Morrisey come to visit me last night?"

"Yes. She came. But you were already asleep, so I sent her
away."

Estelle sighed with relief. At least she hadn't spent an
entire evening with Claudia and been unable to remember it,
although she'd certainly spent many a forgettable evening
with the woman over the years. Still, that didn't explain why
Estelle had fallen asleep so early and why she felt so terrible
now. "I don't understand, Gretchen. I never go to sleep that
early."

"It's nothing to worry about. You just need more sleep

than usual when your body is trying to mend itself. And as I told you, when you spend a long time in bed, your mind sometimes just opts out. Sleep can be a defense against boredom. Or stress. Lord knows, lying in bed day after day when you're not used to it is both stressful and boring. I've seen patients, particularly those over sixty-five or seventy, who completely lost touch with reality after a week or so confined to bed."

For a moment Estelle forgot about her aching head. "What happened to them?" she asked, shocked by what the nurse was telling her.

"Nothing, really. Most of them came back to normal eventually."

Eventually. Most of them. Estelle grasped the coffee cup in both her hands and forced the rest of the hot liquid down her throat. The burning sensation in her mouth reassured her that she was indeed in the real world. No matter how bored or stressed she felt, she vowed not to retire into some kind of fantasy world. Not Estelle Edwards. She had too much to lose. Seth and Paula would like nothing better than evidence—from a qualified medical professional like Gretchen Hedberg—that Estelle was incoherent, living in a fantasy world. By the time she recovered her senses, Estelle had no doubt, she'd find herself living under her son's financial and physical control.

Her stomach still churned, and her head throbbed, but Estelle swallowed her protest. Suddenly she feared that complaining about any physical problems her nurse could not document might be used against her. What if Gretchen mentioned, even casually, to Seth or Paula that Estelle was suffering from hypochondria? She would keep her aches and pains to herself until Cullen visited again. If Cullen ever visited again . . . Estelle wondered whether he really thought her a pest. If he did, could she really depend on him for support?

She no longer knew whom she could count on for help, whose testimony would never be used against her if Seth and Paula tried to gain control over her. Estelle felt very alone. Yet this was hardly the first time in her life that she'd felt that way. There had been dozens of occasions before she'd met Zach and dozens more after he died, and she'd survived all of them. Estelle reassured herself that she was perfectly capable of fighting for her health, and her life, alone.

If that was what was necessary to survive, that was precisely what she would do.

Chapter 21

Adelaide Drive is a residential street tucked away on the edge of the bluff marking the northern edge of Santa Monica. Only a few blocks long, the road is not easy to find unless one knows where to look for it, and Stan Greenwood had had difficulty. By the time he'd located 23 Adelaide Drive last night, it was after dark. He'd sat outside in his rented Oldsmobile for a couple of hours, becoming bored when no one entered or left the three-story structure. Near midnight he'd crept close to the house and attempted to peer in the windows, but he'd been able to see nothing. Heavy draperies obscured his vision, and he could hear no sounds from within. When a neighbor's yard light suddenly went on, Stan had retreated quickly to his motel. He couldn't afford to be asked questions about why he was trespassing on this particular private property in the middle of the night.

He'd returned to his vigil this morning and found himself more impressed with the house and neighborhood by daylight. Now he could see the Pacific Ocean beyond the house, and he realized that the panoramic view increased the property's value by several hundred thousand dollars. Jasmine had found herself a plum this time. This dump had cost real money. If he played things right, Stan might get far more out of that double-crossing broad than he'd hoped.

Attempting to be inconspicuous, to make himself as invisible in the parked car as was humanly possible, he crouched low behind the Oldsmobile's steering wheel while trying to keep his eyes focused on the front door of the huge gray Victorian house. The position was supremely uncomfortable.

He'd thought it over and decided to move in on Jasmine slowly. He'd watch the house, try to judge how many people were living there, figure out what kind of scam Jasmine was running this time. He'd be patient and try to catch her away from the place, far from anyone who might be inclined to come to her assistance. Then—then he'd get his revenge on that bitch.

As noontime approached, the air inside the Olds grew warm and stagnant, and Stan began to feel more and more cramped in his seat. He straightened his body slightly, shifting his legs over in front of the passenger seat, and tried to ward off increasing drowsiness. Rolling down the windows helped cool the car a bit, but Stan was still uncomfortable. This detective routine was downright tedious. Nothing was happening in the house. Nothing was happening on the whole damn street. An Asian gardener mowing the lawn of a Spanish-style house next door provided the only movement in the neighborhood, the drone of his lawn mower adding to the monotony of the day.

Stan felt his head nodding toward his chest. He straightened up momentarily and attempted to focus his eyes on the long front porch of number 23, but his attention soon lagged once more. As the temperature inside the car edged upward he dozed off, his vigil turning into a midday nap.

Faith Sanford had not been reassured by her phone conversations with Estelle. She still felt nagging doubts about Estelle's new nurse-companion despite Estelle's protest that the woman was trustworthy. What, after all, did Estelle really know about her? Maybe she'd checked a reference or two, but there'd been no one local to talk to, so that didn't prove much. Anyone could have a friend supply a recommendation or write one herself. Faith knew kids at her school who had phonied up references to get summer jobs. She'd even heard about cases where people had gotten away with falsely claiming to have college degrees from prestigious schools, sometimes even medical degrees. By the time they were caught they'd sometimes spent years in jobs for which they'd never been qualified.

Faith remained suspicious of this Hedberg woman, disagreeing vehemently with Mrs. Wattman's opinion that Faith was overdramatizing the situation. Why, Gretchen Hedberg could be anyone, maybe even a spy planted by Estelle's son and daughter-in-law so that they could take over Estelle's house and money. What did anybody really know about her? And with Estelle confined to her bed Gretchen had free run of the rest of the house without supervision. Estelle might not think she needed help, but Faith was determined to provide some just the same.

So with time on her hands and an empty summer stretching out before her, Faith decided to begin her own investigation of Nurse Hedberg. She planned to start by entering Estelle's house as she had before, using her hidden key. But this time she would not depend upon chance to see what Gretchen was up to; she would steal quietly from room to room and observe whatever she could.

Dressed in a cool yellow T-shirt advertising the Los Angeles Olympics and a pair of white shorts with double pleats in front—she hoped that the pleats created the illusion of curvy hips where none existed—Faith descended the back stairs. Mrs. Wattman was ironing in the kitchen as she passed by.

"Where you going, miss?" the housekeeper called after her. Since their argument Mrs. Wattman had been cool to Faith, and Faith had been equally chilly in return.

"Estelle's," she replied succinctly.

"Lunch is in an hour."

"I'll be back." Faith let the screen door slam shut behind her. She kicked off her sandals and left them on the steps. Bare feet would better suit her purpose. As she stole around the hedge that separated her yard from Estelle's, she noticed a tan car parked beneath the bottlebrush tree on the boulevard. She hoped that Estelle didn't have a visitor but decided to chance it. She walked quickly down the long driveway and around the back of the big gray house, hoping that the nurse would not glance out a window and see her approaching. She wanted the element of surprise. She stole close to the back door and reached behind the holly bush for her key. Her fingers felt along the ledge but found nothing. Faith pushed the sharp-pointed holly leaves aside and examined the spot where she always kept the key, but it was empty.

Then she bent down and examined the ground beneath the ledge, but the key had not fallen there either.

Faith knew that she had left the key in its usual spot. The only explanation she could find for its absence now was that Gretchen Hedberg had taken it. Obviously the nurse did not want Faith observing what she was doing inside Estelle's house. The missing key further confirmed Faith's suspicions.

Faith swore under her breath and thought about what to do next. She could ring the bell and confront Gretchen about the key. She could go home, phone Estelle, and tell her that the key was missing. Or if Faith's father returned for lunch, she could ask his advice. In her frustration she kicked at the holly bush and pricked her toe. She swore again. Why in the hell couldn't anything go right for her?

As she walked back along Estelle's driveway the tan Oldsmobile at the curb again caught Faith's eye. Noticing a slight movement from within the car, she stopped and stared. There was someone inside. She approached the automobile cautiously, seeing a man asleep in the driver's seat. From six or eight feet away she could tell that he was not bad-looking, maybe thirty, thirty-five at the most, with dark hair cut a little too long to be fashionable. His right arm, braced against the back of the passenger seat, was heavily muscled, bulging under the sleeve of his white polo shirt. He looked strong, like one of the body builders Faith saw at the beach. The man's head was tilted back, and through the open window she could hear him snoring lightly. As she studied his face, she saw something she didn't like about his mouth, a mean twist to the corners that was noticeable even in sleep. "Hey, mister," Faith called to him from what seemed a safe distance, "what are you doing here?"

Stan Greenwood jerked himself awake to find a tall, skinny teenager with a mass of reddish hair staring at him through the car window. Some detective he was, some covert surveillance operation he was running here.

"I asked you what you're doing on this street," the girl said, scowling at him.

Stan sat up and turned the key in the ignition. There was no percentage in prolonging this encounter. "Just catching a few winks, kid," he said. "Not hurting anybody." He hit the gas, revved the engine, and pulled away from the curb. As he drove down the street, he could see the skinny girl standing on the sidewalk, staring after him.

Chapter 22

Gretchen stirred a dash of Worcestershire sauce into the tomato soup she was heating. When steam began to rise from the pot, she poured the soup into a bowl and topped it with some grated Romano cheese. With the addition of buttered crackers and a glass of strong iced tea, Estelle's lunch tray was ready. Gretchen ran tap water into the soup pan and left it to soak, then carried the tray upstairs.

Entering the upstairs bedroom, Gretchen saw that Estelle was sitting up in bed, much of her color having returned to her face. The nurse was relieved; last night she'd obviously overestimated the amount of Dalmane necessary to knock out the old woman. Each patient reacted differently, and Estelle had turned out to be easier to sedate than Gretchen had suspected. It might have been her diminutive size, her age, or mixing the drug with wine.

Gretchen vowed to be more careful in using drugs to control Estelle from now on. And she would abort her plan to drug Estelle again this afternoon so that she could steal away to her storage locker to unload her cache of treasures. Gretchen remained nervous about leaving the old woman alone in the house no matter what excuse she used to duck out for a few minutes. What if Estelle took it upon herself to call Dr. Baxter after all? Gretchen had packed a second suitcase this morning, while her employer was still sleeping, and stashed it in the pantry. In addition to the silverware and coffee service, she now had helped herself to a jade chess set, a collection of genuine Hummel figures, and several valuable ivory carvings.

Keeping these things around the house made the nurse highly nervous. She knew she was risking discovery as long as they remained in her suitcases; she would not be able to relax completely until they had been transported to her storage locker.

Yet Gretchen now realized she couldn't risk cardiac arrest by giving Estelle another hypnotic drug so soon after her bad reaction to last night's. She'd just have to be patient and wait until the right opportunity presented itself.

"You're looking much better," she told Estelle as she settled the tray on her lap. "The roses are back in your cheeks." The old woman did indeed appear improved, although her eyes remained slightly bloodshot.

"My head is beginning to clear," Estelle said. "I think I'm able to try some of that soup."

"Cream soup is nice and easy on a queasy stomach."

Estelle lifted the spoon to her lips and sipped some of the hot red liquid. "That helps. I'm beginning to feel almost human again."

"What did I tell you? You haven't got the flu."

"I guess you're—" Estelle's reply was cut short by the sound of the doorbell.

Gretchen headed toward the stairway. "I'll get rid of whoever that is," she said.

"No need," Estelle called after her. "I think I'd like some company."

Faith, carrying a stack of books she'd taken from her father's den, stood on the porch. "Estelle wanted to borrow these," she said. "I'll just take them on up to her." The girl's manner seemed to dare Gretchen to prevent her from entering.

But the nurse had no intention of keeping Faith away from Estelle this time. In fact, she decided quickly, now that Estelle was feeling better the girl's arrival might turn out to be opportune. "Come in, Faith. Estelle will be glad to see you," she said, smiling and holding the door open widely.

A little confused by this unexpectedly warm reception, Faith climbed the stairway, with Gretchen close behind her. "Here are the books you asked for," she told Estelle, catching her eye and winking. "I think I found them all."

Estelle dabbed at her mouth with a napkin. "Thank you, dear. You're so thoughtful. I've finished my lunch, and I'm in the mood for a nice visit. Sit down and stay awhile."

Gretchen collected the lunch tray and set it on a table just outside the bedroom door. "Estelle," she said, "if Faith wouldn't mind staying with you until I get back, I have a few errands I'd like to run. We're nearly out of milk, and I think some fresh fish would be nice for supper tonight."

"I don't mind sticking around," Faith said, settling herself into a comfortable chair near Estelle's bed.

"Thanks," Gretchen said, sounding genuinely grateful. If Faith and Estelle kept each other occupied here in the bedroom, Gretchen could make a quick trip to the storage locker without interference. "Can I get you anything before I leave?"

The two women declined the offer. Gretchen hurried into her bedroom to change her uniform for a less conspicuous outfit of jeans and a pink cotton sweater. As she picked up the tray of lunch dishes from the hall table, she saw that Faith was still in the bedroom, engrossed in a discussion with Estelle. Keeping an ear perked for sounds from upstairs, Gretchen piled the dishes in the kitchen sink, grabbed the suitcase from the pantry, and hurried out to her car.

Within five minutes of Faith's arrival Gretchen was backing her orange Volkswagen out of the driveway and into Adelaide Drive.

Chapter 23

Sipping coffee from a soggy paper cup, Stan Greenwood resumed his surveillance. After buying a fast-food lunch and an extra cup of coffee to take out, he returned to Adelaide Drive, parking the Oldsmobile on the opposite side of the street, a couple of hundred feet west of the gray Victorian house.

By the time the last of the coffee was lukewarm Stan saw the girl, now carrying something in her arms, emerge from the house next door to the Victorian. His hand reached for the ignition key, ready to start the car if she spotted him. But her eyes never turned in Stan's direction. The girl approached the front door of the big gray house and rang the bell. A moment later the door opened, and she disappeared inside.

For the next ten minutes or so little happened on sleepy Adelaide Drive. Stan watched as the gardener down the street loaded his lawn mower into his pickup truck and drove away, leaving only the sounds of birds in his wake. A small black fly buzzed through the open window, and Stan brushed it back outside. He counted twenty-four white specks—sailboats—dotting the blue of the Pacific beyond the bluff. His kingdom for a magazine or a solitaire deck. A guy could go batty just sitting like this. He wondered if turning on the radio for company would attract too much attention.

As Stan fought against dozing off he saw an Orange Volkswagen emerging from the driveway of number 23 with a black-haired woman behind the wheel. From his position he couldn't see her face, but she seemed to be about Jasmine's size. Jasmine could be driving any kind of car by now; Stan knew she would have unloaded the Chevy she'd had in St. Louis at the first opportunity. The black-haired woman backed the car into the street and headed it toward town. When she reached the corner, Stan started his car and followed her.

The woman's route seemed direct, and she appeared unaware of being followed. She drove along San Vicente Boulevard at an easy pace, braking only when a jogger crossed in front of her car at Seventeenth Street. She turned right on Twenty-sixth, past a quaint shopping area called the Country Mart, and continued another mile south toward the Santa Monica Freeway.

Stan hung back an average of half a block, occasionally allowing another car or two between the Olds and the Volkswagen. At Broadway he missed the traffic light, but he could see the Volks turning left on Colorado, a block ahead. When the light turned green, he gunned his engine and made the same turn, which led him into an industrial district.

But he could no longer see the orange car ahead of him. Damn. The driver must have known she was being followed after all if she'd managed to lose him that fast. She'd have had to pick up her speed considerably while he was stuck at the traffic light to have disappeared so quickly. Stan's eyes combed the side streets as he slowly drove east on Colorado. After about six blocks he made a U-turn and retraced his route. If the woman had driven ahead, he'd lost her. He decided to go back to Adelaide and see what was happening there.

He was almost back to Twenty-sixth when he saw it: The orange Volkswagen was parked on the east side of a red-brick building, nearly hidden from the road. Stan's heart skipped a beat when he saw the sign painted across the side of the building: SELF-STORAGE, WEEKLY, MONTHLY, ANNUAL RENTALS. He'd found her. A smile stole across his face as he congratulated himself. His efforts had finally paid off.

Everything added up. Stan recalled the empty hair dye bottle he'd found in the Seacrest Lodge trash; the color had been black. His original hunch had been right; Jasmine had become a brunette. The storage facility made him doubly certain. She always kept a safe place to hide the things she stole. Stan chuckled to himself. He'd not only found Jasmine Kennedy but found where she'd hidden her loot.

Stan parked the Oldsmobile a few spaces away from the Volkswagen and waited. Except for light traffic on Colorado, there was no one in sight.

She was carrying two suitcases when she emerged from the red-brick building. Stan let her open the trunk of her car before he got out of his car and stole up behind her. "Let me help you with that," he said, grabbing the suitcase she was loading out of her hand.

"Hey!" she protested, turning toward him. "Give me—" She swallowed her words when she recognized Stan. The indignation on her face was quickly replaced by fear.

"What's the matter, Jasmine? Surprised to see me?"

She cowered slightly, and Stan could read the panic in her eyes as she searched for an escape route.

"You ought to be scared, you goddamned bitch." He leaned forward and spit the words in her face. She raised her right hand as if to ward off a blow. Stan grabbed it and twisted her wrist painfully.

"Stop it. You're hurting me."

"What a shame." He dropped the lightweight, obviously empty suitcase and slapped her across the face.

Tears rose in her eyes. "Please, Stan. Please stop it. I—I didn't mean it. I swear I didn't. I'm sorry."

He loosened his grip on her wrist slightly. "You're not going to get away with it this time, Jasmine. You're not going to walk all over Stan Greenwood. I'm not one of your senile old patients."

"I know. I know that, Stan. I was just scared. After Mrs. Pickett died . . . I had to get away, that's all."

"And leave me to take the rap."

"No. Honest, Stan—"

"You wouldn't know honest if it crawled up and bit you. Don't forget who you're talking to." He twisted her wrist again until she moaned quietly and a tear slid slowly down her cheeks.

"Please . . ."

"You're going to make it up to me, Jasmine. Or is it Gretchen these days?" The pain in her eyes receded as panic returned. "How do I know that? That's what you want to know. You want to know how I found out you're using the name Gretchen Hedberg. How I found out you're living at Twenty-three Adelaide Drive. How I found out where you've stashed the stuff you've stolen. Thought you were too smart for me, didn't you?"

"That's not true, Stan. I was going to contact you just as soon—"

Stan slapped her face again, hard. "Don't bullshit me, bitch!"

She tasted blood where the blow had smashed her lip against her teeth. "Okay," she said slowly, keeping her gaze directed toward the ground. "Okay, Stan. You win. What do you want from me?"

Stan loosened his grip on her arm slightly. "You're going to pay, Jasmine. You're going to pay for this. I want half of what you've got socked away. And then I want some of the other half, to compensate me for the trouble you've caused me. I'll just have me a look at what you've got piled up, and then I'll let you know what you can keep. Now let's go back inside, and if you give me any trouble, I'll smash your lying face in."

Inside, Jasmine walked past the attendant and directly to her locker. She couldn't call for help. She'd have to find her own way out of this one. She opened her compartment and showed Stan what was inside.

"This is nothing! Clothes, silverware, knickknacks. What the hell are you trying to pull?"

"For God's sake, Stan, I've been on this job only a couple of days."

"Where's the rest of your stuff, Jasmine? The haul from St. Louis, from Chicago, from Milwaukee, from all the other towns you've worked. All of it."

"What? Did you think I'd have it with me? That stuff is stored in half a dozen different cities, and that's where it has to stay until it's safe to sell." Jasmine could sense that she was regaining some control. Stan could be managed if she played it right. If she soothed his bruised ego and threw a few crumbs his way, she could survive. She could keep him in check without handing over everything she'd worked for. "After Mrs. Pickett died, I was scared. I didn't dare go back to get any of that stuff. You can see that. I didn't know what kind of information about me the cops might have uncovered. The best thing for us to do is play it real safe for a while. A few months down the road, maybe . . ."

He kicked savagely at the locker door. "Huh! Play it safe. On what? I've got about twenty bucks to my name."

"We've got to be patient. I've got a little money. . . ."

"What about your new gig? You get me enough to live on for a few months, and then we'll talk about waiting."

He was swallowing the bait. "Here. Evidence of my good faith." She reached into her shoulder bag. "I've got forty, fifty bucks on me." She handed him her cash.

"Hot damn. This might just cover dinner."

"I can get you more. Not a lot right now, maybe a few hundred. Give me a chance to work this job right, Stan. Be patient, and we'll both be rich. This woman I'm working for now is loaded. You should see the house—"

"I have. From the outside anyway."

"Well, then, you know I'm telling the truth. A house like that is worth over a million bucks in this town. Over a million, Stan. It's packed with things like these." She gestured at the silver, jade and ivory.

"What good is that junk? I told you in St. Louis. Go for the cash, the gold coins, the stock certificates. Forget this artsy crap. I can't pay my rent with a goddamn coffeepot."

"Not now, maybe, but you can once we sell it. That coffeepot's an antique, and it's solid silver. It's probably worth a thousand bucks—to the right dealer under the right circumstances."

Stan picked up the coffeepot and examined it with new eyes. "I still need cash now."

"There'll be plenty for both of us, Stan. Just give me a chance to get in better with the old woman. I've got to gain her confidence to find out where she's hidden her money, where she's got her bank accounts. Give me some time to work on her. She'll eventually hand it all over. I know she will."

"I can help you work on her."

"No way. That's how we got into this mess in the first place. I haven't forgotten that we never did find those securities in St. Louis. That's not going to happen this time. This time I'm running things, and you're keeping out of my way."

"Then you get me some cash. Now. I can't live on sand and sun while you're romancing your old lady, Jasmine."

"I'll get you some cash. A few hundred for now, like I said. There'll be more where that came from if you're patient."

Stan thought it over. "Five hundred. I need five hundred right away, and I'll need at least that much each week until this job is finished." He picked up a box of Jasmine's clothes and emptied it onto the floor of the locker. He began loading the silver pieces into the box. "I'll take this stuff with me, just so I know where it is." He stood up and shifted the box onto his hip. "I want that cash today, Jasmine."

She had perhaps $1,000 of her traveling money left. She'd stave off Stan with some of that, then hurry this job along and get out while he wasn't looking. "I'll get you the money. But it'll have to be tonight after Estelle's asleep. I'm supposed to be shopping now, and I won't be able to get away again without causing suspicion."

"Tonight then, Jasmine."

"Don't call me Jasmine. Somebody might hear you. I'm Gretchen Hedberg."

"Gretchen then. I don't give a damn what you call yourself. Just get me the money tonight. And don't think you're going to get away with any funny stuff this time. I know where you are. I'll be watching you. You try to screw me again, I swear I'll kill you."

They agreed to meet at the Safeway parking lot at eight, then drove away in their own cars. As she headed back toward the north side of town, Gretchen's hands shook slightly on the steering wheel.

Chapter 24

"You know, Faith, sometimes I think we're bad for each other," Estelle said, laughing. "This reminds me of when I was a kid. There was this poor old woman who lived on the corner of our block, all alone in a ramshackle old house. Mrs. Delancy, her name was. Like kids sometimes do, we decided she was a witch. We looked for proof that she did all sorts of weird things: skinning alley cats, making poison potions at midnight under a full moon, putting curses on people—that sort of thing. We used to throw tomatoes on her lawn and write naughty words with chalk on her front sidewalk as our way of retaliating."

"Come on, Estelle. This is not at all the same thing. We're not kids, and Gretchen Hedberg is not some poor innocent old lady. She had no right to steal my key! She's got something to hide, and I think this proves it."

Estelle chuckled again. "When I was a kid, Tim Murphy's dog ran away. He always made a habit of lifting his leg on old Mrs. Delancy's front steps. The dog, not Tim. We convinced ourselves that the dog's running off was concrete evidence Mrs. Delancy had put a spell on him."

"If you don't believe she's got something to hide, then explain why that nurse stole my key."

"Come to think of it, maybe Mrs. Delancy *did* put a spell on that dog. He never came back."

"I'm serious, Estelle." Faith rose from her chair and walked to the window. She opened it and peered down to the driveway below. There was no sign of either the nurse or her car. "You may be in real trouble unless you start taking this seriously."

"Maybe yes, maybe no," Estelle said. "Isn't it possible that Gretchen simply didn't feel safe with a key hidden outside? Maybe she's afraid of burglars."

The girl turned her attention back to Estelle. "Then why didn't she tell you that? Why didn't she give you the key? Or give it to me?"

"I'm sure I don't know, dear. I suppose I could ask her. I just wish the whole thing didn't sound quite so paranoid."

"What do you mean, paranoid?"

"I'm beginning to sound like I'm always expecting disaster. I accused Gretchen of snooping through my things the other day. Now this business about the key. Why, I even thought I was sick this morning, wanted her to call Cullen. It's a good thing she talked me out of it; I'm certainly fine now."

"What do you mean, you felt sick this morning?"

Estelle told Faith about falling asleep early last night, missing Claudia Morrisey's visit, and feeling hung over this morning.

"That makes you feel paranoid? Don't you see, Estelle? She could be making you sick somehow. Maybe she's giving you bad food. Maybe she's drugging you. How do you know?"

"Motivation, Faith. If I've tried to teach you anything about good theater, it's that each character has to have reasonable motivation for his actions. If you can't come up with good reasons why the character you're playing does what he does, your performance is going to fail. The same holds true for life. What possible motivation would Gretchen Hedberg have for making me sick and then refusing to call the doctor?"

Faith thought a moment. "I've got it. Don't you see, Estelle? If Gretchen Hedberg can drive you crazy, Seth and Paula get the house. They want it bad enough. You told me that yourself."

Estelle felt chilled despite the warm summer breeze coming through the open window. "That's just too bizarre, Faith. Even for you to believe."

"Is it?" Faith, warming to her theory, paced back and forth at the foot of Estelle's bed. "What do you really know about this woman? Paula could have hired her to give you the *Gaslight* treatment."

"But I found her through a newspaper ad."

"What does that prove?"

"Well . . . it was *my* idea to look in the newspaper for a nurse, not Paula's."

"I see." Faith stood with her hands on hips, wearing an exasperated expression. "You talked Paula into splitting for Italy so that you could choose a nurse from the classifieds, right?"

"You should join the school debate team, Faith. You've got me so mixed up I can't think straight. I know there's something wrong with your logic, but for the life of me I can't find it."

Faith smiled in triumph. "Look at it this way: Paula tells you she's leaving. So what are your choices? You can go back to the hospital or to a nursing home. She knows there's no way you're going to do that because you're afraid she and Seth will take over your house if you leave. If you'd had a friend or relative who would come and stay with you, that'd be one thing, but you didn't. So what's left? You've got to hire a nurse. Whether you call an agency or answer an ad, either way Paula could easily pull in a ringer, and you'd never know. Not until it's too late."

"I don't think she's smart enough even to think of that, never mind to pull it off, Faith."

"Seth is, isn't he?"

"Lord, I think I'm getting my headache back. Do you realize how crazy we both sound? If anyone overheard this conversation, they'd declare me senile on the spot. Seth would get my property without a fight."

"Well, I think it's time we started to find out a few things about Gretchen Hedberg; that's what I think. What are her credentials? What do you know about her?"

"I called a woman she used to work for. At least she used to work for the woman's uncle, but he died."

"And this woman gave Gretchen a good recommendation?"

"Said she practically walked on water."

"So she could be a friend Gretchen got to vouch for her or somebody Paula or Seth dredged up. One reference doesn't mean much. What about this nursing degree she's supposed to have?"

"She showed me some sort of diploma."

"From where?"

"Someplace in Minnesota. St. something or other."

"St. what?"

"Oh, Faith, I don't remember. It was some odd sort of name. Not St. Mary or St. Matthew or anything common like that."

"Well, I'll see if I can track it down. There certainly can't be all that many nursing schools in Minnesota."

"I suppose it'll give you something to do. In the meantime, Faith, promise me you'll keep quiet about this. I can't afford to have it get back to Seth that I am getting suspicious of everything in my old age."

"You're not suspicious, and you're not old. Now cut that out."

"Please, Faith."

"Oh, all right. I haven't got anybody to tell anyway. But I want you to promise me something too."

"What?"

"Watch yourself. If the food tastes funny, don't eat it."

"You're being silly."

"Promise me, Estelle. I'm not kidding." The girl was not smiling.

Estelle wanted to discount Faith's suspicions. If she could do that, her own might lose their impact, and she would not have to feel frightened and vulnerable. Yet she intuitively felt that there was some substance to what the girl was saying. "Faith, do me a favor," she said.

"Sure."

"In my bathroom, on the shelf over the sink, there's a prescription bottle. Bring it here."

Faith brought the prescription that Gretchen had had filled from the drugstore yesterday and handed it to Estelle. According to the label, it should contain fifteen thirty-milligram capsules of Nembutal. "I can't figure out why Cullen ordered these things for me. Eight dollars for something I have no intention of taking." Estelle emptied the bottle on her lap and counted the pills. All fifteen were there. She sighed with relief. "See, Faith? We're just being paranoid."

As Estelle put the tablets back in the prescription bottle, sounds of a car pulling into the driveway drifted through the open window. Faith walked to the window, looked down, and saw Gretchen's car. "She's back."

"Here, put this away, dear." Estelle handed her the small brown bottle.

By the time Gretchen entered the bedroom Faith was ready to leave. "Glad you're back, Gretchen," she said with barely perceptible falseness. "I've got to go." She kissed Estelle's cheek good-bye and hurried down the stairs.

Chapter 25

With the librarian's help it took Faith only a few minutes to find St. Lucia's School of Nursing listed in one of the college guides. Located in Minneapolis, St. Lucia's had to be the "St. something or other" that Estelle had remembered. Faith copied the address and phone number from the guide and left the library.

Half an hour later she was locked behind her bedroom door, mentally rehearsing how she would handle her telephone inquiry about Gretchen Hedberg. She sprawled on her blue-and-white-checked bedspread and conjured up a character to play. Wealthy, thirtyish, cultured, the sort of person who would be in a social and financial position to hire a private-duty nurse, she decided. As Faith Sanford she would feel shy and tongue-tied. But playing the part of a sophisticated society woman, Faith could be confident and efficient. Like so many actors, she loved acting because it allowed her to become a different, more interesting person from the one she was in real life. She could leave the awkward, too-tall teenager behind and become someone vital, exciting, beautiful.

Prudence Edwards. That's who she'd be. She picked the name Prudence because she believed that making this call was exhibiting prudence. She chose Edwards for Estelle. If there were any way that the nursing school knew Gretchen was now working for Estelle, Prudence Edwards could be passed off as a relative.

Faith got out a pad of paper and a pen for notes, then pulled her white telephone onto the bed. She dialed a one, then the long-distance numbers and listened while the phone rang several times.

"St. Lucia's," a weary-sounding woman eventually answered.

"Hello. This is Prudence Edwards calling from Los Angeles. I'm considering employing one of your graduates, and I'd like some information about her, please."

"You'll have to call back on Monday, Miss Edwards. The office is closed on Saturdays."

"Oh, dear, Monday could be too late."

"I'm sorry. Truth is I answered the phone only because I thought it might be for me. I'm trying to catch up on some extra work, and I thought my husband might be trying to reach me."

"Look, Mrs.—"

"Randolph."

"Mrs. Randolph. This is very important. My elderly grandmother needs a private-duty nurse right away, and she wants to hire this young woman who says she's a graduate of St. Lucia's. Gretchen Hedberg is her name. Couldn't you just look her up in your files real quick? It'll only take a minute. . . . I *am* calling all the way from California."

Faith heard the woman on the other end sigh. "I don't—"

"My grandmother really would be grateful."

"Oh, all right. I suppose it won't hurt anything. Hang on."

Faith smiled to herself. In Prudence Edwards she'd obviously created a believable character.

Several minutes later Mrs. Randolph came back on the line. "Here it is. Gretchen Hedberg. Graduated in 1976. Ranked twelfth in a class of forty."

Faith felt disappointed. She was hoping she'd be told that St. Lucia's had never heard of Gretchen Hedberg or that she had flunked out. "Do you know where she's worked since she graduated?"

"We wouldn't give out that information even if we had it, Miss Edwards. All I'm authorized to release is the student's graduation date and class ranking. You'll have to get her employment record from Miss Hedberg herself."

"Yes. Well, we'll do that. Thanks so much."

The phone call left Faith confused. She'd accomplished exactly nothing, other than to confirm what Gretchen had already told Estelle. She'd learned only that Gretchen had indeed graduated from St. Lucia's School of Nursing.

Yet that confirmation didn't allay Faith's suspicions. She remained convinced that there was something wrong with Gretchen Hedberg. She would simply have to work a little harder to prove it.

Chapter 26

Estelle felt reassured by Faith's report from St. Lucia's. And Gretchen had been wonderful this afternoon. She'd hand-washed three of Estelle's negligees, dusted the bedroom, and still managed to cook a delicious salmon steak with hollandaise sauce for dinner. How could anyone ask for more from a nurse-companion? Estelle felt foolish, even a bit malicious for all the speculations she and Faith had made about Gretchen earlier in the day.

Now the two women sat watching a sitcom on television and sipping brandy. "The quality of drama has reached a new low," Estelle said. "This is worse drivel than anything we used to produce, and let me tell you, some of the old stuff was pretty bad."

As they watched, Gretchen's eyes repeatedly left the television screen and darted to Estelle's face, searching for signs of drowsiness. Then she checked the time. "Here, let me rub your shoulders a bit," she said finally.

"Twist my arm." Estelle smiled, raising her elbow slightly. She took another sip of brandy and relaxed as Gretchen's trained hands worked the knots out of her neck.

"Finish your brandy, and I'll set the glass down for you. You don't want to spill it in the bed," Gretchen said.

Estelle did as she was told, then closed her eyes and enjoyed the massage. The insipid television dialogue seemed to fade and grow distant. Finally it disappeared altogether.

As Estelle's breathing slowed, Gretchen eased her backward onto the pillows. She watched for a few minutes to be sure that the Dalmane she'd dissolved in Estelle's brandy had completely knocked out the old woman. She'd reduced the dosage this time. With luck this morning's hangover scene would not be repeated tomorrow.

Damn Stan Greenwood anyway. If he hadn't appeared out of nowhere and messed things up, Gretchen told herself, there'd be no need to risk drugging Estelle again so soon. There'd be no need for Gretchen to leave the house carrying nearly half the cash she had in Los Angeles—$500. There'd be no need to share her take on this job with anyone.

She pulled the covers up to Estelle's chin, turned off the television set and bedside lamp, and went downstairs. On her way outside Gretchen took the kitchen phone off the hook.

As she drove into the Safeway market parking lot, Gretchen could see Stan waiting in his car near the Seventh Street exit. She quashed an urge to drive past the store, keep her money, and keep going. She resented Stan's tracking her down here in Santa Monica as much as she'd resented anything in her lifetime.

Now, as she thought about Stan, about giving him the money and valuables for which she'd worked so hard, it rekindled all those old feelings she'd had as a girl. She felt as victimized as she had when Aunt Sylvia had stolen things— her time, her youth, her pride—from her. A powerful combination of fear, hatred, and anger—much the way she might have reacted to being raped—threatened to overwhelm her.

Yet, just as during her childhood, Gretchen knew she was trapped. She had no escape. There was nothing she could do to defend herself that would not cause her more harm than her tormentor ever could. As a child she had had nowhere else to go for food and shelter. She could not rebel against Aunt Sylvia's tyranny without risking life on the streets. Now she could not rebel against Stan's unreasonable demands unless she wanted to risk the inevitable results of his wrath—either direct or indirect. If she refused to give him the money she carried in her handbag, he could attack her physically, even kill her, as he'd threatened to do. She'd witnessed what his fists had done to Mrs. Pickett. Or more easily, Stan could make a simple anonymous phone call to the police, instructing them where to find St. Louis fugitive Jane Burden.

If she did not pacify Stan, Gretchen would have to run for her life. She would lose all the treasures concealed in Estelle Edwards's house, as well as the actress's more liquid assets, wherever she had them hidden.

Gretchen pulled her car into the space beside Stan's Oldsmobile and left the motor running. Stan got out of his car, opened the passenger door of Gretchen's, and climbed in beside her.

"Let's see the money," he said.

Gretchen pulled a wad of bills from her purse. "Here. Five hundred, like I said."

Stan counted it out. "Okay." He stuffed the cash into the right front pocket of his wrinkled tan pants. "Now let's get the ground rules straight. I want the same amount every week—five hundred." Gretchen started to protest, but Stan cut her off. "I don't give a damn how or where you get it. I've got to live, and I'm sick and tired of eating eggs and hamburgers. Be grateful that you're getting off this easy."

"I'll do the best I can."

"You'll come up with the money on schedule, and you won't pull any funny stuff on me. I'll be watching every move you make. If I call that house and you aren't there, if I don't see your car in the driveway—"

"You can't do that, Stan! You'll ruin everything."

"All I can't do is trust you. You think I'm going to take this five hundred and crawl back into the woodwork, you got another think coming. I'm going to keep a sharp eye on my investment this time, and my investment is you."

"Stan, be reasonable. If anyone sees you, if Estelle answers the phone and wants to know who's calling me . . . Don't you see that you'll queer the whole deal? For both of us. You can't just intrude yourself into my life like that. Everyone thinks I'm all alone in L.A., that I don't even know anybody here. How can I explain some guy suddenly calling the house, showing up unexpectedly?"

Stan knew that there was truth in what she was telling him, but he also knew that he had to have some way of checking on her. He knew that she'd split on him first chance she had to take the loot with her. "I'll give you this much: I won't call the house as long as I get two calls from you each day. Eight in the morning, seven at night—at my motel." He wrote down the phone number on the back of a gasoline receipt and handed it to her. "The first time your call is one minute late, I'll get you. I'll be watching the house too. You might see me; you might not. But you may as well figure that you're under continuous surveillance. You try to pull something on me, this time you're going to die trying."

Gretchen put the phone number in her purse. "I've got to get back. Estelle may wake up and find me missing."

"We'll talk tomorrow morning. Eight sharp. In the meantime, just figure I'm watching every move you make." Stan got out of the Volkswagen and slammed the door shut behind him.

As she drove back to the Edwards mansion Gretchen's eyes strayed frequently to her rearview mirror. Headlights drifted in and out of her view. Stan might be following her, or he might not be. She did not know.

The one thing she did know was that she could not stand this much longer. She could not live indefinitely under this kind of oppression. She'd have to do something about Stan before long. Something permanent.

Chapter 27

Once again Estelle woke with a throbbing headache and no clear recollection of having gone to sleep the previous evening. She kept her head flat on the pillow and called the nurse.

Entering the room, Gretchen saw that Estelle's face was ashen against the white sheets. "Good morning, Estelle," she said, keeping her voice cheerful. "How are you feeling today?"

"I haven't felt this terrible in the morning since I was pregnant. At my age I know that's not my problem *this* time."

Gretchen placed one hand on Estelle's forehead, the other on her patient's wrist. Although Estelle had no fever, her pulse was slightly erratic. Gretchen recognized the signs: The old woman was reacting badly to the sedatives she'd been given. She could be allergic. Or even the reduced dosage Gretchen had given her last night might have been excessive.

"Let's get you into the bathroom. If you're not feeling better in a couple of hours, I'll give Dr. Baxter a call, Sunday or not," Gretchen promised. If it came to that, she'd make sure that Cullen Baxter could not be reached.

By lunchtime, however, as Gretchen had hoped, Estelle was feeling almost normal. The nurse decided to avoid drugging the old woman again, at least until after the doctor's next scheduled visit.

Over the next few days Gretchen worked tirelessly to ingratiate herself with her employer. She continued to cook elaborate meals; she kept the bedroom and bathroom immaculate; she spent hours chatting with the old woman. She even managed to wash the spilled chicken soup and tea from the quilt that Maisie Gilroy had sewn for Estelle so many years ago and to restore it to its place of honor on Estelle's bed.

On Monday Gretchen arranged a tea party for Estelle and Claudia Morrisey, managing to erase the fat woman's previous animosity. Estelle had seemed bored during the get-together, but Claudia obviously enjoyed both the opportunity to gossip and the variety of sweets that Gretchen had baked for the occasion.

Faith visited daily, bringing enough cut flowers to turn Estelle's room into a garden. Often she and Estelle watched old movies on television together, dissecting the actors' performances and comparing them to today's more special effects-oriented productions.

When Cullen Baxter came by on his way home from the office on Wednesday and pronounced Estelle healthy and healing properly, Gretchen breathed more easily. She knew that if Dr. Baxter had noticed any signs of the old woman's having been drugged, Nurse Hedberg would be finished.

With the signs of her morning illness having disappeared, Estelle did not catalog its symptoms for Cullen. Instead, she focused her attention on improved mobility. "So when do I get my wheelchair, Cullen? I've had about enough of this bedridden routine."

"I don't see why you can't try a wheelchair for a few hours a day as long as you have Gretchen get you into and out of it and you keep your cast elevated. But you've got to promise me that you won't start racing around the halls up here."

Gretchen promised to find a wheelchair to rent the next day. She now regretted ever having mentioned the wheelchair idea to Estelle or Dr. Baxter. It would definitely give Estelle added freedom, but at least she'd have to remain confined to the second floor, and everything Gretchen had taken from the house had come from the first floor. Not that she had finished removing her selections. While Estelle slept or visited with Faith and Claudia, Gretchen had cataloged dozens more valuables she intended to add to her cache. Only because she feared Stan's interference had she not yet moved them to her storage locker or to another, more private hiding place.

Gretchen's revised plan was to wait until she had found everything she wanted from Estelle Edwards, including her stash of jewelry, cash, and securities. With the kind of wealth she saw casually displayed in her house, Gretchen felt sure that Estelle had to have plenty of that sort of thing hidden somewhere, and she thought she knew where. She'd found an old-fashioned wall safe hidden behind a signed Picasso print in the first-floor study. It had a black combination dial and a brass handle that didn't budge when she pulled on it.

In the last few days Gretchen had thoroughly searched everywhere she thought Estelle might have hidden a copy of the safe's combination—in the desk; in the drawers of various tables; in the kitchen. The only place she had not yet searched was Estelle's bedroom. Until she was able to drug the old woman again, the nurse dared not risk searching that room.

In the meantime, Gretchen worked to make herself more indispensable to Estelle with each passing day, gaining more and more of her confidence. On Wednesday, needing cash to pay the gardener and for various other expenses, the old woman sent Gretchen to the bank with a check for $200, made out to cash. Estelle certainly was making things easy for Gretchen. Now the bank would recognize the nurse as an employee authorized to cash checks for Estelle Edwards—a status that could soon prove useful.

Gretchen was also pleased to find that Estelle had minimal visitors. When the nurse first begun her job, Estelle had had a number of telephone calls from her alleged friends. But other than Faith Sanford, only Claudia Morrisey had bothered to visit, and Estelle didn't even like the woman. Now the number of calls had dwindled to almost none. Seth Edwards had called once from Italy, but Gretchen, eavesdropping on the extension phone, heard him engage in a heated argument with his mother over selling her house. Estelle had called him an ungrateful opportunist and "a sad excuse for a son" and slammed the phone down. Now, four days later, neither Seth nor Paula had called again, and Gretchen thought it unlikely that they would. If only Faith could be kept away, Gretchen realized, Estelle would effectively be completely alone—precisely where Gretchen wanted her.

"Lord, I'm going broke fast," Estelle said to Faith. They sat in Estelle's bedroom on a warm Thursday afternoon. While Gretchen was out picking up the rented wheelchair, Faith helped Estelle with her bill paying, a task she'd undertaken often in the past. Estelle made out the checks, and Faith sealed them into envelopes and stamped them.

Writing a check to cover the electric bill, Estelle saw that her bank account balance was dwindling rapidly. The money she'd set aside for the roof repair had already been severely dented. With Gretchen in the house the food bills had risen astronomically. Not that Estelle could complain; she'd been eating as though her meals had been catered by Ma Maison. Now, as she signed a check to Gretchen for her first week on the job, the bank balance dipped to a nervous-making low. Clearly, it was time to begin implementing her emergency financial plan.

"Faith, dear," Estelle said, ripping a check from the book, "run downstairs, and bring up my silver coffee service from the dining room buffet. We'll get a box from the attic and pack it up. You can take it down to Foster's for me." Estelle had called several antiques dealers and determined that Foster's on Fourth Street seemed most likely to give her a good price for the items she'd chosen to sell. She'd start with the silver pieces because the dealers seemed most interested in purchasing them, and they would be relatively easy for Faith to transport without a car. The girl's driver's license exam was still a month away.

By the time Faith returned to the bedroom Estelle had finished her bill paying. "What's the matter, dear?" she asked, seeing bewilderment on the girl's face.

"I can't find it, Estelle. The coffee service isn't there."

"It should be on the buffet. Did you look there?"

"I looked there and everywhere else I could think of. It's just not in the house. I think some other things might be missing, too."

"Like what?" Estelle asked, fear crawling down her spine.

"I'm not really sure what you had. There was so much. Some of the shelves just look a little barer to me."

"Did you look in the kitchen? Maybe Gretchen is polishing the coffee service."

Faith nodded. "I checked every room, every place I could think of, Estelle. It's just not there. The whole set is missing. Maybe we should call the police."

"I wouldn't know what to tell them, not yet. We'd better wait until Gretchen gets back and find out what she knows about it."

"What makes you think she'll tell you?" Despite the nurse's apparently improved attitude over the past few days, Faith had never entirely lost her suspicions of Gretchen. She was still upset about her missing key. When she confronted her, Gretchen had admitted removing the key from Faith's hiding place, but she'd not turned it over to either Faith or Estelle. She claimed that she'd mislaid it. "I think she took your coffee service, Estelle, and maybe a lot more," Faith said. "I think she's been ripping you off."

Estelle could think of no other plausible explanation herself, yet she was a fair person and wanted to give Gretchen the benefit of the doubt. "I'll wait until Gretchen comes back and see what she has to say."

After Gretchen had returned with the wheelchair and Faith had left for dinner at home, Estelle brought up the subject of her missing possessions. Gretchen was momentarily stunned. "What did the coffee service look like?" she asked, stalling for time.

While Estelle described it, Gretchen quickly recovered her poise. "I can't be positive," she said, "but I think it was with the things your daughter-in-law put into that box she took with her when she left."

Estelle was taken aback. "What box?"

"A big cardboard box full of stuff she said you'd given

her. You know, a lot of silver things, some little statues, a few other small things that I can't recall."

"I didn't give Paula anything."

Gretchen appeared to be as shocked as her employer. "You're not serious. She said—she told me that you'd given her some things you didn't use anymore . . . a gift for staying with you after you came home from the hospital. She even asked me to help her carry the box out to the taxicab."

Estelle didn't know what to believe. If Gretchen was telling the truth, she had even more to fear from Paula and Seth than she'd thought. Clearly her son and his wife expected that Estelle would never recover from her injury, at least not well enough to regain the use of her property. Or else they had so little respect for her wishes, for her very dignity, that they thought they could get away with stealing from her.

If Estelle called the police, she wasn't sure how she could prove that Paula had taken anything. The only proof she had was Gretchen's story. In any case, if what Gretchen said was true, Estelle didn't want the police involved. She might be enraged about this betrayal of her family bonds, but she would never turn a relative over to the authorities. Even if she were that hostile toward Paula, the publicity would be devastating. She hated to think what a gossip like Claudia Morrisey would make of a scandal like that.

Estelle realized that she didn't even dare risk calling Paula in Italy to ask about the missing items. Such a phone call might be used to help prove that Estelle was becoming increasingly paranoid, that she was becoming totally senile. Perhaps Paula and Seth planned to return the missing items if Estelle complained, claiming that she had given them as gifts and that she now couldn't even remember doing so. If proving her mentally incompetent was the game her children were playing, Estelle and everything she owned were their ultimate prize.

And if Gretchen was lying? If the nurse was stealing from Estelle while she remained imprisoned on the second floor of her own house? Estelle shuddered as she realized how much power over her she'd willingly placed in this young woman's hands. She might even have put herself in increased danger by confronting Gretchen Hedberg about the missing property. If Estelle ordered the nurse out of the house, would she leave? And if she did, what would she take with her? If Estelle called the police, would they take her seriously in view of Gretchen's story about Paula? Or would her call be used to help build a case that Estelle Edwards had become a crazy old woman?

Estelle realized that the safest course for her, at least for the present, was to appear to be convinced by Gretchen's explanation. She could not threaten the nurse, not from her current position of weakness. To do so could be dangerous.

"Paula must have misunderstood," Estelle said, summoning long-unused acting skills to appear accepting of the story she'd been told. "I suppose I told Paula I would leave her and Seth those things in my will, and she thought I intended for them to have them now." Estelle smiled at the nurse as though laughing inwardly at her own silly overreaction. "I certainly hope you didn't think I was accusing *you* of taking anything. . . ."

From now on Estelle would be more careful. No longer gullible, she would watch Gretchen Hedberg with new vision. In time, she was sure, her observations would show her the truth. And with the right evidence she would move, from a position of greater power, to protect herself.

Chapter 28

Gretchen slept fitfully. She lay awake far into the early-morning hours, fretting about her confrontation with Estelle Edwards. Although she was badly shaken, she was not willing to cut her losses and run. Despite both the suspicions that Estelle had expressed yesterday and the threat posed by Stan Greenwood, Gretchen felt compelled to see this job through to the end. She'd already put in more than a week of her time here, and if she left now, she wouldn't dare find another likely victim in the Los Angeles area. The way she saw it, the treasures in this house, the money and jewelry she believed were in that wall safe—all of them rightly belonged to her. She had no intention of leaving without them. She'd been cheated too often in her life; she would not be now, not when she was this close to financial freedom.

Success with this job would now mean keeping Estelle under constant surveillance. Her patient could no longer be allowed private visits with anyone. She could no longer be allowed to make or receive telephone calls. She could no longer be allowed the slightest opportunity to summon aid.

Gretchen rose early, put on a clean white uniform, and went downstairs to start breakfast. She placed her morning call to Stan while Estelle was still asleep. No sense risking the old woman's picking up the extension phone and overhearing her conversation.

Stan sounded hung over and hostile. "I need more money," he growled at her. "You can give me my next installment today, and make it six hundred this time. I ran short last week."

Gretchen balked. "No. You're not getting six hundred today. You're not getting anything until things calm down around here. The old woman's discovered that some of her things are missing—that silver stuff you've got. She's already suspicious of me. I don't dare leave her alone now."

"That's your problem, not mine."

"Wrong, Stan. It's your problem, too. If she calls the cops on me, there isn't going to be another dime for you."

"Look, babe, you come up with that money, or your old lady won't have to call the cops. I'll save her the trouble."

"Don't be ridiculous, Stan. You turn me in, and you turn yourself in. Even *you* aren't that stupid."

"You bitch. Don't you call me stupid—"

"Okay, okay, I'm sorry," Gretchen said, keeping her voice as low and calm as she could manage. "You're not stupid, Stan. That's why you aren't going to call the police. I'll do the best I can to get you some money, but there's no way I can get away from here for a couple of days. You're going to have to be patient."

"The hell I will—"

"Shut up, Stan," Gretchen said. "I am not asking you; I'm telling you. You are not going to screw this up for me. Or for yourself. Wait a couple of days, and you'll get your money. Good-bye." She broke the connection quickly, then left the receiver dangling off the hook.

She wasn't sure exactly what Stan would do, but she knew that she couldn't chance leaving the house to meet him today, not with Estelle's suspicions already aroused. And if the old woman had somehow managed to summon help already, Gretchen would need the last of her cash to get away. She was not about to give it to Stan. Somehow she would have to keep him at bay until she discovered the combination to that safe.

Chapter 29

By midafternoon Gretchen was exhausted. When she wasn't in the kitchen, she spent nearly every minute with Estelle, flattering and cajoling her patient while she tried to assess how much damage had been done by yesterday's events. Estelle seemed no different, as trusting of Gretchen as she had been since the beginning. Yet, Gretchen reminded herself, the woman was an actress, adept at playing a role.

Now Gretchen had finished bathing Estelle and had carried her back to bed. Wearily the nurse leaned over the side of the old claw-footed bathtub as she scoured it with Ajax. The cold tile floor was hard against her aching knees as she stretched to reach the far end of the tub.

The first time the doorbell rang Gretchen thought it was exhaustion playing tricks on her. But as it rang again Estelle roused her: "Gretchen, that's the door."

She wiped her sudsy hands on a bath towel and hurried down the stairs. The last thing she needed right now was a visitor. She opened the front door to Stan, who was weaving slightly and smelled like a brewery. "Good Lord, what are you doing here?" Gretchen held the door partially closed in an attempt to keep Stan outside, but he shoved his full weight against it and barged into the foyer.

"Stan, you've got to get out of here. Now. You're going to ruin everything."

"I'm here to get my money," Stan said, placing a hand on Gretchen's shoulder. "You won't come to me, I'll come to you."

She pushed his beefy hand away. "I haven't got your

money, Stan. I told you you'd have to be patient. Now get the hell out of here before you get us both arrested."

"Not too shabby," Stan said, surveying the foyer. He sauntered in and deposited himself heavily into the Duncan Phyfe chair beside the fireplace.

"Stan, please leave—"

"You ain't payin' attention, sweetheart. I go when I get my six hundred."

Struggling against rising panic, Gretchen angled for control of the situation. "I haven't got it, Stan. Honest, I'd give you the money if I had it."

"Then you'd better go get it from that old lady. Now."

"You're drunk." Gretchen grabbed one of Stan's arms and tried to pull him out of the chair. "Come on now. Get out of here." Although she yanked at him with all her strength, Stan didn't budge. Gretchen gave up and let go.

"Well, now, that's better," he said, smiling woozily at her. "You gonna get my money from that old lady, or am I? Remember, I don't always ask so nice."

Gretchen cursed herself inwardly for not having gotten rid of Stan Greenwood back in St. Louis. If she'd had the guts to give him a fatal dose of that sedative when she'd had the chance, she wouldn't be dealing with him now. That would teach her to be sentimental. Now she'd have to deal with him. Permanently. It had become a matter of survival.

"Stan," she said, keeping her voice low, "Estelle doesn't keep her money in the house. It's all in bank accounts. But I can get you some money tonight, some of my own."

"Thought you said you didn't have any."

"I don't have six hundred dollars here. But I've got that much hidden away. When I came to L.A., I didn't know where I'd end up living, so I stashed most of my cash in a safe place. I'll take you there tonight, after my patient is asleep."

As he sprawled out, Stan's athletic body seemed too big for the fragile antique chair. He leaned back and sized up Gretchen, who stood within his arm's reach. His hand clenched into a fist reflexively. If he wanted to, he could crush her like nothing. And maybe he would—after he'd had a look at her hoard. Sobering, he fixed her with a gaze and said, "If you're lying, you're dead."

"I'm not lying, Stan. I'll see to it that Estelle is asleep early. We'll meet the same place as last time, and I'll take you to where I've got the money."

A voice drifted down from upstairs. "Gretchen! Gretchen, who's at the door?"

Gretchen glared at Stan and placed an index finger across her lips. "Just a salesman, Estelle," she called up the staircase. "I'll be right up." She lowered her voice and turned back to Stan. "Now get out of here. You'll get the money tonight. Until then I'll keep working on my patient."

Stan pushed himself to his feet and shuffled slowly toward the door. "Eight o'clock. If you're not there by eight o'clock, or if you're lying to me, I swear I'll come after you and the old girl both."

Gretchen closed and locked the front door behind him. She leaned against it for a moment, shivering slightly. She took a deep breath and struggled to regain her poise.

When she returned upstairs, Estelle demanded, "What in the world kept you so long?"

Gretchen fixed an exasperated expression on her face. "Some guy tried to give me a hard sell. Some people just don't know when to quit, but I got rid of him."

Chapter 30

Gretchen wasn't taking any chances. She had mixed the sleeping medicine—Nembutal was her choice this time—into both Estelle's coffee and the applesauce accompanying the grilled pork chop. Even if Estelle claimed a lack of appetite, as she had last night, she would have to eat or drink something. Just a small portion of the powerful hypnotic Gretchen had hidden in her meal would knock the old woman out until morning.

Gretchen forced herself to eat along with her patient. Each chunk of pork, each piece of broccoli tasted dry, although she knew the meal had been expertly cooked. As her fork moved slowly between her plate and her mouth, Gretchen watched Estelle carefully for signs of drowsiness.

Shortly after seven, only partly finished with her meal, Estelle slumped against the pillows and passed out. Gretchen picked up a fork from the floor, where Estelle had dropped it, then tucked the bedcovers under her patient's chin. "Happy dreams, Estelle," she murmured, clearing away the dinner dishes. She pushed the rented wheelchair out of the room, turned off the bedroom lights, and closed the door behind her. With the dose she had ingested, Estelle certainly would not wake for many hours, but Gretchen wasn't taking any chances. If her patient did somehow wake, she'd be confined to her room.

Gretchen put on blue jeans, a dark sweater, and a pair of sturdy walking shoes. She pulled her duffel bag from her closet shelf and tossed it onto the bed. Returning the bottle of sedative pills to her "tool kit," she took out the essential things she'd need for the remainder of the evening: a flash-light and her small pearl-handled automatic. After checking to see that the gun was loaded, she put it into her handbag.

She tried not to think too much about the events ahead of her. Gretchen had cared for Stan Greenwood once; now all that seemed years ago. But he, like everyone else she'd ever tried to love, had betrayed her. Her mother had died. Aunt Sylvia had used her as a despised and overworked servant girl. Friends had gone on to their own lives, leaving her behind.

She now realized that Stan had been a mistake from the beginning, a bad mistake that had become fatal—first for Ellen Pickett and soon for Stan himself. Unfortunate as that was, there was nothing Gretchen could do about it now. Nothing, except whatever was necessary for her own survival.

That included giving herself an alibi for tonight. To any-one who might inquire, she must make it appear that she'd been home, that she'd never left her sleeping patient. On her way out of the house Gretchen made certain that the kitchen telephone was off the hook. There must be no evidence that anyone had called the Edwards house and received no an-swer.

Gretchen arrived early at the supermarket parking lot and waited for Stan to arrive. She watched the shoppers load bags of groceries into their automobiles and thought wist-fully about having a family to shop for, to cook for, to love. Someday, she told herself, she, too, would have that. Some-day, when this life was behind her, when she had what she needed from Estelle Edwards and all her other patients, when people like Stan were part of a distant and forgotten past.

When she saw his tan Oldsmobile pull into the lot, she got out of her car and locked it. Gretchen's plan called for Stan to do the driving.

"Hi," she said, climbing into the Olds's passenger seat. She smiled slightly.

Stan eyed her warily and did not return her smile. "Where to?" Gretchen directed him onto the northbound Pacific

Coast Highway, following the route toward the old picnic place she'd explored her first day in L.A. Traffic was light as they proceeded parallel to the beach. "Where is this place?" Stan asked.

"Topanga Canyon. A friend let me use her cabin for a few days, and I stashed some of my stuff there. I know where she keeps an extra key." She had rehearsed a story in her mind this afternoon.

"She's not home?"

"Uh-uh. I checked. She's a stewardess, and she's on a flight until Sunday."

Stan stared at Gretchen. "I didn't know you had any friends in Los Angeles."

"There are a few things you don't know about me." Beyond Stan's shoulder Gretchen saw the summer sun sinking slowly into the Pacific. Someday she would own a place with a view like that, she promised herself. But first, she must survive, and taking care of tonight's problem would help ensure that.

"Tell me about this old lady you're nursing," Stan said.

Gretchen turned her eyes away from the hypnotizing shoreline. "She used to be an actress, I guess back in the thirties and forties. She's in some of those old pictures on TV. We watched one the other night, with Spencer Tracy and Clark Gable. Estelle wasn't bad. . . . Turn right at the light."

Stan angled the car onto winding Topanga Canyon Boulevard. As they passed the tiny, quaint town of Topanga, dark was falling. "How much farther?"

"Not too far. Take the second road to the right. Slow down, it's hard to see the turnoff." Gretchen directed Stan onto a narrow road that climbed into the mountains, beyond the state park. She remembered a spot just above the park that would do. They drove past a conclave of expensive houses, then entered an open area where construction of another house was under way. The paved street ended, and a rutted dirt road took over.

"You sure this is the right way?" Stan asked.

Clutching her purse tightly with both hands, Gretchen strained to keep her voice casual. She'd had years of practice in the essential survival skill of lying. She'd learned it well as a child, when only a well-told lie could save her from her aunt's frequent and brutal punishments. "It's not much farther now," she told Stan. "It's nothing fancy, just a cabin sort of affair. Jenny bought it cheap a few years ago. She says she's waiting until these high-rent places build up to the edge of her property. Then she figures she'll sell and make a fortune." As the car bumped over the crest of the hill, Gretchen almost wished that such a rustic cabin, that such a friend as Jenny really existed. "There's a turnoff about thirty feet ahead. Pull in there, and park. We'll walk from there."

Stan parked the car, stepped out into the high grass, and looked around. Gretchen opened her own door and emerged from her side of the car, her right hand thrust inside her handbag. She walked around the front of the vehicle until she was facing Stan. He eyed her suspiciously. "This doesn't look right to me."

Gretchen pulled the gun out of her bag and pointed it at him. "It looks fine to me."

"Hey—" Stan lunged for the gun.

She raised it quickly and took aim. Allowing herself no time to think or to falter, she squeezed the trigger firmly and shot Stan directly in the heart. A good nurse always knows where to find the heart. Stan staggered, clutched his chest, and fell backward. His last sound was less a cry than an expression of shock and bewilderment.

While the shot still echoed against the hills, Gretchen took out her flashlight and approached the body. Taking care not to step into the rapidly spreading pool of blood, she put the gun away and felt for a pulse. She found none.

She efficiently removed Stan's wallet and car keys from his pants pockets and retreated to the Oldsmobile. "I didn't want to do it, Stan," she said softly. "You should have stayed in St. Louis. You should have known when to quit."

The drive back to Topanga Canyon Boulevard was the worst part. Shooting Stan had been easier to do than Gretchen had feared. Killing with a gun was in some ways more remote, and certainly quicker, than killing by injection or pill overdose. But Gretchen had been surprised by the loud retort of the gun and its echoing against the mountains. As she drove back along the narrow, winding road, her hands shaky on the steering wheel, she feared meeting a police car summoned by a sharp-eared neighbor.

When she reached the town of Topanga, she breathed a little more easily. And by the time she made a left turn onto the Pacific Coast Highway she began to believe she had escaped.

Forty minutes later Gretchen parked the tan Oldsmobile in an airport parking ramp near the American Airlines terminal. It could stay at LAX for weeks before anyone would wonder about it. She locked the keys inside and walked down the concrete stairs to the cabstand outside.

As she emerged from the cab in front of an apartment building a block from the Santa Monica Safeway store, Gretchen handed the driver a $20 bill for the fare and took $2 in change. She watched him drive away before she turned to walk to her car.

In just a few minutes, Gretchen told herself, it would all be over. She would be back at Estelle Edwards's house, her alibi intact. And Stan Greenwood would never bother her again. Now she would be free to work on Estelle, and Estelle's hidden fortune, without interference.

Chapter 31

Shortly after nine o'clock Faith made the familiar trek between her house and Estelle's for the second time that day. She'd been frustrated for the previous hour, dialing Estelle's phone number again and again and always receiving a busy signal. Estelle almost never talked that long.

The darkness of the overcast, starless night did nothing to slow her pace. Faith could have followed this route blindfolded. Yet it was unusual for the porch lights to be out at the Edwards house. Before her accident keeping the front porch illuminated to discourage burglars had been among Estelle's few financial indulgences.

Now, however, it was clear that the nurse was in charge of the lights as well as everything else in this house. Faith had visited Estelle for an hour this afternoon, but Gretchen had managed to hover over them so successfully that they had had no opportunity for private conversation, no chance to discuss anything Estelle might have learned about her missing property. Faith had hoped that a telephone conversation would be easier; she had formulated specific questions that Estelle could answer with just a yes or no if Gretchen persisted in lingering nearby.

Faith made her way up the wooden stairs of the porch and pressed the doorbell. She could hear it ringing inside, but no one answered it. She pressed the bell again. And again. Still no response.

Now Faith became truly worried as she searched her mind for a plausible explanation. She followed the porch around the side of the house and peered through the French doors.

A crack between the heavy dining room draperies showed
her only the dim, empty room. There was no sign of movement inside. Perhaps Gretchen had gone out, and Estelle
was spending the evening chatting on the phone. Faith decided to try telephoning once more.

Sitting on the edge of her bed, the white telephone in her
lap, Faith again got a busy signal. She dialed the operator
and asked him to check whether the line was in service.

"I'll try that number for you, ma'am."

Faith again heard the busy signal. "Can you check to see
if the phone's out of order?" she asked. "That line's been
ringing busy since eight o'clock."

"If this is an emergency, I'll verify the line. Do you want
me to do that?"

Faith thought for a minute and decided to follow her intuition. "Yes. Please do." She gave the operator her name and
was somehow not surprised to be told a moment later that
there was no conversation on the line; the telephone was off
the hook. "Thanks for trying," she said, now feeling certain
that something was very wrong at the big gray house next
door.

If she had her key, she could go in and check to see that
Estelle was all right. But that nurse had stolen the key. . . .
Faith didn't know what to do. Her father was in Palm
Springs for the weekend—with which one of his girlfriends
she didn't care to know. Mrs. Wattman, carrying her ever-
present "coffee mug," had gone to bed; by now she'd be
beyond any ability to help.

Estelle could be in trouble. She could be sick, even dying.
And that damn nurse was nowhere to be found. Anger rising
in her, Faith decided that the lack of a key could not keep
her from helping Estelle. She located a sturdy flashlight in
the kitchen and retraced her steps next door.

When there remained no response to her renewed assault
on the doorbell, Faith returned to the French doors outside
Estelle's dining room. She shone the flashlight through the
crack in the draperies and again saw no movement inside.

She rattled the doors, but the lock held. Using her flashlight to guide her, Faith carefully inspected each door and window within her reach—every one on both the main floor and the basement levels. But someone had been efficient in securing the big gray Victorian against intruders. Frustrated, Faith tried the doorbell once more, then returned to the French doors outside the dining room.

"Forgive me, Estelle," she said under her breath as she swung the flashlight in an arc toward the glass pane nearest the door handles. The sounds of shattering glass disturbed the nearly total silence. Faith pushed the last of the glass shards into the room with the end of her flashlight, reached inside and released the lock on the French doors.

Bits of glass crunched under her shoes as she stepped inside. She closed and locked the doors behind her, then crept through the massive room, guiding herself with the flashlight. Faith's eyes darted about the shadowy room, halting a moment at the bare spot on the buffet, where the silver coffee service once had been.

Reaching the foyer, she called up the stairway, "It's just me, Estelle. It's Faith." The house responded with an eerie silence.

The hairs on the back of her neck standing on end, Faith crept slowly up the stairs to Estelle's bedroom. She opened the door and saw the old woman lying as still as death on her bed.

"Estelle," Faith called once quietly, then again in a louder voice. She turned on the bedside lamp and saw that the old woman was pale and breathing slowly and shallowly. "Estelle, wake up." Faith's voice took on increasing anxiety.

She leaned over the bed and took hold of Estelle's fragile shoulders, shaking her gently. "Estelle, wake up. *Please* wake up."

Settling Estelle back against the bed pillows, Faith touched her forehead, then her cheeks. The old woman seemed unnaturally cool. Was she dying? What was wrong with her? "Estelle, talk to me," the girl pleaded.

Tears brimming in her eyes and hysteria rising in her voice, Faith called to the old woman over and over again, but there was no response.

Chapter 32

Using only the parking lights to guide her, Gretchen maneuvered the Volkswagen into its parking spot in the garage at the back of the Edwards property. With the garage door still open, careful not to do anything that might call a neighbor's attention to the fact she'd been out, she crept up to the back door of the house.

She went into the kitchen, closing and locking the outside door behind her. Once she was inside, weariness and a faint feeling of loss began to replace her nervous-energy high. She slumped into a chair at the kitchen table and sat for a moment in the dark. For the first time Gretchen felt as though she'd really committed a murder. With her elderly patients, she often rationalized, a slight overdose—just enough to hurry an already inevitable death—was not really murder at all. Most of them probably welcomed death's release from pain.

Ellen Pickett, of course, had been Stan's doing, not hers. She had begged him to stay away from that poor old woman. Gretchen felt adamantly that Ellen Pickett's death had not been her fault.

But Stan was different. He had posed a threat that had to be removed. Gretchen had attempted to do that by leaving him, but he'd forced her to take stronger measures. Stan Greenwood had turned her into a murderer.

As she sat at the table, her head in her hands, Gretchen suddenly heard a noise from somewhere in the house, a faint sort of cry. She straightened up abruptly. It didn't seem possible that the old woman could have awakened so soon.

Given her rapid and complete reactions to sedation last week, she should be asleep for hours more. Gretchen rose from the table and walked through the pantry into the dining room, toward the front of the house. As she passed through the massive room, a small gust of air ruffled her hair. She turned toward its source. In the dim light, she could see pieces of broken glass scattered across the parquet floor in front of the French doors.

Placing her handbag on the dining room table, Gretchen removed her flashlight and gun. She shone the light on the shattered glass, then raised it to illuminate the missing pane next to the door handle. Someone had entered the house.

The noise she had heard a moment ago was repeated. Now Gretchen could tell that it was coming from an upper floor of the house. She hurried silently through the foyer and up the stairs. As she reached the landing she heard the noise again, coming from Estelle's bedroom, where a light was shining from under the door.

Indignant, Gretchen had visions of a burglar attempting to rob the old woman. . . .

She burst into the bedroom, holding the gun out in front of her. A tall figure in dark clothing was bent over Estelle. "Get away from her!" Gretchen shouted, pointing the gun. As the figure turned, Gretchen recognized that troublemaking teenager from next door. Faith's face was streaked with tears, and she was close to hysteria.

"Help me. You've got to help me," Faith cried. "There's something wrong with Estelle. I can't wake her up." The girl seemed unaware of the gun pointed at her.

Gretchen assessed the situation rapidly. "What are you doing in here?" she demanded.

"Something's wrong with Estelle," the girl repeated. "You've got to do something."

Gretchen lowered the gun. "There's nothing wrong with her. She's just sleeping."

"No, she's not. I've been trying to wake her for ages, and she won't come to. I think she's in a coma or something. We'd better call the doctor." Faith wiped her face with the back of her hand.

Gretchen moved closer to the bed and observed Estelle.

She was clearly heavily drugged, her breathing slow but even. Placing a hand against her patient's ashen face, Gretchen said, "There's nothing wrong with Estelle. The doctor prescribed a sleeping pill for her, and she's in a deep sleep. There's nothing to worry about. She'll get a good night's sleep and feel better for it in the morning."

Faith backed away from the bed and for the first time noticed the gun in Gretchen's hand. "What are you doing with that thing?" she asked, repulsed and fascinated.

Gretchen straightened up, pointing the gun at the floor. "I'm protecting my patient. What do you think I'm doing? I come home, find that the house has been broken into, what am I supposed to do?"

Faith retreated slightly, keeping her eyes on the nurse. "Where were you anyway? Why did you leave Estelle alone?"

Gretchen thought quickly. If she weren't prepared to kill Faith and to find some way to dispose of her body, she'd have to get rid of the girl until she could strip the house of its valuables, find the combination to that safe, and escape with its contents. "Not that it's any of your business," she said, "but I had some errands I had to run. For Estelle. Now you get out of here before I call the police."

"What do you mean, call the police?"

"I don't care who you are, Faith, you're guilty of breaking into this house. You frightened me half to death. Now get out of here and let my patient sleep in peace before I call the cops to get you out."

Faith glanced at Estelle. The tiny woman shifted her position slightly. Was her movement a sign that she was indeed just sleeping? Had Faith been a fool to come barging in that way? She'd only wanted to help Estelle. . . .

"Come on," Gretchen said, gesturing toward the door with the gun. "Just get out. You hear me? Just get out."

Faith glared at the nurse with unveiled resentment. "I still think there's something wrong," she said.

"You're just going to have to take my word that Estelle is perfectly fine. Now go home."

Gretchen reached to take Faith by the elbow and lead her out of the bedroom, but Faith jerked her arm away. "Don't you touch me," she said. "I'll go, but I want to talk to Estelle first thing in the morning, and she'd better be all right or I'll be the one calling the police."

"You're not going to do anything that foolish, Faith. I am a trained nurse following doctor's orders with my patient, and you—you are guilty of a felony. Think about it. Estelle might not want to press charges against you, but I wouldn't mind. I might even enjoy it."

Faith muttered under her breath as she walked downstairs. Although she remained suspicious of the nurse, she felt impotent to do anything about it. Gretchen was right: Faith dared not call the police. If there truly were nothing amiss here, Estelle would never forgive her. Having the police barge in to check on her health and safety might even work against Estelle in her fight to retain control over herself and her financial affairs.

As the nurse started to close the front door behind her, Faith said, "Tell Estelle I'll be back tomorrow morning."

"No, you won't," Gretchen replied. "I've seen enough of you for a good long while. You harass either me or my patient again, and I'll press charges against you." She slammed the door shut, leaving Faith standing alone and looking forlorn on the front porch.

Despite a bone-aching exhaustion, Gretchen knew she had no time for resting. She might be able to intimidate that snoopy Faith, but if the girl brought adult help tomorrow, the results could be totally different. Gretchen would have to take the things she wanted from this house and get that safe open quickly. Then she would head north, perhaps drive to Monterey or to San Francisco. With what she was certain she would find in that safe, she'd be rich enough to leave all her false identities behind, to become Jasmine Kennedy once again. She would be rich enough so that she would never again be forced to play nursemaid to a sick old person. She would find somewhere she could rid herself of this constant fear of discovery, a place where she could relax and be free for the first time in her life.

Gretchen found boards, a hammer, and nails in the cellar and used them to close up the broken section of the French doors. Then she set about packing the objects she would take with her when she left Estelle Edwards's house. Now past making any effort to hide her thefts, she packed every cardboard box she could find with small valuables: a nineteenth-century Persian lacquer pen case, a set of silver tankards, two small oil paintings by Renoir and Monet, a gold filigreed cigarette box, a pear-shaped Japanese porcelain vase in the Kakiemon style, a Louis XV gold and mother-of-pearl snuffbox, and dozens of other costly pieces. Using her practiced eye for quality, Gretchen efficiently stripped each room in turn of its wealth, leaving behind only things of questionable worth and those too large for her to transport. She moved everything into the pantry and closed the swinging door. Tomorrow, by daylight, she would find more boxes in the attic in which to pack and remove her treasures.

Only Estelle's bedroom remained unsearched when, well after 4:00 A.M., an exhausted Gretchen fell into a troubled sleep.

Chapter 33

Estelle awoke gradually, drifting in and out of sleep for at least an hour before she opened her eyes. She shut them again quickly. The throbbing headache, the dry mouth, the nausea she'd suffered last week had returned to plague her, as badly as before. Holding her head steady on the pillow and her eyes shut tightly against the painful light, Estelle tried to sort out her thoughts. If she were suffering from an illness, surely it would not come and go so arbitrarily. And after a week's freedom from this brutal discomfort she felt certain that her mind was not playing tricks on her. Estelle Edwards had never been a hypochondriac, and she didn't believe she was one now, no matter what Gretchen Hedberg implied.

Gretchen Hedberg. Even with her temples pulsating and bile rising in her throat, Estelle realized that her nurse represented the final possible reason for her strange discomfort. Each bout had come when she awoke in the morning. On each prior evening, Estelle realized, she'd been unable to recall falling asleep. In fact, she'd been unable to remember even finishing her dinner. If she were not losing her mind, there was only one logical conclusion: Gretchen was drugging her—or, worse, slowly poisoning her.

Unlike last week, now Estelle could see some possible reasons why her nurse might do that, and those reasons no longer seemed to be evidence of her own paranoia. Seth and Paula's desire to gain control of her money was one. Much as she didn't want to believe it, Estelle knew that her son and daughter-in-law could have bribed Gretchen to make Estelle think she was going crazy or even to feed her some drug that would actually result in insanity. Estelle believed that such drugs existed. She'd read about people who'd jumped off buildings while under the influence of LSD and about others who'd run naked through the streets and fought off the police with superhuman strength after smoking angel dust.

The missing silver constituted another motive. Estelle's headache increased as she realized that Gretchen might be stripping the house of her beautiful, richly sentimental possessions while she lay helpless in her bed. If the nurse were stealing, she might intend to keep Estelle drugged so that she could not summon help. Or she might be poisoning her to assure that she would never recover.

Estelle attempted to raise her head from the pillow, then quickly lowered it again, praying that the throbbing pain would cease. Whatever was happening to her, she realized, she had to get help soon. She was losing her desire to fight back. The main thing she wanted to do was go back to sleep so that the pain would stop. Somehow she knew that if she gave in to that impulse, she was finished. She had to find help. Perhaps she should call the police, even if she risked their thinking she was a senile old woman. If she called the police, they'd have to come. She would tell them that Gretchen was poisoning her, that she was stealing from her. They would arrest Gretchen and take her away . . . wouldn't they? But if they believed Gretchen instead of Estelle, then what?

There must be someone else who could be counted on to believe Estelle over her nurse, no matter how things looked, someone who would rescue her without question. Of course, Estelle thought, the doctor. She would call Cullen. He would see that her suffering resulted from some sort of chemical Gretchen had put in her food. She'd known Cullen Baxter since he was a child; he would believe whatever she told him. He would help her.

Estelle pushed herself slowly and carefully to a half-upright position, keeping her eyes closed. She opened one eye at a time, then reached for the bedside telephone and pulled it onto the bed. She winced as the slight exertion reverberated through her aching body. She pushed herself into a sitting position and put the receiver up to her ear. But instead of a dial tone, Estelle heard only the shrill sound of an off-the-hook signal. She jabbed several times at the phone's disconnect button, but the dial tone did not return. In frustration she replaced the receiver and leaned back in her bed.

For the first time in years Estelle felt her aloneness as if it were a physical pain. She realized how vulnerable she had become, trapped in this room, unable to communicate with anyone but her nurse-companion—a woman about whom she knew nearly nothing, a person who might well be her persecutor. Her beloved house had become her prison, her possessions a motive for her incarceration, possibly even for her execution. She shuddered as she considered her possible fate.

Yet, as alone, ill, and trapped as she felt, there was something in her that refused to give up. Until now Estelle Edwards had seldom felt fear or intimidation. She'd always prided herself on not being the "victim type," despite her diminutive size and her sex. She'd once read a story about cops who could pick people out of a crowd and predict which ones were probable mugging victims just by the way they carried themselves. Those who walked tentatively, fearfully—no matter what their age, their size, their sex—far more often became crime victims than those who walked as though they were fearless and in charge of every situation. Estelle had always placed herself in the latter category. She might be small, she might be female, she might be seventy-three—although she prided herself on not looking anywhere near that old, or had until she'd become confined to bed—but she was nobody's patsy. So much depended upon one's attitude, upon one's bearing, and lying here in bed, feeling sorry for herself, Estelle had begun to lose her sense of personal powerfulness. Getting it back would require a conscious effort, but she vowed that she would manage it somehow. She simply would not let Gretchen Hedberg get away with whatever it was she was doing.

"Gretchen!" Estelle called as loudly as she could. "Gretchen, come in here!"

Gretchen entered the bedroom, looking unusually haggard. "Good morning, Estelle. Ready for breakfast?" she said.

"Not quite. I've been trying to make a phone call, and the phone is off the hook downstairs. Please go fix it," Estelle said in her most assertive manner.

"The phone's out of order," Gretchen replied. "It won't be fixed before Monday. The phone company says they can't send anyone to repair it on the weekend."

Estelle examined Gretchen's expression for a sign that the nurse was lying, but she couldn't detect one. Realizing that Gretchen looked no different from the way she had since she'd started working here was chilling. Estelle lifted the receiver off the hook and held it out to Gretchen. "I know an off-the-hook signal when I hear one, and that's what this is. Now you go check the phones in the study and the kitchen. I'm positive one of them has been left off the hook."

Gretchen stood her ground. "I've already checked. The phone is not off the hook; it's out of order." Although her words were benign, Gretchen's tone became menacing. "I'll get your breakfast." She turned and left the room.

"Wait—"

"I'll get your breakfast, Estelle," Gretchen repeated, continuing her progress downstairs.

Estelle swallowed the reprimand that rose to her lips. She wanted to remind this young woman which of them was in charge here, but she realized that practically speaking, Gretchen was now in charge. Because Estelle lacked both mobility and communication, her status as employer was essentially worthless. She was at the nurse's mercy . . . for now. Estelle realized that her best move would be to make Gretchen believe she intended to go along with whatever the nurse proposed, that she posed no threat . . . until someone who could help her arrived. Surely Faith would visit, or Cullen, or perhaps Claudia Morrisey. Then, fortified by her friends, Estelle would order Gretchen Hedberg out of her home. In the meantime, however, she'd have to avoid being drugged or poisoned again. Unconscious, she'd never be able to help herself. And although her headache and nausea were not abating, she had no desire to repeat them.

Gretchen reentered the room, carrying a breakfast tray.

"Here you go, Estelle." She set the tray on the old woman's lap and stood over her for a moment.

Estelle looked over the offering: a sectioned half grapefruit, a bowl of oatmeal, toast, and coffee. She decided that it would be hard to tamper with a grapefruit. As Estelle ate it Gretchen opened the draperies, letting sunlight into the room. Then the nurse seated herself in the chair at the foot of the bed and watched her patient.

"You needn't wait for the tray, Gretchen," Estelle said. "I'll call you when I'm finished."

"I don't mind. I'm tired today, and it feels good to sit for a few minutes."

Estelle finished the grapefruit and nibbled on a piece of toast. "Guess I don't have much of an appetite this morning," she said. "You can take the tray now."

The nurse's expression was rigid. "You've got to do better than that, Estelle. Your leg's not going to mend unless you eat a healthy breakfast."

"Just the toast will be fine."

Gretchen shook her head. "No. Leave the toast, and have the oatmeal if you're not hungry. It's better for you. I made a new pot of coffee special for you, too. Have some of that."

Estelle felt certain now that the food *was* drugged. She could think of no other reason why her nurse would be so interested in seeing that it was eaten. She would have to go along with her. She raised the coffee cup to her lips and feigned a sip. "This *is* good, Gretchen. My appetite certainly has perked up since you've been doing the cooking."

"Thanks. I do try."

"Do me a favor, dear. Run downstairs and get me the newspaper, will you? I like to read while I eat my breakfast."

Gretchen hesitated a moment. "All right. Get started on that oatmeal, and I'll be right back."

When Gretchen left the room, Estelle pulled the tissue box from the bedside table, quickly dumped the oatmeal into it, poured the coffee on top, and shoved the soggy mess under the bed. By the time the nurse returned with the newspaper Estelle was visibly yawning. "Thank you, Gretchen," she said, accepting the newspaper. She stretched and yawned again. "All of a sudden I'm so sleepy I don't know if I can stay awake to read it."

Gretchen picked up the tray and smiled slightly at the empty bowl and cup. "A good breakfast will do you good. If you feel like napping, that won't hurt either. Want me to close the drapes?"

"Doesn't matter . . ." Estelle laid her head on the pillow and closed her eyes.

"Have a nice nap, Estelle," Gretchen said, carrying the tray out of the room. She glanced at Estelle, smiling in self-congratulation.

Estelle lay in bed for more than an hour, patiently feigning sleep. She listened for the nurse's footsteps, pondering how soon she dared appear to awaken. Finally her patience was rewarded; she heard Gretchen enter the bedroom. Estelle kept her eyes closed and consciously slowed her breathing as much as she could tolerate. She felt, rather than saw, the nurse standing over her. She tried not to tense her body and reveal her deception. *Just pretend you're playing a part in one of Zach's movies,* she told herself. She did indeed have a part to play; only this time her role was in real life.

She heard Gretchen's footsteps moving away from the bed, then faint sounds of objects being moved and drawers being opened. Estelle opened her eyes a slit and peered through her lashes. She could see Gretchen searching the room, looking through each of the dresser drawers. The nurse moved Estelle's clothes—sweaters, nightgowns, stockings, slips, and panties—and inspected them, then examined the drawers themselves. What was she looking for? Estelle watched surreptitiously while Gretchen picked up each of the silver-framed photographs and inspected the back of it, as though she were looking for a hidden message.

When Estelle saw her property being touched and handled by a woman she now knew was a thief, she felt violated. Enraged, she wanted to strike back, to hurt Gretchen as she was being hurt. Yet she stifled her impulse.

Estelle felt her body stiffening as she lay rigidly in position. She longed to move her muscles, to shift her head on the pillow, but she was afraid that doing so would reveal that she was awake. As she lay in bed, she gained a new appreciation of what it must be like to be paralyzed.

When Gretchen moved away from Estelle's view, the old woman agonized about what the nurse was doing. She could hear the sounds of objects being moved but could not tell which things were being touched or what was being done with them. She decided to risk shifting her position slightly. She shut her eyes tightly, then carefully moved her body and head a few inches. She kept her eyes closed until she heard the noises resume, then opened them a crack. Again she could see Gretchen searching. Now she was rifling through the jewelry cabinet. Estelle watched as the nurse took out several pieces, inspected them, and returned them to the cabinet. Then the old woman went rigid, choking back a protest as she saw Gretchen take out a strand of cultured pearls and slip them into her uniform pocket. The pearls were quickly joined by three gold flower-shaped pins and an antique opal brooch. *Let help come soon,* Estelle prayed, *or all my beautiful things will be gone forever.*

Gretchen pulled open another tiny drawer in the jewelry cabinet, and Estelle held her breath. The nurse held up a dainty emerald and pearl necklace in the morning light, examining it carefully. The gems in the necklace—the gift Zach had given Estelle for their twentieth wedding anniversary—glowed green and white. Gretchen slipped the delicate strand into her pocket with the other jewelry.

Estelle felt as though Gretchen had stolen not a necklace but her husband. She had observed more than she could bear. Her fear forgotten, she sat upright in bed and shouted, "Put that back, you thief!"

Gretchen whirled and faced Estelle. "You sneaky old bitch! You've been lying there watching me, haven't you?"

"You're damn right I have. You put my things back and get out of my house before I call the police."

Gretchen laughed mirthlessly. "You do that, Estelle. You just do that." She took a ruby ring from the jewelry box, held it up briefly, and slipped it into her pocket.

"Stop it!" Estelle cried impotently. "You won't get away with this."

"But I *am* getting away with it, you rich bitch. People like you think you can order around people like me, drive us twenty-four hours a day, treat us like slaves." She added a strand of jade beads to the jewelry in her pocket. "You're the one who's not going to get away with your threats. You're going to give me what I want, and then, if you don't give me any trouble, I may be generous enough to let you live."

Estelle straightened her shoulders, refusing to be intimidated. "You won't get away with this, Gretchen. If you harm me in any way, my son will come after you. He'll find you."

"Ha! Who do you think you're kidding? Your precious son will dance on your grave. With you out of the way Seth will inherit this house. That's all he cares about, and you know it."

Estelle cringed. "I have friends—"

"Your *money* has friends, Estelle. Nobody gives a damn about you."

"That's not true. I don't even have any money, not anymore."

Gretchen approached the bed threateningly. "Don't lie to me. You live in a million-dollar house packed with wealth. Why, this stuff alone is worth thousands." She pulled Estelle's jewelry out of her pocket briefly, then put it back again. "You know who you remind me of?"

Estelle was silent.

"Well, I'll tell you. You remind me of the skinflint old aunt who raised me. Aunt Sylvia kept claiming she was broke, too, so broke that I had to wait on her day and night. She swore she couldn't afford to *pay* for care. I, of course, was expected to work without pay, out of gratitude for her not throwing me out in the street. But let me tell you, there was plenty of money she left to her damned church when she finally died."

Gretchen's eyes took on a not-quite-sane fire that frightened Estelle far more than her words did. She realized that she'd made a mistake by letting Gretchen know she'd been observed. Estelle shuddered, wondering whether the nurse was serious in her threat to kill her. "You're making a big mistake, Gretchen. Think about what you're doing. If you put back my things and leave the house, I promise I won't press charges."

Gretchen laughed cruelly. "That's really big of you, rich bitch." She sobered quickly and pointed her finger at Estelle. "Let's get one thing straight here. I am in charge, and you are going to do whatever I tell you to do. Is that clear?"

Estelle glared at her, swallowing her instinctive reply.

The nurse advanced toward the bed. "We will start with the combination to that safe downstairs, Estelle. I want it."

Estelle had to think a moment to realize what Gretchen was talking about. It had been years since she'd even thought about that old safe. Zach used to keep scripts in it.

"The safe, Estelle," Gretchen repeated. "What's in it? Cash? Negotiable securities?"

"Cobwebs, most likely. Gretchen, I'm telling you the truth. I live on income from a trust fund. I haven't had enough cash for years. Why do you think that I haven't even got a housekeeper here? Why, I was going to have to sell some of my things to pay your next week's salary. Not that I intend paying you anything now—"

"Lies! You're a liar, Estelle. I want the combination to that safe." The nurse advanced toward the old woman, her fist clenched and threatening.

Estelle flinched reflexively. "I don't know it. I don't remember. It's been years—"

"You must have it written down somewhere. Just tell me where. I'll check for myself what's inside."

"I don't have—"

Gretchen grabbed Estelle firmly by the shoulder and glared at her. "Listen to me, woman. You had better remember the combination to that safe, and there had better be plenty of cash in it because that's all that's going to keep you breathing." She released her grip on Estelle's shoulder. "Take your time, and think it over." Gretchen turned and abruptly left the room, patting the uniform pocket that held Estelle's jewelry.

Estelle was thoroughly shaken. The look in Gretchen Hedberg's eyes convinced Estelle that the nurse was deadly serious. Estelle now believed that Gretchen intended not only to steal Estelle's beautiful things but to find cash that Estelle didn't even possess. Gretchen planned to strip her of everything she had and leave her behind here, alone and helplessly confined to bed . . . or dead.

Chapter 34

Faith walked on the hard sand along the water's edge, watching as the hypnotic waves lapped closer and closer to her sandals. The tide was coming in. She often came to the beach when she wanted to sort out her emotions or make a decision. She'd paced the sand for days when her mother died and for countless hours at times when lesser crises had invaded her young life. There was something about the vastness of the sea, the beauty and grace of the gulls soaring against the sky, the freshness of the air that always helped her put her problems into better perspective.

On this sunny June afternoon thousands of other people were at the beach, although Faith imagined that all but she were carefree and happy. The other beachgoers played in the surf with boogie boards, frolicked on the sand with Frisbees, doused themselves with tanning lotions, and ate endless picnic lunches. And to Faith's self-pitying eyes, only she had come alone.

She grew warm in the brilliant sunshine—Faith wore a long-sleeved shirt and jeans to protect her fair, lightly freckled skin from the sun's burning rays—but she continued to walk northward from the pier. She had to decide what to do about Estelle.

In the cruel light of morning Faith had felt a little silly about last night's panicky escapade. In preparation for an early visit next door she had nearly convinced herself that she would find Estelle well rested, eating a hearty breakfast, and laughing with Gretchen Hedberg over Faith's breaking-and-entering stunt. Despite her adolescent dread of looking

foolish, Faith honestly wished things had worked out that
well.

Instead, when she'd gone to the Edwards house before
nine this morning, the nurse had refused to let her in, claiming that Estelle was still sleeping and Faith was making a
pest of herself. Gretchen also had repeated her threat to
press charges against Faith: "You're disturbing my patient,
and I won't have it. If I have to have you arrested to keep
you away from this house, that's what I'll do."

Feeling intimidated, Faith had retreated. She'd tried phon-
ing Estelle about noon, but the line still rang busy. Now she
was more confused than ever.

Faith's intuition told her that Estelle was in some kind of
trouble, that the nurse was pulling something strange and
perhaps dangerous. But she had no proof. At best Estelle
must not know that Gretchen was keeping Faith away from
the house. She would never have approved of that. Estelle
had been a second mother to Faith for years. It was because
of that bond that Faith could not abandon her friend now.

Faith bent down and picked up a smooth stone the tide
had washed in. She tossed it sideways expertly and watched
it skip three times before it disappeared in the blue-gray
water. The question, she knew, was not whether to help
Estelle but how to help Estelle. Because she was only sixteen, she knew that the police probably would not be inclined to believe her story over the nurse's. A call to the
police might bring them around to check on Estelle's safety.
But such a call could also result in the police's finding out
that Faith had broken into the Edwards house and in
Gretchen's making good on her threat to press charges.
Faith wasn't sure what the consequences of that might be,
but she could guarantee that they'd mean trouble for her
when her father found out. More important, Faith knew that
Estelle had decided against involving the police in looking
for the missing silver pieces. She had feared that the publicity could cost her her freedom. Now Faith couldn't ignore
Estelle's wishes because of a hunch.

Faith kicked a discarded beer can out of her path. Her
father would be home tomorrow. Their relationship was becoming increasingly strained these days, but he had always

seemed fond of Estelle. If Faith told him the whole story, would he help? Or would he say Faith was acting like a silly child? She wondered if she'd have to confess that she'd broken into Estelle's house and had had a gun pointed at her. If she did, her father might be more tempted to punish Faith for last night's dangerous excursion than to investigate Estelle's health and safety. She sighed with discouragement.

Three teenage boys sharing a joint of marijuana ran in front of Faith, laughing and shoving each other. One boy, fully clothed, staggered, tripped, and sprawled in the surf. He and his buddies found his pratfall hilarious. Their ludicrous behavior reminded Faith of the only other source of help that had occurred to her. But she might as well ask these boys for help as to go to Mrs. Wattman.

She strolled a hundred feet past the rowdy boys and sat down on the sand beyond the water's reach. She'd walked a long way, and her knees had begun to ache. Sitting with her knees folded under her chin, Faith stared at the incoming waves.

Whom else could she ask for help? She hadn't felt so completely alone since her mother's death.

Chapter 35

Estelle pulled herself back into bed and lay exhausted and gasping for breath. Of urgent necessity she'd managed to half hobble, half drag herself to the bathroom and back again. With the wheelchair nowhere in sight, that process had taken her a good fifteen minutes plus most of the little strength she still possessed. She was chagrined to realize how physically debilitating her days in bed had been. She'd thought herself in good shape prior to the accident, but nearly two weeks flat on her back, without exercise, had weakened her tremendously.

It had been hours now since Gretchen Hedberg had searched Estelle's room and stolen the jewelry. Estelle had quenched her thirst with two glasses of water from the bathroom sink, but she was very hungry. She hadn't eaten the drug-laden breakfast, and there had been no lunch. Now it was approaching the dinner hour, and she had no idea whether the nurse would bother to feed her. After all, she'd left Estelle lying here all day without so much as help to the bathroom. If dinner did arrive, Estelle wondered whether she dared eat it.

She'd spent her hours of solitude trying to think of ways to survive until help arrived. She had no money to give Gretchen, and the thought that if the nurse left, she would take most of the valuable things from the house with her made Estelle livid. Yet lying here wondering whether she had been abandoned or whether she would soon be killed helped put material possessions into perspective.

She'd heard Gretchen's footsteps on the stairs a number of

times today as she'd lain imprisoned in her bed. Without the television or telephone, noises seemed to echo in the old house—odd thumps and scrapes from downstairs; occasional creaks from the floors above; sounds of breezes drifting through the cracks around the windows. Now, though, she'd heard nothing of human origin for an hour or so. Had the nurse gone off and left her here alone? Suddenly the sound of footsteps resumed. Estelle heard them approaching her bedroom door and tensed.

Gretchen Hedberg, now wearing soiled jeans and a shirt in place of her uniform, entered the room. She'd spent the past several hours packing Estelle's valuables into cardboard boxes she'd found in the massive cobweb-laden attic. Now she was bone tired and out of sorts, in no mood for trouble from Estelle Edwards. "You've had enough time to remember that combination," she demanded harshly.

"There's really nothing in that safe, Gretchen," Estelle said. "Believe me, if I could open it and show you that, I would."

Gretchen didn't—wouldn't—believe that. Acquiring the old woman's jewelry and artworks and silverware was one thing, but Gretchen might not be able to sell them for months, possibly even years. In the meantime, she needed cash or something easily converted into cash in order to get away from this town. "I don't believe you, Estelle. I've given you plenty of time to cooperate with me. I wouldn't like to get nasty with you."

Estelle cowered as the nurse moved slowly toward the bed, her hands clenching compulsively. Gretchen stopped near the edge of the bed and said slowly, "I want that combination."

"I don't have it."

Suddenly Gretchen raised her hand and slapped Estelle hard across the face. Reflexively Estelle's hand covered her stinging cheek, and tears rose in her eyes. The shock was almost greater than her pain from the blow. She didn't recall ever having been struck before.

"Now, tell me that combination," Gretchen repeated coldly.

Estelle cringed as her mind raced in search of a solution.

She truly did not remember the combination to that safe. And even if she did, she wondered how Gretchen would react when she opened the safe and found it empty. She might well kill Estelle in revenge or to keep her quiet. "I haven't got it here—" Estelle turned her head when she saw Gretchen raise her hand once more. She blurted out, "It's written on a paper in my safe-deposit box at the bank."

Gretchen lowered her hand slightly. She observed her patient closely. Was Estelle lying? She appeared to be terrified, but that didn't mean she was telling the truth. "What safe-deposit box?" she asked.

Estelle straightened up a bit. She realized that she was succeeding in diverting the nurse. "Years ago, before my husband died, we had an attempted burglary. Zachary decided that it wasn't safe to keep anything too valuable in the house safe, so we got a safe-deposit box at the bank." That much of the story was true. "Once he died, I wasn't about to begin keeping cash or securities in that old safe, so I just left that sort of thing at the bank—along with important papers, like birth certificates, insurance policies . . . and the combination to that old safe. I never open the thing—why bother when there's nothing inside?—so there's no need to keep the combination handy."

"What else is in that box?"

"I'm not actually certain," Estelle said. Frantically she tried to remember the things that had once been there, the things she'd sold over the years in order to pay the expenses her trust fund income no longer covered. "I know there's a coin collection, some stock certificates, that sort of thing."

"How much cash?"

Estelle tried to choose a believable amount. "Perhaps a few hundred, maybe a thousand. Most of my cash is in interest-bearing accounts." She read dissatisfaction on Gretchen's face and quickly added, "There are some gold ingots, too, and some bearer bonds Zach bought years ago. They may be worth quite a bit by now."

Gretchen sized up the situation. It was logical that Estelle Edwards had transferred those valuables to a bank safe-deposit box; an old woman, living alone, might not want them in the house. Gretchen turned away from the bed and

walked to the window, where she looked out at the jacaranda tree, its purple blossoms littering the driveway and the
surface of the swimming pool. She weighed her options. She
could leave here now, taking the items she'd already packed.
And then what? What would she use for getaway money?
She'd given too much of her ready cash to Stan Greenwood.
Once she was gone, Estelle would quickly call the police. Of
course, she could kill the old woman; but that, too, would
soon be discovered, and Gretchen Hedberg would be the
only suspect. Without enough cash to buy a new car or to
hide out, her chances of permanent escape were poor.

With enough cash, some gold, some bearer bonds, however, Gretchen felt she stood a good chance of pulling off
this job the way she'd originally planned—despite Stan
Greenwood's interference. A chance was all she needed. If
she could get far enough away from Santa Monica, if she
could get enough money to hide out even for a few months,
she could begin discreetly liquidating some of Estelle's property as well as that of her previous employers. In a year or so
she might even open that shop she'd thought about.

Gretchen turned and observed the woman on the bed. She
thought Estelle Edwards was a rather ridiculous figure, lying
there in her wrinkled peacock blue nightgown, gray roots
starting to show in her dyed auburn hair. Hardly a formida-
ble opponent . . . or was she? Given the dangerous position Estelle was in, would she have the nerve—or the stupid-
ity—to lie? "Where's the key to the box, Estelle?" Gretchen
demanded.

Estelle breathed more easily. She leaned over to her bedside table and pulled open the drawer. She took out a red
and silver key with the number 33 engraved on it and
handed it to Gretchen.

"Which bank?"

"First Seaside, same as my checking account."

Gretchen had been there to cash a check for Estelle and
had been given no trouble. "How do I gain access to the
box?"

"Normally I'd have to open it myself. But my banker
knows about my accident. I think he'll give you access if you

have a handwritten note from me and I call him on Monday morning before you go over there."

Gretchen turned the key over in her hand. It was now six o'clock on Saturday evening. The bank would not be open before Monday morning, probably at ten. She put the key into her pocket and turned to Estelle. "I'll get you some paper and a pen. You can write that letter right now."

As Gretchen left the room in search of the writing materials, Estelle calculated her odds. She realized that she'd bought herself perhaps another forty hours. Now it was up to her to find a way to use those hours to save herself from probable death at the hands of her nurse-companion.

Chapter 36

Estelle strained to hear the grandfather clock in the
foyer chime three times. Her empty stomach growled. After
she'd written the letter to the bank, Gretchen had given her
a light supper, but all Estelle had dared eat was an apple and
a piece of unbuttered bread. Gretchen had laughed at her
caution and said tauntingly, "If I want you knocked out,
Estelle, I don't have to put anything in your food. I've got a
nice little syringe and an entire selection of drugs that will
take care of that quite efficiently. All I have to do is stick
you right *there!*" She jabbed her finger roughly against Estelle's upper arm as the old woman cringed against her pillows.

Fighting off sleep, Estelle had formulated a plan to summon help. Now, when Gretchen must surely be asleep, was
the time to implement it. Estelle sat up in bed and lowered
her good leg, then her cast over the edge. Clutching the old
quilt Maisie Gilroy had made for her, she lowered her body
gently onto the floor. Her earlier trip to the bathroom had
taught her that trying to walk—or hop, to be more precise—
would be far too noisy. But with something soft wrapped
around the hard cast, Estelle thought she could pull herself
along the floor quietly enough to make it downstairs without
waking Gretchen. Once on the main floor, she'd locate that
off-the-hook telephone and use it to call the police.

Sitting on the floor, Estelle wrapped the quilt around the
cast to soften any clunking sounds it might make when she
dragged herself along. Her progress was slow as she pulled
herself to the bedroom door, opened it carefully, and peered

into the hall. The door to Gretchen's room was open a few
inches, but Estelle saw no light and heard no movement
from within.

Taking her time and listening intently for any unfamiliar
sounds in the creaky old house, Estelle crept toward the
stairway. She was grateful for the old, frayed ruby-colored
carpeting that softened her journey along the hallway. Estelle had never had much flesh cushioning her bones, and
after her days of forced inactivity she was stiff and sore as
well.

When she reached the top of the staircase, she paused to
readjust the quilt around her cast and to tuck up her nightgown so that it would not trip her. This would be the most
difficult part. She'd slid downstairs on her fanny a thousand
times as a girl, Estelle reassured herself. She could do it
again. She positioned herself perpendicular to the staircase,
then lowered her good leg and her hips onto the first step.
She lifted the leg with the cast and pulled it after her slowly
and quietly. She repeated the process four or five times, then
paused to rest. Straining to hear any sounds from above,
Estelle slowly made her way down another half dozen steps,
then rested once more. Clearly she was no longer a girl. Now
her body ached and complained with the effort of moving
herself so short a distance. The stairway in her beloved
house had never seemed so long.

Estelle reached down to the next step with one arm and
her good leg, then braced herself to lower her hips again.
Flinching as a sharp pain suddenly shot through her hip and
reverberated through her broken leg, Estelle's arm doubled
up under her. She momentarily lost her balance, failed to
catch herself quickly enough, and toppled forward down the
staircase. Each step, as she bumped against it, inflicted a
painful blow to her body. Her left arm flailed wildly in an
effort to break her descent until it struck the banister on the
landing halfway down the stairs. Estelle knew at once that
the arm was severely bruised, possibly even broken. Her
body landed hard against the railing and crumpled into a
pain-racked heap as she swallowed her sobs of emotional
and physical defeat.

The upstairs lights went on. A demoralized Estelle looked

up to see Gretchen, tying the sash of a yellow bathrobe around her waist as she descended the stairs. The nurse's mouth was set in a firm line, and her eyes were frigid. Her silence as she reached down and grabbed Estelle under the arms was more frightening than threatening words could possibly have been.

"Please, you're hurting me," Estelle begged, to no avail, while Gretchen dragged her back up the stairs. Several times Estelle came close to fainting from the pain as her fresh wounds bumped against the steps, but she was not so lucky. By the time the nurse lifted her onto her bed, tears were streaking Estelle's face, and her moans had turned to shrieks.

As Estelle continued to sob, Gretchen grabbed a pillow from the bed, removed the pillowcase, and efficiently ripped it into strips of fabric. She pulled Estelle's hands roughly behind her back, immune to the old woman's screams of "My arm! I think it's broken. Don't, please, don't!" The nurse bound her patient's hand tightly with the strips of sheeting.

Then Gretchen wadded the remainder of the pillowcase into a ball and stuffed it into Estelle's mouth, effectively stifling her cries. Still without a word, Gretchen turned and walked out of the room, closing the door firmly behind her.

While Estelle suffered—now quietly—on the bed, she heard the key turn in the lock on her bedroom door.

Chapter 37

Faith pierced her fried egg with a fork and watched the golden yolk seep over the egg white and onto the bacon. She cut off a bite-size piece, chewed it slowly, and washed it down with a gulp of orange juice. As she ate her breakfast, she tried to focus her attention on the Sunday *Times,* normally the pleasurable start of her week. Today, sitting alone at the kitchen table, she didn't even have to share the paper with her father. Still, she was having trouble concentrating on what she read. She was troubled about her friend Estelle.

As she nibbled on a piece of toast and finished her egg, Faith's eyes skimmed over the newspaper sections in order of her interests: first the Calendar section, with its entertainment news; then View, with its features; the news and Metro sections; and finally, the Westside section. As far as she was concerned, the remainder of the *Times* did not exist.

She paid slight attention to a story about singer Michael Jackson, an editorial piece against the violence in a new Steven Spielberg-George Lucas film, a feature about political wives, and an item about a family that had won half a million dollars in an East Coast state lottery. If she won half a million dollars, Faith thought, she'd . . . what? Move out of this house, for one thing. Put some money away to study acting at college, for another. Then she'd find some way to help Estelle with her financial problems. If Faith were rich, she thought, people would have to stop treating her like a child. Or maybe the trick was that if she were financially independent, she would stop feeling so much like a child.

When she turned the pages of the Westside section, an

artist's sketch caught Faith's eye. She took another bite of bacon and read the brief news story accompanying this drawing of a man's face. "The body of an unidentified man who had apparently been shot to death was discovered in Topanga Canyon yesterday. . . ." There was something familiar about that face. Faith studied it carefully. She mentally colored the hair and eyes on the drawing and tried to remember where she had seen that man.

As she wiped the last of the egg yolk off her plate with a piece of toast, the answer came to her. The picture looked exactly like the man she'd seen sleeping in his car . . . when was it? About a week ago. Several times since then Faith imagined that she'd seen the same man driving slowly down Adelaide Drive, watching the neighborhood. She'd found him a sort of creepy type and wondered if he'd been planning to burglarize some of the houses on the block. Faith decided she'd probably caught him "casing the joint," as it was called in all those old gangster movies. Now he'd evidently been murdered. Was there a connection?

The news story asked for anyone who had information about the man to call the Los Angeles Police Department. Faith thought it over. Assuming that she was right, that this really was the same man she had seen in front of her house, she still wouldn't be able to tell the police very much. She didn't know the man's name, only where he'd been for a time. The car he'd been driving . . . She closed her eyes and tried to visualize her confrontation with the sleeping man. His car had been a light color—silver, beige, maybe blue. An American make, although Faith couldn't remember which one. If she called the police, she didn't want to look like a fool. . . . If only someone else had seen him, if only someone else could corroborate that this was the same guy, she'd feel more confident in calling the police.

Estelle, Faith thought. Estelle had spent several afternoons last week sitting in her rented wheelchair on her second-story balcony. If this man had been lurking around the neighborhood while she'd been sunning herself, Estelle might have seen him. In any event, the newspaper sketch was as good an excuse as any for Faith to approach the house next door and to attempt to see Estelle one more time.

Faith carried her breakfast dishes to the sink and rinsed them. Mrs. Wattman always complained whenever Faith let egg yolk dry on a dish. She stacked her dishes on the drainboard, then wiped her hands on a terry-cloth towel. She was ready to do battle with the nurse next door.

Faith folded the newspaper so that the sketch of the murdered man was on top, slipped on her shoes, and went out the back door.

Chapter 38

"I'm sure you're not stupid enough to try that again," Gretchen said as she untied her patient's hands.

During the night Estelle had managed to spit out the wad of fabric that had been stuffed into her mouth, but she had not been able to free herself from her bindings. The pain had been too intense for sleeping, and now it peaked again as she tried to move her left arm forward. Rapidly turning a hideous purple, the arm was swollen almost double in size.

"I brought you some breakfast," Gretchen said, as though this were a typical morning and her patient were not battered, bruised, and in excruciating pain. The nurse appeared rested and insensitive to Estelle's obvious suffering. Over time Gretchen had become quite tolerant of suffering, as long as it was not her own.

"I don't feel like eating," Estelle murmured, moving her throbbing body as slowly as possible into a slightly more comfortable position.

"Suit yourself. I'll leave the tray in case you change your mind." She set the tray on the bed next to Estelle. "You want one of your codeine pills?"

Estelle was tempted, but she didn't trust Gretchen to give her the right medication. And she felt she must stay awake and alert. Her only hope of survival lay in someone's coming to visit before she made that call to her banker tomorrow. Gretchen would have to keep her alive until then if she hoped to gain access to that safe-deposit box.

Her only hope of survival. Lying against the pillows, Estelle considered whether survival was worth the cost. At the moment death would almost seem a welcome relief. She didn't know how much more of this pain she could endure.

Gretchen emerged from the bathroom, carrying a glass of water and a small white pill. "Here, swallow this, and you'll feel better," she said, holding it out.

Estelle eyed the pill and slowly shook her head. "Uh-uh."

"Afraid? I told you, Estelle, if I want to drug you, I've got plenty of ways to do it. I don't have to trick you into swallowing—" Her sentence was cut off by the ring of the doorbell.

Estelle quickly pulled herself into a sitting position and began to shriek at the top of her lungs, "Help! Help! Help me!"

"Shut up, you old bitch!" Gretchen reached back, made a fist, and slugged Estelle squarely in the jaw. The old woman slumped over in the bed, upsetting the breakfast tray. Gretchen grabbed her by the hair and lifted her head out of the spilled food. She shoved Estelle roughly against the pillows, then lifted one of her eyelids. She was out cold.

The doorbell rang again, more insistently. Gretchen dared not ignore it, not without determining whether Estelle's screams had been heard by whoever was at the door. She hurried out of the bedroom, shut the door tightly behind her, and ran to answer the door.

Faith stood on the porch, holding a newspaper in her hand.

"What is it this time?" Gretchen asked her coldly.

"I want to see Estelle."

The nurse shook her head. "Estelle is sleeping."

"Then I'll come in and wait until she wakes up."

Faith made a move forward, but Gretchen blocked her entry. She glared at the girl. "You certainly will not. I told you not to come around here bothering Estelle, and I meant it. She's not feeling good and—"

"But this is important!" Faith held her ground.

"Estelle's health is what's important. Now go away."

As Gretchen began to close the door in her face, Faith shoved the newspaper at her. "I have to find out whether Estelle saw this man around here," she blurted out. "She might be able to help solve a murder."

Gretchen glanced at the folded paper and caught her breath involuntarily. Stan Greenwood's likeness stared at her from the page. For a moment she didn't trust herself to reply. She kept her eyes lowered as her thoughts raced frantically. What did Stan have to do with this girl or with Estelle? Was it possible that they suspected Gretchen of murdering him? Gretchen chose her words carefully, trying not to betray her mushrooming panic. "I'll take the newspaper and ask Estelle when she wakes up." She reached for it.

But Faith pulled the paper away. "No. I want to talk to Estelle about it myself. You—you have her call me when she wakes up."

"Our phone is out of order. If she feels up to it, she'll call you tomorrow, after the phone's been repaired." Gretchen closed the door, leaving Faith standing on the porch, forlornly clutching the sketch of the murdered man.

As Gretchen stood alone in the foyer, her heart started racing with fear. She hurried into the kitchen, where she'd left this morning's *Times* on the table, still bound together with string. She tore off the string and frantically turned the pages of the news portions, looking for the sketch of Stan. Finally she located it in the center of the Westside section and read the accompanying brief story about the unidentified man found murdered in Topanga Canyon. There was little to be learned from the article, only that the body had been found. Evidently the police had no information that would connect Stan to Gretchen Hedberg, to St. Louis, to Jane Burden, or to Jasmine Kennedy.

Yet that young snip from next door obviously saw some reason to connect Stan to her, and the old woman upstairs might as well. What was it? Had Faith seen Stan lurking about? The fool had refused to stay away even after she'd warned him. Had Faith seen him enter this house? Or, even more unthinkable, could she have seen him with Gretchen at the Safeway store, at the storage locker, or in Stan's car?

Gretchen could see that she had to get away from here as quickly as possible. She couldn't risk waiting another day, not when Faith Sanford might have evidence linking Gretchen to the murder of Stan Greenwood. Not when the girl might take the newspaper's advice and contact the police. Even if Faith could testify only that she'd seen Stan on this street, the police would soon start questioning residents. They might well insist on talking to Estelle. . . .

No, she couldn't risk staying here until tomorrow. Yet without enough cash how could she possibly escape? There would soon be an alert sounded on behalf of Estelle Edwards, whether the old woman was dead or alive when Gretchen left. If only there were money in that safe . . .

Gretchen walked to the study, pondering the question of the safe. She removed the framed Picasso print from the wall, set it on the floor, and pulled once more on the safe handle. It still didn't budge. She spun the combination dial fruitlessly. If there really was nothing of value inside, she thought, why hadn't the safe been left unlocked? And in any case, why wouldn't Estelle have kept the combination in a more accessible place than a bank safe-deposit box?

The reason, Gretchen suddenly realized, was that everything Estelle had told her about the safe was a lie. Certainly, if Gretchen were in the old woman's position, she would play for as much time as possible. She, like Estelle, would invent a ploy—such as a bank safe-deposit box that couldn't be opened for days—to postpone the loss of her money. With a long enough delay help would inevitably arrive, and Estelle would be saved. With a long enough delay Gretchen, not Estelle, would become the prisoner.

She should have trusted her original instincts about that safe, Gretchen concluded. There was something in it that Estelle had not wanted her to have. She'd been a fool to allow the old woman to convince her that she couldn't open it.

Gretchen would not be fooled a second time. She mounted the stairs quickly and entered Estelle's bedroom. The old woman lay unconscious on the bed, her bruised and swollen body covered with the remnants of the ruined breakfast. Gretchen was repulsed by the sight of the battered and filthy old woman. If it had not been for Estelle's lies, Gretchen would now be well on her way away from this town.

She went to her room, brought back a small vial of smelling salts, and held it open under Estelle's nose. As the sharp ammonia scent drifted into her nostrils, Estelle flinched and slowly regained consciousness.

"Now," Gretchen said menacingly, "you're going to tell me the combination for that safe."

Chapter 39

Feeling defeated once more, Faith wandered around the back of Estelle's house, still clutching the newspaper. She plopped herself down on one of the white metal chairs beside the swimming pool and stretched out her long legs. Not long ago she and Estelle had sat here, drinking tall glasses of iced tea and watching the sun set over the Pacific. That was—what?—only a little more than two weeks ago. Now . . . now, Faith realized, Estelle might be dying. And she felt at least partially responsible.

As she watched the last of the jacaranda blossoms drop from the tree onto the surface of the pool, Faith could not shake her feeling that Estelle was in crisis and that Gretchen Hedberg was the cause. She examined what she had learned in the past two weeks, compiling a mental list.

On that first day Faith had caught Gretchen Hedberg searching Estelle's desk.

Although there had been a time of reprieve, since Friday the nurse had refused to let Faith see Estelle.

Or talk to her, for that matter. Gretchen claimed the phone was out of order, but on Friday night the telephone operator had said it was off the hook. Gretchen could have taken the receiver off the hook to prevent Estelle from communicating with the outside world.

Estelle has told Faith that she suspected she might have been drugged against her will.

On Friday night, when Faith had broken into the house, Estelle clearly had been drugged into a heavy sleep.

Faith had heard some faint noises this morning as she'd

stood outside the front door waiting for the doorbell to be answered. They might have come from a cat somewhere in the neighborhood or perhaps a radio. Or they could have been cries from within the house, cries for help.

Faith felt she had to do something quickly. In frustration she swatted her knee with the newspaper, then tossed it down on the patio. As it fell the sketched face of the man who'd been watching the street caught her eye once more. Could he be connected in some way to Estelle's plight? Faith picked up the newspaper and reread the news story. According to the police, the man had probably been killed Friday night. *Friday night*—the night Faith had broken in and found Estelle alone and nearly comatose. Friday was the night that Gretchen Hedberg had threatened her with a gun.

Faith noted that the man in the newspaper picture had been shot. Gretchen had a gun. She'd been away from the house on Friday night. Not only that, Faith realized, but the nurse had reacted oddly this morning, when she'd seen that newspaper. Faith recalled that Gretchen had seemed surprised, perhaps even shocked. Then she had tried to grab the paper out of Faith's hand. Could she— Was it possible that Gretchen Hedberg had actually murdered this man?

Faith's thought frightened her. If Estelle was being nursed by a woman capable of shooting a man to death . . . But Faith caught herself. She couldn't jump to conclusions like that without proof. She knew that there could be a plausible explanation for every "fact" on her list.

Back to the desk incident—Gretchen's story about looking for a phone number could be the simple truth.

And Estelle's being drugged against her will? Perhaps a touch of the flu or a reaction to the long, dreadfully boring days in bed. Faith knew that the elderly often developed pneumonia and died after breaking a hip. Estelle's feeling ill in the morning might not be unexpected for a woman in her condition.

Gretchen's reluctance to admit visitors might be explained if Estelle were, indeed, developing a life-threatening illness of some kind. No good nurse would want her charge exposed to additional germs.

And the telephone—was it out of order or off the hook?

Faith had had enough experience with the local phone company to know how inefficient it often proved to be. Gretchen could be telling the truth there too.

Then there was the dead man. Faith looked at the sketch again. She could be mistaken. It had been more than a week since she'd seen his face close up, and the newspaper had run only a sketch, not even a photograph. Faith certainly couldn't swear that the murdered man was the same person she'd seen on her street. And even if he were, what did that prove? He could have come to an unfortunate end for a dozen reasons, none of which had anything to do with Gretchen Hedberg or Estelle Edwards or Adelaide Drive.

Owning a gun didn't make Gretchen a murderer either. As a nurse who often lived with and cared for helpless elderly people, many of whom were quite rich, she might own a gun merely to protect her patients and herself. Coming home to a house that showed obvious signs of a break-in, of course she'd use a gun if she had one.

And Estelle's condition on Friday night? Perhaps, Faith considered, Estelle really was sedated according to doctor's orders. Yet why would a doctor order such a heavy dosage? Although Faith had had no personal experience with sleeping medications, it seemed strange to her that she'd been unable to rouse Estelle. Surely the doctor would not have prescribed such a large dose. . . .

The doctor. Faith sprang to her feet. Of course. She should have thought of him earlier. The one person whom the nurse would have to let into Estelle's house, the one person whom Estelle could trust to be discreet about her family problems, the one person who could help Estelle if help was necessary, was the doctor.

Faith grabbed the newspaper and ran around the corner of the gray Victorian house, heading toward home. Somehow she would manage to locate Estelle's doctor, explain the situation to him, and convince him to come to Estelle's aid.

Chapter 40

Cullen Baxter pulled on a T-shirt over his swim trunks while his two-year-old daughter, Margaret, bounced enthusiastically on the queen-size bed and baby Jessica practiced standing up by clutching the hairs on her father's leg. "Watch out, Meggie. You're tearing the newspaper," Cullen said. The *Times* was strewn across the rumpled bed, where Cullen had lain reading it for the past hour. Sunday was the one morning a week he allowed himself to be lazy.

"I'm back!" Laura called, coming through the front door of the apartment, a bulging brown paper bag in her arms. "They were out of chicken salad, so I got tuna. Okay?"

"Okay with me if the kids will eat it."

"Daddy, look at me!" Meggie shrieked, jumping as high as she could and landing on her fanny in the center of the bed.

"Be careful, muffin. You jump too high, you might fall off the edge."

"Not me." She jumped again, this time landing flat on her round belly, her elbow piercing the *Times* sports section.

Cullen hobbled over to the dresser, impeded by Jessie's grasp on his leg. He leaned over and peered at his pale face in the mirror while applying suntan lotion. "What do you think, Jess? You going to have a good time playing in the waves with your old man? Huh?"

The baby smiled at him, worked up her courage, and let go of her grip on his leg. She teetered for a moment, then sat down with a plop on the carpet.

"Nice try, kid," Cullen said, reaching down to smear a

drop of suntan lotion on her button nose. "Don't give up the faith. You'll get it right eventually." The telephone rang.

"I've got it," Laura called from the living room. She picked up the receiver. "Baxters'."

"Mrs. Baxter?"

"Yes?"

"May I speak with Dr. Baxter, please?"

"Who's calling?"

"Faith Sanford. I live next door to Estelle Edwards, Dr. Baxter's patient."

"Dr. Baxter is busy at the moment. He'll be in the office tomorrow."

"This is an emergency. He's got to come over to Estelle's right away."

Laura tensed. She'd had enough of Estelle Edwards and her demands to last her a lifetime. "If it's a medical emergency, you'd best take Miss Edwards to the hospital. I'm sure they'll be able to help her."

"But you don't understand—"

"This is Sunday. Dr. Baxter does not work on Sunday. If it's *really* an emergency, take her to St. John's Hospital." Laura's tone demonstrated that she did not believe an emergency existed.

"I—"

"Otherwise, call Dr. Baxter tomorrow, at his office. Goodbye." Laura hung up the phone, then removed the receiver to ward off a second call. She had no intention of allowing the one day Cullen had promised her and the girls to be interrupted by that dried-up old movie star and her broken leg.

"Who is it?" Cullen called from the bedroom.

"Nothing. Just a salesman. I got rid of him."

"You almost ready to go?"

"Give me ten minutes. You get out the beach towels and see if Jessie's diapers need changing. I'll finish packing the picnic basket."

Chapter 41

Faith quickly redialed Dr. Baxter's phone number. The line rang busy. She tried again, got the same result, and slammed down the phone in frustration. She was certain she could convince Dr. Baxter to help Estelle if only she could talk to him and not to his wife. She dialed a third time. Still a busy signal. Obviously Mrs. Baxter had no intention of allowing another call through.

It wouldn't be so easy for that woman to prevent Faith's talking to Dr. Baxter if she went to his home. . . . That's exactly what she'd do. She wouldn't leave until she'd seen the doctor. Once he heard the whole story, he couldn't refuse to help.

Faith checked the doctor's address in the phone book. It was on San Vicente Boulevard, a little more than a mile away—too far for her to walk in a hurry. The buses ran infrequently on Sundays. A cab would require cash she didn't have. If only her father were home . . . But then, if her father were home, she might not need Dr. Baxter.

Faith walked down the hall and peered through the open door into Mrs. Wattman's room. The housekeeper was slumped over in an overstuffed chair, her head sagging toward her chest. Her light snoring rose above the sound of the television set. As Faith crept into the room she noticed the smell of stale whiskey.

Mrs. Wattman's handbag lay open on the dresser. Faith eyed it briefly, tiptoed over to it, and removed the housekeeper's keys. This was, she rationalized, an emergency.

The key ring in her hand, Faith skipped downstairs and

hurried to the garage. She paused for a moment, looking at Mrs. Wattman's old green Chevy with slight apprehension, then screwed up her courage. After all, she reassured herself, she had a learner's permit to drive, and she'd had three lessons behind the wheel. She could do it. She climbed into the driver's seat. At least this old boat had an automatic transmission. She found the ignition key, started the engine, shifted the gear lever into R, and pressed on the gas pedal. The car lurched into reverse. Cringing, Faith heard the sound of scraping metal as the side of the car made contact with the wall of the garage. She braked, shifted, and pulled the car forward, then turned the steering wheel sharply and tried backing out of the garage once more. This time she made it without mishap.

Faith drove along the streets carefully and at a tediously slow speed, mistrustful of her skill in maneuvering the big old car. She prayed that she would not encounter a police car before she reached the San Vicente Boulevard address.

Approaching the apartment building where Cullen Baxter lived, Faith drove into the driveway leading to the underground garage. She shoved the gear lever into P and turned off the motor. Her driving lessons had not yet progressed to parallel parking.

As Faith emerged from the Chevrolet she saw Dr. Baxter loading a large wicker basket and some beach toys into the back of a Honda parked in front of the building. She ran over to him. "Please, Dr. Baxter, you've got to help me— you've got to help Estelle, I mean. She's in terrible trouble." Faith quickly outlined the events of the past few days for him.

"Let me get this straight—you actually shook Estelle and couldn't wake her?" he asked.

"That's right. I thought she might be dead. But then that nurse, Gretchen, came in, and she told me that you'd prescribed this sleeping stuff for Estelle—"

"That's ridiculous. I would never . . ." Cullen was both puzzled and alarmed at what he had heard.

"You'll come, won't you? Gretchen'll have to let *you* in. And if she won't, we'll call the police." Faith breathed more easily now that she'd found an adult to take charge.

Laura emerged from the front of the building, carrying Jessica and leading Margaret by the hand. She stared at Faith suspiciously. "What's going on?" she asked Cullen.

"Sorry, honey. I've got to go for just a little while. There's an emergency with Estelle Edwards. You go ahead to the beach without me, and I'll catch up later."

Laura glared venomously at Faith. "I told you to take her to the hospital!"

Cullen whirled on his wife. "You told who what?"

"Her," she said, pointing at Faith. "When she called, I told her to take Estelle to the emergency hospital. I'm not going to give up my one day with my husband for—"

"You had no right, Laura. You lied to me!"

Tears rose in her eyes. "If I hadn't, you'd have gone running off to that has-been actress. I'm your wife. Don't *I* have some rights?"

"Come on, Dr. Baxter," Faith begged. "Estelle could be dying while we're standing here." She took hold of his arm, trying to pull him into action.

"It's Sunday afternoon, Cullen. Sunday!" Laura shrieked, like a spoiled child in the throes of a tantrum. "This is *my* day!"

Cullen gave his wife a contemptuous look and swallowed his retort. He was too angry to trust answering her. "Let's go," he said to Faith. "We'll take your car."

"Here," Faith said, handing him the keys. "You drive." She looked sheepish. "I haven't got a license."

As Cullen backed the green Chevy out of the driveway and headed it toward the Edwards house, Laura Baxter stood on the curb, biting her quivering lower lip.

Chapter 42

When waves of pain weren't completely overwhelming her mind, Estelle felt confused and frightened. She could not imagine what had changed so quickly, why Gretchen no longer believed her story about the safe-deposit box. For much of the past hour the nurse had been slapping her, shaking her, threatening to kill her unless she revealed the combination to the study safe. At one point, when one of Gretchen's blows had fallen on her injured arm, Estelle fainted from the pain, but the nurse used the smelling salts and returned her to consciousness unwillingly.

"I don't know the combination," Estelle insisted exhaustedly. "I've told you and told you. It's at the bank. . . ."

"You're lying!" Gretchen screamed, an irrational glint in her eyes.

"Please. I'll help you get it tomorrow. I promise . . ."

"Huh! I'm not going to wait until tomorrow." Gretchen paced the room as though it were a cage. "You're trying to trap me, and it's not going to work."

"I swear I don't remember the combination. Please, Gretchen. I just don't know it." Huddled against her pillows, in severe physical pain, and humiliated beyond anything she had imagined possible, Estelle began to sob quietly.

"Shut up! Stop that sniffling!"

Estelle continued to cry, her tears flowing onto her soiled nightgown. She had become incapable of controlling her tears.

Gretchen looked at her contemptuously. A phrase from her childhood, something Aunt Sylvia had often said to her, leaped into her mind: "Stop crying or I'll give you something to cry about!" Invariably the exclamation had been followed quickly by a hard slap across the face or a rap of knuckles on the head. Gretchen's fists clenched involuntarily. Her anxiety level was becoming intolerable; much more of this, and she would lose control. She would beat the old woman to death. She would do to Estelle Edwards what Stan had done to Ellen Pickett . . . and then she'd never get that safe open. She forced herself to breathe more slowly. Time out. She—both of them—needed time out. She'd give Estelle a minute or two to regain her composure, to consider the futility of her continued refusal to cooperate.

Gretchen walked into her bedroom and grabbed her bag of drugs from the half-packed suitcase she'd left on her bed. She removed a large syringe and a vial of clear liquid. Inverting the vial, she filled the syringe, then carried it into Estelle's room.

Estelle was slightly calmer. She still cowered against the headboard, but her tears no longer flowed as freely. Now her hysteria had given way to exhaustion.

"Well, now," Gretchen said, "that's over. I hope you've decided to be sensible."

Estelle neither replied nor looked up.

"See this?" Gretchen held up the syringe; Estelle raised her eyes and looked at it. "This is Ketaject—chemical name ketamine hydrochloride. Very interesting stuff. Ketaject is a fast-acting general anesthetic, and there's enough in this syringe to knock out two women your size—permanently. All it takes is an easy little injection with enough of this stuff, and it's all over."

Gretchen advanced toward her patient and stared at her coldly. "We're not going to have any more yelling or hitting, Estelle. We're both going to be very calm and rational. I'm going to give you five minutes to think about whether you want to live." She tossed a pad of paper and a pencil onto the bed, within Estelle's easy reach. "I'm going to go finish my packing. While I do that, you will write down the combination to that safe. The trade-off is very simple. If you come up with the combination, I'll let you live. If you don't, I'll inject you with this"—Gretchen waved the syringe under

Estelle's nose—"and you'll be dead within minutes."
Gretchen turned on her heel and started out of the bedroom.
She glanced over her shoulder. "The decision is yours, Es-
telle. Life . . . or death."

Alone once again Estelle tried to marshal her thoughts.
Much of her now found the idea of death almost appealing;
it would be a release from pain, from fear, from trouble. Yet
a spark still cried out to live. Two weeks ago she'd still felt
like a young woman. Seventy-three was not old. Not nowadays. Not for a woman like Estelle, who'd always taken care
of herself. She'd figured on counting the remainder of her
life in decades, not in minutes.

Yet the truth was she didn't know the combination to that
safe. She stared at the blank paper. Think, she chided herself, think of something to do. She picked up the pencil and
poised it over the pad. She closed her eyes and concentrated.
It was no use. No numbers came into her mind. If she'd ever
known that combination, she'd forgotten it years ago.

The old windup alarm clock on her bedside table ticked
ominously. *Buy some time,* Estelle told herself. *Find some
way to gain time.* She scribbled three random numbers on
the pad of paper. It would take Gretchen a few minutes, at
least, to discover that they were not the correct combination.
Perhaps those few minutes . . .

Gretchen came into the room, gripping the syringe in her
right hand. She grabbed the pad of paper with her left. "So.
You've come to your senses, have you?" She ripped off the
top sheet and stuffed it into her pocket as the doorbell rang
once, then quickly rang again. Panic flitted across Gretch-
en's face. She thrust the syringe toward Estelle. "Any noise
out of you, and I'll use this."

Gretchen ran into Estelle's sitting room and peered
through the window onto the front porch. It was that girl
again, but this time there was someone with her . . . a
man. Good Lord, it was the doctor! She felt the trap closing
on her. If she refused to answer the door, the doctor would
summon help. If she answered it, she could hardly refuse
him entry. And if she let him in, Estelle would tell him
everything. . . .

She returned to Estelle's bedroom, still clutching the syringe. As the doorbell sounded again Gretchen's glance darted around the room frantically, as though she were searching for an escape route. Her eyes landed on the syringe. It represented her only chance.

Grabbing a whimpering Estelle's arm, Gretchen efficiently inserted the needle. She depressed the plunger on the syringe partway, trying to estimate how much of its contents would knock out the old woman without killing her. As Estelle moaned, then slumped, Gretchen removed the needle, quickly gathered up the food-covered quilt, and pulled it off the bed. She covered her patient to the neck with the blanket. There. She would try to bluff Cullen Baxter that Estelle was asleep, try to convince him to come back later. It was a long shot, but it was the only shot she had. The doorbell rang again, this time accompanied by energetic pounding on the door.

"I'm coming, I'm coming!" Gretchen called out as she ran downstairs. She opened the front door. "Cullen," she said, forcing a smile. "What a surprise."

"I imagine so. I want to see Estelle." His expression was cool.

Gretchen opened the door wider. "What a shame. Estelle had a bad night. She's been having terrible trouble sleeping. She finally gave up, oh, maybe an hour ago and took a sleeping pill. She really shouldn't be awakened."

"I'll make that judgment." Cullen pushed past the nurse and headed up the stairs, with Faith close behind. Gretchen hurried after them, cautioning again against disturbing her patient.

Cullen barged into Estelle's room and drew in a breath at what he saw. "Estelle," he called, but received no response. He pressed a finger against an artery in the old woman's neck and felt a feeble pulse. Her breathing was shallow. He pulled back the bedcovers and looked at her. "My God! What's been going on here?" The abuse Estelle had endured was obvious.

At Cullen's statement Gretchen slipped out of the room.

Cullen turned to Faith. "Call an ambulance," he instructed her. "Then call the police."

"Not so fast," Gretchen said. She reentered the room,

holding her gun in front of her. "Nobody's going anywhere."

"I bet that's what she shot that guy with—" Faith said, pointing.

Gretchen turned to the girl. "I'm going to use it to shoot you with it!"

As the nurse raised the gun and aimed at her, Faith dived for the floor. Gretchen lowered her weapon, trying to follow her moving target. While she squeezed off a first shot, Cullen dived forward, striking Gretchen's hand. The shot went wild as the gun flew out of the nurse's grasp. The smell of gunpowder rank in her nostrils, Faith lunged for the spot where the gun had fallen and grabbed the weapon. She rolled out of the way, clutching the gun to her body, as the nurse dived after her. Faith kicked frantically at Gretchen, refusing to relinquish the weapon.

Cullen moved toward the scuffling women, reached down, and grabbed Gretchen by an arm and her hair, lifting her off Faith. The girl struggled to her feet, holding the gun out in front of her with two shaky hands.

"Stay back," Faith said to Gretchen, her hands shaking violently. "Here." She handed the gun to Cullen. "I'll go call for help."

Cullen aimed the gun at Gretchen. "You stand right there until the police get here," he told her.

Gretchen stood quietly for a moment, sizing up the doctor. Then she turned her back and moved toward the door.

"Stop where you are," Cullen ordered, raising the gun higher. "Stop or I'll use this."

Gretchen turned and looked at him. "No, you won't," she said. "You haven't got the stuff." She walked out of the room, quickly grabbed her suitcase and handbag, and ran downstairs.

Cullen contemplated the gun in his hand for a moment, then set it down on the dresser. Gretchen was right. He was a lifesaver, not a life taker. He turned his attention to Estelle. Keeping her alive until the ambulance arrived would require all his medical skill.

Chapter 43

Estelle sat upright in her adjustable hospital bed, holding a mirror in her right hand. She was instructing Faith as the girl brushed her hair for her. "Good Lord!" Estelle exclaimed, peering into the mirror. "With this face and body maybe I should go back into show business. I always did play a great traffic accident victim, and once I was a really terrific gun moll. Bogart played my lover—beat the hell out of me four times in that picture." She mugged at her reflection. "Now, though, now the sky's the limit. I could even play a battlefield survivor. . . ."

"I bet you could get a part on *General Hospital,*" Faith said, delighted to see Estelle's sense of humor reemerging after four days in the hospital. "They'd save a fortune on makeup and bandages."

The face Estelle saw in the mirror had a greenish yellow bruise along the jawline, and the shadows underneath her eyes testified to the harrowing ordeal she'd barely survived. Her left arm was now in a cast matching the one on her leg, and her rib cage was firmly bandaged to support her three cracked ribs. After four days in the hospital Estelle's pain was diminishing, and she could begin to think about other things. At the moment her attention was focused on her hair, which was rapidly showing gray at the roots. It might be weeks before she'd be able to get to the beauty shop. Perhaps some sort of turban, she thought. Bright colors, a combination of pinks and lavenders and blues—the effect could be quite stunning.

"There," Faith said, putting down the hairbrush. "You're as gorgeous as ever . . . almost."

"What's this 'almost'? She's never looked so beautiful if you ask me," added Cullen Baxter, walking into the room. "The fact that she's sitting up and breathing is a living testament to my superior medical skills. I can't imagine anything more beautiful than that."

"At least your mother taught you modesty," Estelle said, tilting a cheek for Cullen's kiss.

He gave her a peck. "There's someone here you've got to meet," he said. He gestured to a thin dark-haired man in a three-piece suit who had followed him into the room. "Estelle Edwards . . . Faith Sanford . . . here's Bill Schmidt. He's the assistant district attorney who's going to be prosecuting the Gretchen Hedberg case."

Faith nodded a greeting while Estelle made an effort to straighten her back, then smiled and held out her good hand. "Mr. Schmidt. How nice to meet you."

Schmidt shook her hand gently. "I've been a fan of yours for years, Miss Edwards."

"Nonsense. You're much too young for that."

"Maybe for the first runs, but I'm an old movie buff. I practically live at the art theaters on my days off. My mother was a makeup artist before she married my father, and I guess she gave me an appreciation for the business. You were just great in *The General's Lady.*"

"I'm flattered, Mr. Schmidt. That was one of my favorite films."

"Your performance was wonderful." The tall, hollow-cheeked DA smiled at her and pulled a chair up to her bedside. He sat down and leaned forward earnestly. "Miss Edwards, I'm afraid I have to ask you to give a few more performances . . . in court. We need you to testify for the prosecution in Jasmine Kennedy's trial for fraud, assault, robbery, murder—"

Confusion lodged upon Estelle's face. "Murder? Who's Jasmine Kennedy?"

Cullen broke into the conversation. "All Estelle knows so far, Mr. Schmidt, is that the police arrested Gretchen Hedberg in Santa Barbara. You'll have to fill her in on the rest of what's happened."

"Jasmine Kennedy is the real name of the young woman who worked for you under the name of Gretchen Hedberg," Schmidt said. "From the evidence we've gathered so far, it appears that the Kennedy woman pulled the same scam in a number of states—"

"But murder? What murder?" Estelle asked.

Faith's excitement showed. "The guy in the newspaper. The one who was murdered in Topanga Canyon. I knew it!"

Schmidt turned to the girl. "That's the one. Preliminary ballistics tests indicate that the gun the nurse left at Miss Edwards's house was the same one that was used to kill the man whose picture you saw. He was Stanley Greenwood, from St. Louis. There's another murder charge against Jasmine Kennedy, in Missouri. She went under the name Jane Burden there. She and Greenwood, who was apparently her boyfriend, beat one of her patients to death. An old woman." Schmidt noticed Estelle's shudder. "And there are indications that similar charges may be filed by other states."

"A murderer . . ." Estelle said, realizing once more how lucky she had been to escape the clutches of her deadly nurse-companion.

"How did she get away with it for so long?" Faith asked.

"Oh, she had quite a system worked out," Schmidt replied. "She used a different name and different credentials— all of them verifiable—for each job."

"Like that nursing school diploma?"

"Yeah. She really did have some nurse's training. Went to school in Minnesota, at a place called—"

"St. Lucia's," Faith filled in.

"Right." Schmidt rose and began to pace the small hospital room as he spoke. "While she was a student at St. Lucia's, there was a series of thefts in the dormitory where she lived. Several students' purses were stolen, including their driver's licenses, credit cards, that sort of thing, along with whatever cash they'd been carrying. Our speculation is that Kennedy used the identities of her fellow students— young women named Jane Burden and Gretchen Hedberg, along with half a dozen others—to gain employment as a private-duty nurse or companion. That way, if anyone checked with the nursing school—"

"They'd be told that the person whose name she was using really was a graduate."

"That's right, Miss Sanford. Besides that, Kennedy stole some blank diplomas and some of the school's stationery. There wasn't much she didn't think of. She managed to fool a lot of people into believing her credentials were genuine."

"At least I tried." Faith shrugged.

Estelle patted her hand. "You succeeded too, Faith. Without both you and Cullen I wouldn't be alive. Don't think I don't realize that."

"Miss Edwards is right," Schmidt said. "The two of you saved her life. Some of her other patients weren't so lucky. Kennedy's MO was to work for wealthy older people, then to steal valuable property from them. In the process she apparently helped a few of them to their deaths."

"But how could she get away with it?" Estelle asked, appalled.

"Nobody seems to have caught on until the St. Louis death, mainly because that one was so messy. Most of her patients were on their deathbeds anyway, so there wasn't much surprise when they died. And most were so well-off that the thefts weren't discovered until probate, several months after Kennedy had left town and taken on another new identity. In St. Louis her scheme started to fall apart, but we suspect her boyfriend was responsible for that. Stan Greenwood had a prison record for assault."

"This Stan Greenwood," Faith said, "if he was her boyfriend, why did she kill him?"

"St. Louis PD reports that she walked out on him. My guess is that he didn't like that much, so he followed her out here."

"Bad luck for him," Cullen said.

"Bad judgment more likely," Schmidt said. "And greed. There was a load of stolen goods in his motel room. A silver coffee service, a set of sterling—"

"Those are *my* things!" Estelle said. "So that's where they went."

"You'll get them back once they've all been cataloged as evidence," Schmidt said. "But the reason I'm here is to make sure that you're willing to testify in court. All of you."

"Just give me a time and place, and I'll be there," Estelle said. "As long as my doctor here says I'm in good enough shape."

"You've got to realize the trial could last a long time. And testimony can be grueling. Don't kid yourself that it will be an easy experience." Schmidt's expression was grave. "However, without your testimony we may not have enough to convict—"

"I'm no softy, young man," Estelle said, offended. "If I were, I wouldn't be alive today, I can tell you that. I'm not about to be responsible for Gretchen Hedberg—or whoever she is—treating some other poor person the way she treated me. I'll testify for as much time as it takes to put her in prison. For good."

Schmidt, Cullen, and Faith all smiled at the tiny, battered woman in the bed. Despite her size and condition, Estelle Edwards's basic core of steel was still obvious.

"Count me in," Faith said.

"And me," Cullen added.

"That's what I wanted to hear," Schmidt said. "I'll let you get some rest now, Miss Edwards, and I'll check with Dr. Baxter as we get closer to the preliminary hearing. If you're not ready to appear in court, we'll ask for a postponement. If we all work together, no one else will ever have to suffer at the hands of Jasmine Kennedy."

When Schmidt left the room, Cullen shrugged his shoulders and said wistfully, "You know, it's kind of sad."

"That we'll have to testify?" Estelle asked.

Cullen nodded. "I guess so, but what I really meant was that Gretchen—I mean, Jasmine—is obviously a very bright young woman. She'd have to be to pull off this sort of thing in city after city without getting caught. The reports I've heard indicate that she was a pretty decent nurse, too, when she wanted to be. But somewhere it all fell apart . . . or maybe there was always something missing in her. She viewed her patients not as an opportunity to help but as things to be used. . . ."

"We'll probably never really understand what made her that way, Cullen," Estelle said. "Maybe she came from an unfortunate family life . . . who knows? But eventually that young woman made her own choices, her own decisions, just as we all do. In fact—" Estelle raised her chin, preparing to make an announcement. "I have made a few decisions myself in the past few days." She gave an awkward nod, as close to a bow as she could manage, given her casts and bandages.

Cullen and Faith smiled at her.

"Well, aren't you going to ask me what they are?"

"I'll bite," Faith said. "What decisions have you made?"

Estelle's voice took on a sense of excitement. "First of all, I'm thrilled that my things have been recovered. Now I can sell them."

"Sell them? But, Estelle—"

"Yes, Faith, sell them. If Gretchen did one valuable thing for me, it was alerting me to how much money I've got stowed away in knickknacks all over my house, things that are just gathering dust. I can use that money for other things, more important things."

"You shouldn't be worrying about money now, Estelle," Cullen said. "I'm sure insurance will pay most of your bill here. . . ." He gestured at the utilitarian green hospital room.

"It's not just that, Cullen. It's . . . well, I've had plenty of time to reassess my priorities since I've been flat on my back—it's getting to be hard to remember being able to walk around!—and I've discovered that there are things I don't like about the way I've been living. I've selfishly kept my house like some sort of personal museum. I've guarded my privacy until it's turned into hermitlike loneliness—"

"You're being too hard on yourself, Estelle."

"No, Faith, I'm not. What I'm doing is looking at reality. I'm not too old to change either. Not now that you and Cullen have given me a second chance."

The girl stared at the floor and blushed while Cullen, too, looked embarrassed.

"Well, it's true. You have, both of you. And I'm going to show my gratitude. As soon as I sell those things that will bring the best price, I'm going to take some of the money and set up a college scholarship for you, Faith. I'll see to it that you can study drama, or whatever you want to study, at the school of your choice. Then whether your father approves won't matter." Estelle raised her right hand to silence Faith's automatic protest. "And you, Cullen, will have an equal amount to help you purchase your medical practice."

"We can't accept—"

"Hush! Both of you. You're interrupting me. Weren't you ever taught respect for your elders?" Estelle smiled, enjoying herself for the first time in many days. "Now, gifts for some other people, too, gifts that will result in a gift for myself. I'm going to open up my house to other people like me, people who are getting along in years and who can't afford to live alone decently. I've already located my old friend Maisie Gilroy, and she's dying to move in with me. Your mother might like to share my house too, Cullen. She's miserable in Toledo, from what she writes, and if she lived here, she'd be available to help with baby-sitting—"

"Estelle! That's a wonderful idea," Faith said.

Cullen nodded thoughtfully. If his mother could provide a relief shift with the babies, it might just help save his marriage to Laura, he thought. That and some serious marriage counseling.

Estelle continued. "I figure I can accommodate six or seven besides myself. Men as well as women—the hell with what the neighbors think! Times have changed. We can pool our incomes; each of us will pay what we can afford. There's no argument that I'll be better off with some money coming in. And my friends will be better off living with me than in shabby single rooms somewhere, cooking their meals on hot plates. Or bunking with their children and making everybody miserable. By pooling our resources, we can afford to hire a housekeeper, we can buy food cheaper in quantity, and we all can pitch in on cooking and chores."

"I don't want to be a wet blanket," Cullen said, "but how are Seth and Paula going to react to these plans?"

Estelle smiled wryly. "In the immortal words of Clark Gable, 'Frankly, Scarlett, I don't give a damn!' My ungrateful son and his devoted wife will just have to wait until I die to get their hands on my money—*if* there's any left by then."

"There's your privacy to consider too, Estelle," Cullen said. "You're not used to living with other people."

"Nothing can be as bad as living with that so-called nurse-companion I hired," Estelle said. "Truth is I've been alone too long. I've been selfishly concerned with only myself. It's about time I thought about somebody else for a change. I've been given a chance—a second chance really—to help other people and help myself at the same time. It will require some big readjustments. I realize that. But I also know I can do it." She patted her hairdo with her right hand. "I'm a pretty tough old bird, you know."

Cullen shook his head. "You can say that again."

"My last companion turned out to be pretty deadly . . . but that's changing, as of now. From now on it's nothing but loving companions."

"Just promise," Faith said, stifling a laugh, "that you won't go looking for them in the classified ads."